3/16

AFTER THE WOODS

AFTER THE WOODS

KIM SAVAGE

FARRAR STRAUS GIROUX
NEW YORK

Farrar Straus Giroux Books for Young Readers
175 Fifth Avenue, New York 10010

Text copyright © 2016 by Kimberley Haas Savage

fiercereads.com

Library of Congress Cataloging-in-Publication Data
Savage, Kim, 1969–
    After the woods / Kim Savage. — First edition.
        pages cm
    Summary: "On the eve of the year anniversary of the Shiverton Abduction,
two former best friends grapple with the consequences of that event" —
Provided by publisher.
    ISBN 978-0-374-30055-5 (hardback) — ISBN 978-0-374-30056-2 (e-book)
[1. Kidnapping—Fiction.   2. Psychic trauma—Fiction.   3. Friendship—
Fiction.]   I. Title.

PZ7.1.S27Af 2016
[Fic]—dc23

                                                                    2015005287

Our books may be purchased in bulk for promotional, educational, or
business use. Please contact your local bookseller or the Macmillan Corporate
and Premium Sales Department at (800) 221-7945 ext. 5442 or by
e-mail at MacmillanSpecialMarkets@macmillan.com.

For Jackson,
whose quiet bravery never makes headlines

Keep her down, boiling water.
Keep her down, what a lovely daughter.

—"Seether" *by Veruca Salt*

Truth has rough flavors if we bite it through.

—*George Eliot*

AFTER THE WOODS

PROLOGUE

November 22, 2013
In the Woods

How can something so bright be so cold?

There's no use sharing my ironic observances about the sun. Liv's been barely responsive today, all aimless energy and distraction. I didn't want to run in the woods, but she insisted. Leaves crunch under my sneakers. A tingle in my earlobes warns of pain to come. We'll run like jackrabbits, like banshees, like Diana through the trees, with only an hour left of light.

Liv will. I'll do my best to keep up.

I finish my last quad stretch and find her staring at the trailhead. "We're losing light. Maybe we should bag it," I suggest.

Liv throws back her shoulders. "I need you with me."

"Of course. I'd never let you go alone." I bend at the waist and yank my laces tight, clumsy in gloves. "Aren't you going to warm up? Oh right: you don't need to." I say it softly, tucking the envy behind a gentle chide.

"Have you ever felt like your heart is swollen inside your chest?" she asks.

I rise fast. "You *are* into him! You said it was just a party hook-up!" I exclaim.

"I'm not talking about Kellan MacDougall." The low curves of her cheeks flush. "What I mean is, did you ever feel like you were on the brink of something?"

I follow her eyes past the poker-burned entrance sign, past the kiosk with maps under glass. Despite the desolation—no one runs at four p.m. in November after weeks of rain—the woods pulse. The canopy shatters fast-dropping light into glittering shards. A chipmunk skitters close to my foot and ducks into a hole. I know what Liv means. All day, I've felt a fullness, as though there's something waiting for me, today, tomorrow, soon. I start to say this but my words are lost to geese barking overhead.

Liv shakes off her trance. "We should go," she says, as she leaps up the railroad-tie steps like a deer, flashing pale calves. Speed is easy for her. We come to a puddle buzzing with damselflies and thick with icy rot. Liv jumps over and keeps going. The cold slows me, and I call for her to wait. Liv tosses a grin over her shoulder, the smile that forms her cheek into a shiny rubber ball. She's about to leave me. While I fight to match my breathing with my pace, Liv goes from zero to ten with no effort. We meet another pocket of water. Leap over, dig deep, keep going. She sprints ahead of me as I track her powder-blue jacket, leaves crackling in her wake. We're supposed to stay together. It's the only way my mother allows me to run in the woods, with its overgrowth and lonely trails winding across town lines and Indian ruins. But we run on, longer and farther than we should. I fight to catch up, and I get faster. Liv makes me faster.

Before the flat Sheepfold lies the Hill, a lump of stone and shrub covered by gravel. Today, the gravel will be frozen in the earth, making an ankle-turning hobnailed path. I'm about to call out, tell her to stop, but she breaks into a full-on sprint. I dig in, watch my footing, hop, and weave. My phone falls from my jacket pocket and lands with an ominous clap.

"Wait!" I call to Liv.

I squat. My quadriceps tingle and itch. "Got it!" I raise the phone to my nose; the earbuds dangle. A spiderweb of cracks spreads across the screen. I'm screwed. We need to go home. I wrap the cord around the phone and stash it away in my jacket. No way of avoiding the Hill. I throw my weight forward, and drive myself up, up, up, mounting the crest.

"Liv!"

Sunlight flashes between trees and blinds me. I blink through the pain until I see the man on top of Liv. She writhes, kicking up gravel and leaves. The man shifts his weight rhythmically to keep her pinned.

Liv is screaming.

I am screaming.

"Let her go!" My voice is strangled.

His eyes are red-streaked aggies.

"Who are you?" he bellows. He braces Liv with his forearm and reaches up his pant leg. Metal glints near his hand.

I scream, an animal sound.

He holds a knife at Liv's throat, eyes darting between us, but lingering on Liv. When she squirms, he pulls the knife away from her neck.

"Walk away and forget what you saw! Now, or her blood's on your hands!" His pitch wavers.

I shake my head slowly.

"I'll end her life, right here!"

I don't believe him.

He has a baby face and his head is small for his body. A slice of forehead, pink and smooth, peeks from under a black knit cap, and the buckles on his camouflage jacket clang as he fights to keep Liv from escaping.

Liv sobs. "Julia, please don't leave me!"

I feel my front pocket for my phone, the phone we take turns carrying in case someone gets hurt and we need help. Then I remember: my phone is cracked.

She's been my best friend since she gave me her cherry cola ChapStick in the sixth grade.

If I grab the scruff of his jacket and yank, I might move him, a little, maybe. Just enough so Liv can roll and run. We can run.

I step closer. A light flickers in his eyes. Greedy. He wants us both, but he can't hold two of us. He imagines we'll fight.

Liv's eyes flit over my face. Pleading.

ChapStick.

I rush him.

My fingertips graze his jacket as a glove clamps down on

my ankle. I fall. My ankle snaps. The pain fills every space in my body. I hear someone howling. Me.

I turn my head. The view is different from the forest floor.

Liv rolls and scrambles to her feet. Liv is a powder-blue smudge, running and falling and running, until the crashing fades.

The man stands over me, smiling. He has small teeth like a child.

"You'll do."

ONE

353 Days After the Woods

Statistically speaking, girls like me don't come back when guys like Donald Jessup take us.

According to my research, in 88.5% of all abductions, the kid is killed within the first four hours. In 76% of those cases, it's within the first two hours. So when they found me alive after nearly two days, the reporters called it a miracle.

They liked it even better when they found out Donald Jessup didn't want me at first. He wanted Liv. But I took her place. Not only did they have a miracle, they had a martyr. In the eleven months since the abduction, more than half of the *Shiverton Star*'s stories (so, thirty-two of them) have been about us. And Paula Papademetriou, who lives right here in Shiverton and anchors the evening WFYT News, still won't leave us alone.

Liv says we must move on.

It had rained a lot that November, and everyone's basement got water, and the high school gym flooded. The track warped in places where the water underneath forced it up, so the track team had to run in a pack all over town. Off hours and against coaches' rules, we trained in the woods.

I think Liv reminded Donald Jessup of a deer, all knees and angles and big brown eyes. In his sick mind he thought he was the Greek hunter-god Zagreus, his avatar in Prey, which he played 24/7 in his mother's house. *Zagreus* is the ancient Greek word for a hunter. My theory is Donald Jessup couldn't get enough of virtual Prey and decided to bring the action to life.

Liv doesn't let on that she used to be a bit of a gamer. Liv would never cop to knowing more about Prey than I do. It doesn't fit the perfect-girl image, the maintenance of which is her mother Deborah's full-time job. What little I know about Prey comes from my research—research that Liv wants me to stop. If Liv had her way, I'd have spent the last eleven months forgetting the woods ever happened.

Dr. Ricker, on the other hand, wants me to remember. Ricker is my new therapist, for better or for worse. The jury's still out on that one. Mom secured my first appointment the day we got home from the Berkshires. The trip started out as "a little time off" and lasted through the second half of sophomore year and the whole summer. I felt like one of those nervous Victorian ladies hustled by my mother to the English countryside for a rest cure. Less than a week after the woods, and as soon as the cops gave us permission, Professor Mom announced a sabbatical, pulled me out of school, and closed

9

up the house. We hightailed it out of Shiverton in time for Thanksgiving for two at the vacation home I hadn't seen since I was nine due to Mom's workaholic tendencies. Mom said holing up 135 miles away from Shiverton would allow the media frenzy to die down. Also, it would give me time to get myself together: stop melting down at the sight of trees and such (for the record, Western Mass was the last place I should have been. So. Many. Trees.). But clearly it was a reflexive act. She was verging on a breakdown of her own, and needed to feel I was safe. After a while, between the homeschooling and our mutual lack of any friends, I actually looked forward to my visits with Patty Petty, RN, MS, CSW. Dr. Petty (Call me Patty!) was supposed to cleanse me of the trauma that I don't totally remember. Her expertise is expressive arts therapy, which involved staging interpretative dances of my feelings about Donald Jessup (I refused). We mostly ended up making masks out of paper and chicken wire, and drawing in what she called my art journal. I went along with it, mainly because Mom, in a weak moment during one of my crying jags, gave me her word this would be the extent of my therapy. But her word is weak. Because here I sit, as I have for all of September and October, on Elaine Ricker's cliché of a couch, deciding how to screw with today's template for Fixing Julia.

At least Patty Petty didn't make me play with dolls. "Seriously?" I groan as Ricker reaches for the basket under her desk.

Ricker is convinced Donald Jessup did something to me that I can't talk about, so I'm supposed to show her. That's where the anatomically correct dolls come in.

The basket rests on her lap. There are girl dolls and boy dolls.

"I know this is an unorthodox approach for someone your age. But I'm asking you to be open-minded," Ricker says.

"Open-minded means willing to play with dolls?" I ask.

"Uncovering lost memories is key to developing a plan for treatment. It may take a long time, and it may be painful. This is a marathon, not a race."

I want to ask if she's ever met a cliché she didn't like. But I stuff it, deep into my bowels, feeding the thing I think of as the black in my belly. I don't want to rouse the black because I actually like Ricker, with her glossy bangs, funky glasses, and big man hands. But that's not for her to know.

Best simply to remind her who's in charge.

"So I've been thinking about Newton's Third Law. Of Motion. You know: for every action there is an equal and opposite reaction," I say.

Ricker tucks the basket under her desk. "You can't touch without being touched."

"Exactly. Here's the thing. Two people, call them X and Y, are pushed by another person. Call him . . . D. No wait: call him Z." I smile and continue. "We'll call the push 'force A.' If person Z exerts force A on persons X and Y, then persons X and Y exert an equal and opposite force A back on person Z. $Axz = -Azx$. And, $Ayz = -Azy$. You get pushed, you push back. Follow me?"

Her mouth parts, then shuts.

"Cool. So according to Newton's Third Law, how can Person Y not exert an equal and opposite reaction?" I say.

"You cannot compare individual responses to trauma," Ricker says.

"Work with me here."

She exhales through her nose. "Y wasn't pushed with the same force as X."

I sigh, throwing my boots up on the couch. "If you're more comfortable with dolls . . ."

"Let me be clearer then. Only one of you was abducted."

"A psychopath dropped into our lives. Mine and Liv's. It was worse for me, I get that. But is it healthy to just go on, with no questions? *Que sera, sera?*"

"There is no useful outcome for comparing your recovery to Olivia Lapin's."

"I'm not talking about recovery. I'm talking about basic, everyday behavior."

Ricker scans her desk and settles on a small legal pad and a pencil. Her mouth twists as she scribbles for a second, then two.

I lean over my knees. "Are you sure that's how you spell *'que sera, sera'*?"

I am a monster. She is trying to help me, and is probably the only person who can. Gosh knows I have a better chance talking with her than by mask making with Patty Petty, with her silver ponytail and turquoise and Wellies that smelled of manure.

"The most important thing to remember is that when an

evil act is committed, the shame belongs to the perpetrator. Donald Jessup's shame is not your shame—"

"And my strength is my survival. I covered that with Patty Petty," I interrupt.

Ricker folds her swishy pant legs and leans back until her chair creaks. Dramatic leg swoops signal a change in tactic.

"It might help our progress to put a name on what you're experiencing. The clinical term is post-traumatic stress disorder, or PTSD."

"That happens to me every month. I bloat and break out. One word: Motrin."

Ricker doesn't blink. "When a person experiences a physical threat, and the person's response involves intense fear, helplessness, or horror, certain side effects can result for that person. I'd like to explore if you're experiencing any of these side effects," she says calmly.

"As a person?"

Her face is blank.

"Just checking."

"Sometimes, the traumatic event is re-experienced over and over, in the form of dreams, or during the day, as intrusive thoughts. Do you have thoughts, Julia?"

"Never. I never think," I say, grinning.

"Another feature is avoidance of stimuli associated with the trauma."

Liv thinks I have the opposite problem.

"Julia?"

"Still here. Not thinking."

"Perhaps it would help if I gave you a specific example. Because the abduction happened during track practice, you might avoid running."

"I still run. Like a madwoman. Like someone's chasing me. Doh, bad joke. And in case you're keeping count in your little notebook of the PTSD markers that I don't have, that's like the tenth negative."

The cell phone on her desk buzzes.

"Restricted range of effect? That means you're unable to have loving feelings where they previously existed," Ricker says.

"Are you going to pick up? It might be one of your kids."

She holds my eyes and turns the phone facedown. "Are you having difficulty feeling affection, Julia?"

"I'm as loving as ever. Ask my mother. You, I'm not so sure about, seeing as your kid might have an emergency and you're not answering your phone."

She pretends to write words, but draws small squares. "Irritability? Outbursts of anger?"

"Zen as ever. Ask my therapist."

She blinks at the phone.

"Maybe I'm projecting my own experience, but you are freaking me out by not answering that phone. Answer it. Seriously. I don't care."

"Normally I would never allow an interruption on our time. But that was my emergency ringtone. I promise this will only take a second."

"I won't tell," I stage-whisper.

Ricker says a deep hello, pressing the curve of her hand into her top lip as she listens. She sets the phone down and stares at it for a second.

"I was just yanking your chain about your daughter. Is everything okay?" I ask.

She smiles tightly at her lap, and when she looks up, she's the composed Ricker again. "I apologize. Where were we? Oh yes. We know for sure that you have the final symptom: inability to recall aspects of the trauma. That said, I'd like to hypnotize you."

"Whoa! What?"

"It will be like falling asleep. When you're fully under, I'll regress you to those lost moments."

"Can't we just wait for my memories to return?"

"It doesn't always work that way. Repressed memories can stay repressed for a lifetime. They're not like seeds. Shoots won't rise from the ground without some nurturing," she says.

"I'm not so sure of that. Ever hear of the yellow tansy? It's the worst invasive plant in North America, and it grows better when ignored. Pretty, fragrant, and totally poisonous."

"Once we understand the past, we can move forward."

My master plan—to humor Man Hands while secretly rejecting her textbook dogma—suddenly seems wrongheaded. If she wants to understand what happened in the woods, we're on the same page.

"I'm all for understanding," I say.

The secretary's light tap at the door signals Ricker's next

appointment is waiting. I lean across the couch, reaching for my bag on the floor.

"Julia," Ricker says suddenly. "The reporters. They'll be back."

I sit up slowly, frowning. "Why would you say that?"

"Slow news cycle." Ricker rushes over her words. "Or they might try to make a big deal out of the one-year anniversary. It's less than two weeks away."

"I'm aware."

"You need to be prepared to reject them completely."

"You make it sound as if I actually like the attention."

"I simply want to be clear about where you should put your energy in the days ahead. The media is in the business of selling stories. Our business is healing you."

I consider pointing out that, unlike the media, not one of the persons supposedly concerned with my healing has used the word *brave* to describe what I did. As in, *Brave Teen Saves Friend*, *Brave Girl Fights Off Predator*, or *Lucky Teen Escapes Attacker Because of Brave Friend*. Nor do they take advantage of the delightful wordplay my name affords: *Meet Julia Spunk, a teen whose name suits her perfectly*.

"If your business is healing me, then isn't it in your interest that I stay broken?"

"Maybe I'm not being clear. I'm advising your mother that you should stay away from all press."

Deep in my belly, the black thing shifts. "I can handle it," I insist.

"When it comes to the press, it's your mother's job to

handle it. I know it's hard to hear this, but the work we have to do is here, in this room." She sits back and sweeps her hand in front of her head—"Here"—and her chest—"And here."

She's losing my favor fast. I roll my eyes so hard I see stars. "We're done, right?"

Ricker nods, tucking her lips. I scramble off the couch and yank my cuff down to cover the metal doorknob, one of many tricks for never being cold again. The door opens and there is Mom, a shudder through her springy, dark curls.

"I apologize! It was me knocking," she calls to Ricker, then leans in and says in her shrink-shop undertone: "I need a few minutes to catch up with Dr. Ricker, and I wanted to make sure she had time for me before her next appointment."

"Sorry I used every minute. I won't do it again," I say.

Her smile falls. "You can't think I minded."

"I didn't. I was teasing."

"Oh!" She reaches to smooth my hair, then stops. "I won't be long."

I watch Mom slide through the door, a sliver of a woman, birdlike, with a small head and hollow bones. I take over her chair, feeling ungainly, stretch my legs, and scan the room, daring someone to say something. A fat kid with emo hair and a mole on his cheek points his phone at my head and takes a photo.

"For real? I'm right here!" I lean over my knees. "I. Can. See. You."

He jams the phone into his jacket and rises, shuffling over

to a receptionist talking into a headpiece. He begs her for the men's room key, which she shoves through a glass arch. The last thing I need is this loser posting my photo for his pals to ogle. I trail him into the bathroom and kick open the door.

"Give me your phone."

"This is the men's room, freak!"

The black thing in my belly flicks. "Give it or I'll send that mole to the other side of your face."

"Here." He holds it up. "Look, I'm deleting it."

I swipe the phone from his doughy hand and pitch it over the stall wall. His eyes widen at the porcelain clatter, followed by a plop.

"What the . . . ?"

I harden my gut. "Now it's deleted."

His mouth opens and shuts soundlessly. Finally, he stalks into the stall, reappearing with his dripping phone. "What do you even care if I send your picture to a couple of my friends?" He pulls paper towels from the holder on the wall. "It's not like your face isn't going to be back all over the news by the end of the day."

I remember Ricker's weird warnings. What are she and this dork talking about? I squint at him.

He wraps his phone inside a mealy towel wad, shaking his head. "Who would ever guess that in person, you'd be such a bitch?"

"Excuse me?"

"I mean, if anything, I'd expect you'd be super happy. Grateful, even."

"Grateful?" I hiss, my breath hot behind my teeth. "That's rich."

"Yeah, grateful. Most people would feel lucky they got out alive."

I snort, an ugly noise that echoes off the stalls and lingers. "Thank you so much for putting everything into perspective for me, Moleman. What am I even seeing Elaine Ricker for? I could just come see you! But here's the thing." I poke his soft shoulder. "Dr. Ricker isn't a fan of her patients showing up on the Internet. Pictures of them at her office and whatnot. It's a violation of patient confidentiality. I wonder how she'll take your little transgression. Drop you as a client, I imagine."

He jabs his sausage finger in the air at me. "Oh man. Now I get it."

"Sorry, too harsh? You prefer your abductees with cream and sugar?"

"You haven't seen the news, have you?"

"I've *been* the news, Dough Boy. And I can tell you, it sucks. So no, I don't watch much of it these days."

The mole slides toward his ear in a sickening grin. "Then you don't know about the body."

The video is at the top of the WFYT Web site. I tap Play on my phone's touchscreen. Hometown gal–slash–glamorous ladyanchor Paula Papademetriou ticks her voice down a notch, the way she does when she's talking about Nor'easters, school shootings, and Liv and me: "A couple out walking their dog early this morning stumbled upon a body police believe to be eighteen-year-old Ana Alvarez, who went missing while jogging in the Sheepfold section of the Middlesex Fells Reservation in August of last year. Many are wondering about the involvement of a man arrested for an attack on two local girls in these same woods nearly one year ago."

The cold and nausea come at once, like they sometimes do, and prickles erupt on my chest. I jam my phone deep in my pocket and take the back stairs one floor up, duck into the women's room, and lock the door. I tug my cuffs down before pressing my palms against the chilly walls, and sway over the toilet, willing the black, or lunch, or anything to expel itself so I will feel better. Nothing comes.

Get ahold of yourself, Julia. A body in the woods is just another fact.

To normal people, researching facts about abductions, and then your own abduction, labels you all kinds of morbid. But research soothes me. The methodical ordering of gathered facts is a beautiful thing, especially when I order them in ways that make me feel safe. If I put my hand over my heart while I reread the facts I've collected in my Mead wide-ruled black marble composition notebook, my heart beats slower. I sway out of the bathroom and down the stairs, leaning outside Ricker's waiting room. I slide down the wall. The carpet smells of cleaning chemicals and mud from shoes, but it's not a totally unpleasant spot to sit. "You are good," I whisper to myself, rubbing my knuckles across my chest with one hand and feeling through my messenger bag with the other. I touch my notebook's hard taped spine, then a pencil. On a clean page, I draw a circle. Next to it, I draw a second overlapping circle of equal size.

My shoulders fall. I bury my head in the notebook, ignoring passing shins and murmurs.

In the the first circle, I write JULIA. In the second circle, I write LIV.

The seed shape in the middle stares back at me, no longer a seed, but the pupil of a cat's eye. I draw a third circle above the first two, overlapping. It bisects the cat's eye. Inside the third circle, I write BODY. The three of us share a space, the bisected cat's eye, and it is small, but there's still room to write.

I wriggle my hand into my pocket for my phone and click on Paula Papademetriou's live feed. I'm too impatient to listen to her, though her perfect aubergine lipstick transfixes me for a second. Besides, I'm a faster reader than listener. In the transcripted story below, I scan for the word *pit*, but it's not there. In Ionian Greek, the word *zagre* means a "pit for the capture of live animals." The important word here is *live*. You can debate back and forth whether it's better to be killed or kept, but either way, a body popping up in the Sheepfold means old Zagreus was tweaking the mythology.

Liv is alive. I am alive. The body is irrelevant, Liv would say.

At the bottom of the page, I write PROBABILITY.

The probability of Liv and me stumbling across a deranged maniac in the woods was low: 1 out of 347,000. And stranger abductions are the most improbable, at 24% of all abductions, versus 49% by family members and 27% by acquaintances. So

Liv's right when she insists what happened in the woods was a fluke, just a forgettable, little thing.

But if Paula Papademetriou is right, and Donald Jessup killed before? That makes us part of a big thing.

After PROBABILITY, I add a question mark.

TWO

354 Days After the Woods

I am disappointing naked.

Since the woods, kids stare at my naked body parts, hoping to spot scars that will reveal the things Donald Jessup did to me. In gym, they stare at my arms and legs. I imagine it's a letdown that the marks aren't visible. But the real reason I prefer to dress in Sherpa layers is what I call cold-avoidance. For me, cold—the kind that slips down your collar and swirls down your spine like a frosty helix—is unstoppable. It sends me right back to the woods, and that can be inconvenient during, well, everything. In my first ten weeks back at school, I've concocted some excellent excuses to avoid changing into my standard-issue gym shorts and tee. Today, Ms. Dean isn't having it, possibly because today's excuse, Kuru disease, is found only among cannibals in remote New Guinea.

Liv warned me that my crazy clothes only fuel the gossip.

Gossip, I will add, that doesn't seem to plague Liv. You'd think she'd get her share of stares, though I guess because she never took a break from school, and maybe because she wasn't *actually abducted*, she never generated my brand of buzz.

Lucky for me, something else has everyone's attention.

A bustle near the bleachers. Kellan MacDougall is getting shoved by his hockey pals into a pretty freshman. He shoves them back. The girl giggles, knuckles pressed against her upper lip. Kellan barely makes eye contact with her, twisting the toe of his sneaker like he's grinding something into the parquet. She puffs her chest and tips her chin, spilling flat-ironed hair down her back. Her cheek is the color of a pink apple. Kellan's a player; he even hooked up with Liv at a party the weekend before the woods, then never spoke to her again. It had to be awkward for him when his detective dad was assigned our case.

Kellan spies me as I end my walk to the door marked GIRLS. I hold his stare, making my eyes vacant. Apple Face follows his gaze, her eyes lashy Os. He's probably thinking we have some connection because his dad captured my abductor. Those days were smeary. I didn't deny myself hits off the morphine pump meant for my ankle. By the time my head cleared, I was settled in my ivory tower on Mount Greylock, and Detective Mac-Dougall had made his career by locking up Donald Jessup. I wonder how he felt when Donald Jessup killed himself by swallowing a pen spring in jail.

I lean my shoulder against the door with the GIRLS sign. GIRLS are flouncing creatures with satin bows in their hair who circle maypoles and use their eyelashes to charm—a luxury for people who assume other people won't hurt them. I have let my charm shrivel. GIRLS are weightless, without black things in their bellies that coil and spring. Apple Face is a GIRL. Somehow, Liv is still a GIRL.

The door moves beneath my shoulder. I fall into Liv, pulling the door open from inside.

"I've been looking for you!" she says, stepping back and tugging her shirt down over her flat belly.

"Just giving the fans something to stare at," I say, righting myself.

"You skipped lunch."

"Not exactly. I had a strategically timed guidance office appointment–cum–wellness check-in."

Liv smiles. "I'm familiar. But you're going to have to face lunch someday. Like, tomorrow." She parts a pack of wispy, wan girls—friends of my next-door neighbor, Alice Mincus—and stakes out a corner. They change clothes and tie their sneakers fast. I try to decide if it's Liv they're intimidated by or my weird factor, but Liv seems not to notice either way. When the last few scatter, she circles the locker room, yanking back shower curtains and checking under stalls. I watch, mystified. Liv usually pooh-poohs my paranoia, but here she is, feeding it. It's like a minivindication. Satisfied there are no spies, she turns to me.

"They found a dead girl in the woods," she says.

"I know. My mother told me last night." After Moleman did. But no sense mentioning that.

"You knew? Why didn't you call me?"

"I figured your mom talked to you about it." As soon as it comes out of my mouth, I realize how ridiculous that sounds. If Liv glosses over what happened, Deborah Lapin shellacs it. Being preyed upon by a man who played dress-up in the woods is not in line with the image she has cast for Liv. "I mean, I was trying to be better. More like you. Not get hung up on the past," I add. That last line is a direct quote from one of our weekly e-mails while I was in the Berkshires, the ones that kept me sane and tethered to reality. While Patty Petty said let it all hang out, Liv gave me permission—really, more of a directive—to let it go.

Liv brushes her hair back roughly behind one ear. It's Liv's hair, cornsilk-fine and aggressively highlighted, that guys always notice first. That and her boobs, full-blown by sixth grade. "I think that's great," she says, her eyes skipping around the room. "Moving forward and all."

"Right? Ricker wants me to do hypnosis. She says unlocking my repressed memories is the way to heal. But then she avoids answering questions that might actually help me heal. To me that's a contradiction. It's like she wants me on one path: hers."

Liv slides her jaw from side to side.

"I'm pretty sure Ricker got a call about the body right in the middle of our session yesterday. She tried to pretend it was her daughter, but I knew something was up," I say. "So do you think Donald Jessup killed that other girl?"

Liv's face goes dark. After the woods, my mother spun into

action, jetting me out of town and hooking me up with Patty Petty, then Ricker. Deborah's sole effort at supporting Liv was dragging her to speak with a local priest exactly once before signing herself into Valium rehab. I can be bitter about my forced removal, but at least what my mother did was in the realm of appropriate reactions for a mother.

Of course Deborah isn't a mother, but a hedgewitch.

"How are things with your mo—"

"Eighteen is hardly a girl," Liv says suddenly. "She was old enough to vote."

"Everyone out!" Ms. Dean booms as she rounds the corner, sporting an unfortunate choppy new haircut. She stops short and knits her brows, making a lumbering mental calculation. I imagine she's recalling what she learned during meetings of the school's Incident Management Team.

"Are you ladies okay? Do you need, um, support?" she says.

"We are so okay!" Liv says, already out the door when Ms. Dean plants her ham-hand on my shoulder.

"You're not dressed." In her other hand is a balled-up pair of jersey-style Shiverton shorts and a T-shirt, my punishment for wearing jeans to gym. I accept them as Ms. Dean says that while she respects my need for time to readjust, there are no exceptions to the sweats rule. She's a softie for anyone with issues, always letting the cutters wear long sleeves to hide their razor scars. Still, I give her a nice piece of cold back, waiting until she leaves to drop my sweatercoat with a thump. Next, I shimmy out of my hoodie, unzip my fly, and yank off my jeans.

A Henley button-down is the last layer standing before bra and bare skin. The locker room might be warm, but the gym is a drafty space with exposed beams that stretch to the ceiling like ribs. I tear the Henley over my head and wriggle into my shorts and extra-large tee. My white legs and arms make me look spectral. The Shiverton High girls' locker room is exactly the same as when it was built in the 1960s, with its faint smell of mildew and decades of bad energy that lingers. Echoes of teasing banging around lockers, inadequacies stuck inside mirrors. Special pains inflicted by GIRLS onto GIRLS. But I'm not a GIRL anymore. I shake my hair out, press my lips together, and stride out, hand on belly, willing my serpentine friend—the black thing in my gut that Liv doesn't have and doesn't need, but I do—to rise and get me through this, the real, indoor, after-the-woods world.

Ms. Dean nods as I join the far end of the line for stretches. Liv has been absorbed among the slouchy-loud girls. I will not be absorbed. She smiles at me, hard and tight. I smile back anemically, hugging my elbows and rocking slightly, just enough to feel better and not look catatonic.

So. Cold.

My hands float up and bat at my ears, burning, as though I am outside, in the woods, but I'm not, I'm in the gym, with its faint smell of mold from last year's flood, and still the snowy flash spreads until the gym is white. The smell of night air and woodsmoke blooms around me. Now the rush, the sensation of plunging down a hole. I'm going and I can't stop.

What Ricker doesn't know is that I don't need hypnosis. Not when there's a trigger.

The joint shakes in his hand as he winds it. His tongue flashes to lick the paper. It falls in his lap.

"Shhhit!" His hands flutter.

"Are you okay?" I say. Begging, reasoning, and crying haven't worked. Empathy is the only thing I haven't tried.

"Been off-line too—too long—long," he stammers, patting his lap. "In the six hours I sleep sleepy-time raiders plunder my camps, destroy my weapons, and take my prey. I set traps, everything, but nothing does any good. I hardly have any girls left. What's gonna happen when I'm gone for days? Can't play 24/7, I just can't. How'm I gonna get ahead after this? Phew, there it is." He lights the fat white pupa at his lips, a flame dancing at his trembling fingers, his inhalation like a long sip of water.

I take tiny breaths. Being a pot virgin, I have no idea if just being near the smoke will make me high, and the thought of losing my wits terrifies me. I wiggle away from the downwind. The movement triggers pain in my ankle, and I cry out. He looks at me quizzically.

He holds out the joint. "Want a hit?"

I shake my head wildly.

He shrugs. "Might help."

He takes softer drags, puffing and sucking, intimate sounds that make my privates clench. I'm hit with a wave of revulsion. I stare hard at the outlines of trees and hills, trying to get back into my head, match their silhouettes with the woods I know in daylight. The fire between us burns a low flame, but it's enough for me to imagine my rescuers will see it and come. How long ago did Liv run away? Seven, eight, nine hours? Why hasn't anyone come?

"This was a mistake," he says.

I shift in my spot. If I am a mistake, I am less valuable to him. That feels dangerous.

"If you free me, you could go back to your game," I say, my voice small.

He giggles, teeth flashing in the dark like little pearls.

I force myself to mirror his laugh, but I sound like a hyena.

"What are you laughing at?" he says.

I stop laughing. "I'm not."

"Oh, what, was that an owl?" He laughs again, uncontrollably this time. "Was that an owl laughing in the woods?"

I become very still, trying to make myself shapeless so he'll forget I am a GIRL, because that feels the most dangerous of all.

If only there were stars to count. Math, then.

1,133 divided by 2 equals 566.5.

8,349,179 divided by 7 equals 1,192,739.8 . . . 6.

"Funny, isn't it?" he sputters, taking a last drag and flicking the orange stub into the darkness.

"Yeah!" I say, unconvincing.

"Here we are, you and me. Not what I expected. But something."

"What happened to you?" Liv cries, her hand out, warding off others.

In nine months of e-mails, she never did ask me what happened in the woods.

Ms. Dean mouths my name in slow motion. A ring of pale

faces crowd in over my crumpled body, their voices drifting, but I make out "swallow tongue" and "orange juice" and "so sad." Liv plants herself to avoid being shoved. Now she's arguing with the guy next to her. Ms. Dean's mouth moves again, but I can't hear her over my own breaths, loud as shotgun blasts.

I sit up. "I think I have a fever."

Ms. Dean dings my forehead with the nugget on her college ring. "You're burning up. Off to the nurse." She yanks me up light as paper and tosses me toward the exit.

The pack collapses, and Liv runs after me, grabbing my arm and whispering close to my ear. "It was like you went somewhere else. Where did you go?"

I look at her meaningfully.

"My God. You're remembering."

"Lately, yes."

Ms. Dean turns to the crowd. "Nothing to see here but a girl with Kuru disease. Lapin, back in line. Make teams for dodgeball!"

I smile lamely at the floor. There's something grounding about having a gym teacher straight from central casting screaming about dodgeball, the purest form of Darwinian selection in any high school. Shane Cuthbert, slouched on a bleacher until now, rises on loose legs and strolls over. He wears the required sweats and a ratty T-shirt with a smiley face, its eyes Xs, its tongue hanging out. Some girls think Shane is hot, with his inky hair and unnaturally blue, Siberian husky eyes, but never me.

31

He stands behind Liv, thumbs jammed deep in his pockets. He's always had a creepy thing for her. I glare at him above her shoulder.

Liv's eyes flicker all over my face.

"A-hem," Shane says, his nasal pitch cartoony.

Liv spins and he catches her wrist in the air, grinning, his eyes popping white.

"What do you want, Shane?" I say his name like a swear.

"Nothing you can give me, nutters. Weren't you heading to the nurse?"

I check Ms. Dean's coordinates. She's already heading back toward us, overdeveloped forearms pumping.

"Whatever you've got, it better not be contagious. I don't want my girl here catching it," he says, snaking his hand around Liv's waist.

I wait for Liv to twist away. Instead, she giggles.

My *girl*?

"Liv?" I rasp.

Shane's lank hair brushes Liv's cheek as he whispers something in her ear. She pulls away with a sour look, which he catches. She smooths it over with a quick smile. "You have a filthy mind," she says, swatting his chest with a fist. He explodes in a pratfall, sharp knees and elbows, a bug on its back. He grabs her ankle. She squeals and tries to shake him off, like it's the funniest thing in the world, so funny to get grabbed, but he'll let go before the ankle snaps, because it's Shane Cuthbert and not Donald Jessup and the panic lacing round my throat can stop now.

I've known Shane since kindergarten. He lives on the other side of Shiverton, where the walkways to tidy houses are lined with pansies in the summer and chrysanthemums in the fall. Every so often, you pass by one where the windows are glazed yellow and a car sits on the lawn. Donald Jessup lived in one of those houses. His mother still does. Shane's house is pretty nice, and by all accounts he's lucky to have it, because he was adopted from a Russian orphanage where prostitutes dump their unwanted babies. His real name was Alexei, but his parents renamed him Shane. In elementary school, Alexei-Shane couldn't sit still, so by seventh grade doctors put him on a rainbow of pills. When he missed half of sophomore year, everyone said he'd been sent to McLean Psychiatric Hospital, and got thrown out when he stabbed an orderly in the hand with a jackknife.

Shane clambers up, shaking hair from his eyes. He laughs, at me or at nothing, and his lips peel above a tooth lodged high on his gum. His hand settles on the small of Liv's back, steering her away. I cry, "Wait," but it's barely a whisper.

Slowly, his hand moves to his left pocket, so much bigger than the right, to a rectangular bulge, so much like a folded knife. My throat tightens.

"Liv!"

They turn, his smile in profile with that one misgrown tooth.

Her eyes are worried. Is she afraid of what I'm going to say? Or that I'm remembering again?

"What is it?" Liv says.

What is it? What?

"I'll see you after school," I say. "I'll come over. We'll do . . . statistics."

She cocks her head and squints like I'm daft. Then she laughs, not a real laugh, but like she knows other kids are watching. "Awesome. You can help me with independent and dependent events." As they turn back around, Shane slaps her hard on the butt.

Her shoulders clench. They stay. They do not fall.

I squeeze my elbows and hustle to the nurse's office. The nurse is missing, and this is good, because I'm learning the memories might surge fast, but they also cool and crust. It's best to record them fresh. Except my notebook is in my locker.

I look around the sterile exam room wildly. Stealing a pen from the nurse's desk, I tear a sheaf off the roll of exam table paper, and write:

Things I Know About Donald Jessup:
- Dopehead
- Losing his game
- Not what he expected (me)

THREE

Later

Lamplight burns the side of my face. I close my stats book and flatten my cheek against the cool nubs of Liv's white crocheted bedspread.

"They're hard to explain. I think of them as nightmares, only during the day," I say.

"A daymare," Liv says.

"Right. And it's not like watching a movie. I smell what I smelled. Sweet smoke and leaves. Alive and dead things underneath the leaves; that's a musty smell. The rain smelled like metal. I taste things, too. The beef jerky he gave me. Blood."

Liv winces. "What were you remembering in the gym?"

"That first night. The night he and I were together. The night I escaped. The next day and night I spent being hunted . . ."

Liv exhales loudly.

"Right. Sorry," I say, trying my best to "move forward and

all." "It was after we stopped. We couldn't go farther because it got dark, and he was tired of dragging me. I could barely walk. And he wanted to smoke a joint."

Liv twists her hair hard near her ear. "Did the joint make him, you know, talky?"

"Mainly he was jonesing to play his video game. He was worried other players would steal his weapons and his prey." I raise myself on my elbows. "You know about Prey better than I do. That's what he was playing, in his sick mind. But you know that."

Liv ignores my mild dig, releasing her hair and winding it around her fingers again, tighter. "How do they happen? The daymares."

"A trigger sometimes. Sometimes nothing at all. This last time, it was the cold."

She drops her hair. "This last time? How often do they happen?"

"Too often. In Ricker-speak they're called intrusive." I don't mention that I haven't gotten around to telling Ricker I have them.

"Can you make them stop?"

I shake my head. "I haven't been able to yet."

"You never told me about them in your e-mails."

The back door slams and the old Victorian house quakes. Keys clatter in a china bowl, the antique rimmed with gold Greek keys on the hall curio. Liv groans and rakes her hair with both hands.

"Olivia!" Deborah screams up the stairs.

"Should we go?" I say.

"I need a minute," she says.

"Then it's your turn," I say quickly. "Speaking of things unmentioned: Shane Cuthbert? When did that start? And why?"

She tips her head forward until her hair waterfalls onto the desk, and kneads her scalp. "I'm just fooling around." Her voice is muffled. "It's not serious."

"With Shane Cuthbert? You could have anyone!"

"Shane Cuthbert happens to be an exceptionally effective way of pissing off Deborah."

"I heard he got thrown out of McLean for stabbing an orderly. Is that true?"

"How would I know?"

"You're seeing him! He called you his girl."

"You're making a big deal out of nothing."

"Seeing Shane Cuthbert is not nothing. He's always been obsessed with you. Even if it's nothing to you, it's something to him, I'm sure of that. What happens after you use him to piss off Deborah? How will you ever get rid of him?"

She draws her hands through her hair hard. "I know exactly what I'm doing with Shane."

"Olivia! I know you're up there!"

She flips her hair back. "Down in a second!"

Deborah murmurs something sharp below. Liv fans her fingers in front of her, examining hair like floss—lots of it— threaded through each set of fingers, catching the desklamp light.

"Liv?"

She shakes her hands above the wire trash can under her desk.

"Your hair!" I say.

"Come down now, we have no time!" Deborah's voice is clearer now; she's moved to the gilt mirror at the bottom of the stairs. Liv slowly pushes away from her desk and trudges down the bare stairs, her steps hollow, the runner long ago stripped to wood and staples and left that way. I wait, wondering if I should bother to come, wondering if I want to. Slanted rain pelts the quarter moon–shaped window. Barring Deborah's box-of-chocolates persona (never know what you're gonna get), I've always felt at home here, especially in the cool, quirky attic bedroom, with its secret eaves and its *Amityville Horror* window. Now the house seems as if the rain might poke straight through. Before the woods, Deborah constantly renovated the Victorian like it was another whole being she cared for in reverse proportion to how much she cared for Liv. Now the repairs have ground to a halt. Curlicues of yellow paint speckle the tops of shrubs overtaking the porch, worn silver in spots. Today, the front doorknob fell off in my hand.

I stash my book in my backpack and head for the landing.

"That idiot hairdresser took forever and it was pouring by the time I left, and I had to wear my hood, and now I have static." From my spot, I can see Deborah leaning toward the hallway mirror, glaring at hair plastered against her cheek. "How will I ever fix this?"

"It gets worse if you touch it," Liv says, taking the last few stairs.

"I'm going to have to leave it alone, because we have less than two hours, and I still need to write down what I'm going to say to that reporter. I am so perpetually *rushed*. You could have started your own hair while I was out; you know how to mix the chemicals by now. Honestly, everyone on the planet is so selfish with my time."

Liv follows her into the kitchen and leans against the doorframe. The TV on the kitchen wall plays a commercial. I recognize the sounds: a savvy mom whips up a fancy chicken dish using a jar of mayonnaise, and the teenage son goes from dour to amazed. My stomach rumbles. In most homes in the Northeast region, it is the dinner hour.

"I had a terrible day at work. No one is satisfied with the schedule—the dentists want it full, the hygienists want breaks, and the assistants want time to clean the instruments. I have no energy left and a million things to do in less than two hours." Deborah pauses her rant. "Do not expect me to make some lavish dinner right now."

Liv sinks against the wall. "I do not expect you to."

Deborah heaves a dry sigh. "You know, you can be very difficult to love." I come from behind Liv just as Deborah reaches for a bottle of pinot noir from the lattice rack above the fridge.

"Olivia!" she exclaims. "You didn't tell me Julia was here." She sets the wine on the counter and swoops me in her arms, her chest hot through her blouse. "I thank God every time I see you." I feel her shove up her sleeve to check her watch behind my back.

Box of chocolates. Right after the woods, Deborah was grateful that I saved Liv. In the news footage of Mom pleading for my return, Deborah was right there, holding Mom up (though the opposite scenario was true: Deborah took Valium and could barely lift her eyelids). The news stations made a lot of the two-attractive-single-mothers angle, but the reporters cared mostly about Dr. Spunk, who managed to look elegant and calm during the worst two days of her life. Besides, Deborah had her daughter back, and Mom was still in that bad place. After I got home, the *Today* show asked Mom to host segments on missing children (she declined). For a while, Deborah was all about girl power and hugs. But then the frost set in. She never visited our house between the time I was released from the hospital and when we left for the Berkshires. Liv blamed it on her Valium detox, but finally she slipped that Deborah thought Mom and I liked the media attention a little too much.

"Liv probably didn't tell you that there's a reporter from the *Shiverton Star* coming over at seven thirty to interview me about being Catholic Woman of the Year, and he'll be photographing Liv and me together. I want to make sure she looks her best, so I planned a little pampering session. You should probably be heading home . . ."

Liv stares past Deborah to the TV. I follow her stare, and Deborah follows mine.

A reporter with a snub nose and a pancake face rests his foot on the railroad-tie stairs that mark the main entrance to the woods. His suit jacket flaps over his crotch in an unseen breeze. Behind him, yellow caution tape flutters between two young trees. The sign says MIDDLESEX FELLS RESERVATION: GATES CLOSE AT DUSK.

"I'm at the Middlesex Fells Reservation in Shiverton, where a couple out walking their dog yesterday afternoon stumbled upon a body many believe to be eighteen-year-old Ana Alvarez, who went missing while jogging in a remote section of this enormous wooded area in August of last year."

A thud, then *glug-glug-glug*. The wine bottle lies on its side, its nose pointing to a scarlet puddle. A rivulet makes its way to the middle of the island. No one moves to clean it up. The scene cuts to two women, Paula Papademetriou and a generic blonde, sitting in the WFYT studio.

"Ryan, has the body been positively identified?" Paula asks the on-scene reporter.

"That's what police are working on right now, Paula."

"Is this a murder investigation?" Paula asks.

"The police will not yet say. But many are wondering about the involvement of a man who attacked two high school students in the same area nearly one year ago. That man has since died in jail awaiting trial."

"You're referring to Donald Jessup, a man on parole at the time for earlier attacks against women in those same woods," Paula says.

"That's right, Paula. It sounds like the police may be explaining once again why a parolee was loose in these woods. This time, perhaps, with fatal consequences."

Paula folds her brow and leans in to ask more questions as

Deborah cuts her off with a wave of the clicker. She rushes toward Liv. "My baby!" she cries, pulling back and grabbing Liv's jaw. "Do you know how lucky you are to be alive?"

I wrinkle my nose at the smell of damp earth and cherries and turn away, embarrassed for Liv, embarrassed for Deborah for being the only person in the world who hasn't heard this story in the last forty-eight hours, and embarrassed for me, because hello, I'm pretty sure I was in the woods, too.

"Should we clean up the wine?" I ask.

Deborah releases Liv and flutters her hand at the TV. "But for the grace of God! The mother of that girl could have been me!"

"If we don't have time to do my hair, it's all right," Liv says.

"It's most certainly not all right! There's no chance those reporters aren't going to be sniffing around again now. We have to prepare, Olivia. What do you want, roots on live television?" She unravels a trail of paper towels and goes at the wine spill with a grunt. "This body in the woods is going to be a great big distraction, that's what it's going to be."

"You're telling me," I pipe up, just to say something. "Once in the Berkshires, a reporter camped out next to us on the concert lawn at Tanglewood."

"I'm talking about my award! This honor was planned last November, before the incident happened. It's like the world is out to thwart me. You need to promise me that you will not speak to any reporters about this latest bit of ugliness, even if that Ryan Lombardi comes around again, flattering you, Olivia." She drops the wine-soaked towels into the trash and turns to clear coffee mugs from the sink. "I'm sure your mother will say the same to you, Julia."

"What happened in the woods is over," I say, for Liv, even if I don't believe it for a second, because it's what Liv wants to hear, and she needs me on her side, having to deal every day with this big bag of crazy.

Liv smiles weakly. "Exactly."

Deborah tears open a box with a flaxen-haired girl on the front and expertly combines the contents of the two plastic bottles. The ammonia smell is acrid and instantaneous, and it singes my nostrils. I hold my breath.

"So, I'll see you at school tomorrow. Stay well, okay?" Liv says, then turns to Deborah. "Julia got sick in gym."

Deborah raises an eyebrow as she peels thin clear gloves from a sheet of directions, the tearing sound a perfunctory note of dismissal.

"Right." I glance back to say "You stay well, too," but Deborah already has her hand on the back of Liv's neck, drawing perfect rows of poison down her scalp.

I've been rinsing the salad greens for minutes before I notice they're wilting. The oven timer is buzzing, which means the chicken is nice and crispy, but I ignore that, too. I was determined to have dinner ready by the time Mom changed out of her wet clothes, a little dig for being later than she said she'd be, on a rainy night when she should have known I wouldn't want to be alone, because I despise rain nearly as much as trees, the cold, and sociopaths. But then I got to thinking about Liv's perverse interest in Shane, and the body, and whether what happened in the woods is really over, and suddenly the mesclun was mush. And the phone's been flashing. Voice mail can wait, because surely it's Ricker, the only person who calls the house phone, asking how does the news of a body in the woods make me feel, exactly? Also, what were my thoughts before collapsing in gym? I wrinkle my nose at the phone and reposition the remaining grocery bags, so Mom will see them when she hustles downstairs and act sheepish because her work is creeping right back in where it was before the woods, to that place that comes before me.

Blink after spastic blink. "Easy, Ricker," I murmur, wiping my hands on my jeans. Raindrops thrum the skylight over my head. I glance up warily as I cross the room to the phone and press Play.

"This is Paula Papademetriou calling for Julia Spunk." The voice is husky and confidential.

I run from the kitchen to the bottom of the stairs and look up. A crack of light glows under Mom's bedroom door.

"I'd like to talk with you about the recent developments in the Middlesex Fells Reservation," she says, and then she leaves her personal cell phone number.

I tear back to the kitchen and scan the counter. The glazed clay fish I made in fifth grade to hold pencils contains only lead dust. Mom's door squeaks open; her feet thump down the stairs, quick, like a child's. I grab a box of aluminum foil off the counter, tear off a sheet, and lay it flat, using my fingernail to scrape digits into the silver as she enters the kitchen.

"Honey, the timer," she says.

I hunch my shoulders, fold the foil into a triangle, and drop it into the fish's mouth. "Give it five more minutes."

"Is everything all right?" she asks me.

I catch her gazing into the sink at the colander of green mush. "The mesclun was dirty. Gritty dirty." I rush to the stove and bang at the timer, avoiding her eyes. I'm acting crazy, speaking way too fast, but I can't slow down. "Better safe than sorry. Did you know a woman found a black widow spider in a bunch of supermarket grapes?"

Mom unlatches her silver bead necklace and sets it on the granite counter with a pretty click. "Can't say that I did." She meets me at the stove and pushes my hair behind my ear, frowning. "How are you handling the awful news?"

"News?"

"About that poor girl."

"Oh that. I don't know. Aren't I supposed to wait for Elaine Ricker to tell me how to handle it?"

"Chilly night." She turns away and rubs opposite arms, heading for the sink. "We can talk about it later. If you want to. Or not." She covers the lettuce with a paper towel and pats it carefully. "Who called?"

"Oh, the voice mail? That was a reporter." I hold my breath.

"Leaving their personal number? Pushy."

She heard more than I thought. "It's just the same old," I say.

"If only it were. Dr. Ricker warned me that this new discovery in the woods would rekindle the media's interest in you. I didn't want to do this during Girls' Night, but that call makes it clear: we need to talk about how we'll manage intrusions into our privacy."

As if having reporters crouching in the bushes outside our house last fall, or setting blankets next to ours on the Tanglewood lawn last summer, was manageable. That's the special talent of Gwen Spunk, biomedical engineer. MacArthur Genius Award winner at the tender age of thirty-five. Survivor of Having Your Child Abducted. Other moms pop Valium. Mine strategizes.

"Dr. Ricker advises a no-tolerance policy when it comes to the media," she says. "I agree."

"She mentioned that. I don't see how local news reporters are the enemy. In fact, to hear Paula Papademetriou tell it, the police are the ones who screwed up by not watching Donald Jessup in the first place."

"Dealing with reporters isn't useful to your healing. In fact, quite the opposite."

I consider pointing out that spending hours alone after school during torrential downpours is not useful to my healing. Instead, I grunt.

She sticks her index fingers into the ends of her eyes and stretches them into slits. "By the way, which reporter was it?"

"Ryan Lombardi," I lie, tossing out a name less likely to ping Mom's radar, since Paula was way aggressive last time around.

"Is Ryan a woman?"

"Ryan is a man."

"That's odd. I thought I heard a woman's voice."

"Nope."

"Male or female, we aren't letting a reporter ruin Girls' Night," she says.

Every night is Girls' Night. From a medical perspective, Erik Meijer is my father, but that's pretty much the extent of it. I'm not even supposed to know Erik was Mom's sperm donor, but I figured it out around age ten, and since then it's been a silent understanding among the three of us, along the lines of Santa Claus. I know the truth, Mom and Erik get that I know the truth, but talking about it would spoil the magic. My discovery is based on our identical looks (Erik is half-Japanese and half-Dutch, which for us translates into being tall, with blue almond-shaped eyes, oval faces, and pale skin, for me, with a dusting of freckles), and, more directly, the legal paperwork Mom keeps on the family desktop outlining said sperm donor's parental rights (none). Keeping my knowledge on the down-low saves me from taking a stand if vague tensions erupt, as they inevitably do, when Mom feels Erik is overstepping. Despite all this unspoken weirdness, Erik's always been devoted to Mom, especially when she didn't get tenure, and apparently that's some kind of learn-who-your-real-friends-are moment. It's mutual, because when Erik was being wooed away from her lab by the big Ivy across the Charles River, Mom was beside herself until he rejected their offer.

How she resists an übersmart, ridiculously fit hottie who's

devoted to her and gave her his guys to produce a fabulous kid like me is another question entirely.

Mom circles behind me and reaches up to give my shoulders a gentle squeeze. "What's in the oven? It smells like chicken."

"Bingo."

"Really lovely, Julia."

I should admit it's precooked supermarket rotisserie chicken, but she's already yelling into the fridge. "Thanks for getting dinner going! The rain had traffic at a standstill! Did you know the Aberjona overflowed and they closed Main Street?"

"I notice rain, yes," I say.

She produces a bruised onion triumphantly. "This should perk up the salad."

I take the onion and set to work at the cutting board. The knife gets stuck in the mealy layers. "I don't care that you were late," I lie. It's a fine line, wanting Mom around, but not wanting Mom around as much as in the Berkshires.

"I care." She cups her hand over mine. "I'll slice. You finish the salad."

I drop the knife and move to the sink. Mom chatters about a dating epidemic among her latest crop of postdocs while I squint through the window. Somewhere in that purple darkness is an improbably gorgeous, rolling grass lawn. We are the last people in the world who should have a backyard, given that Mom spends most of her life under artificial light and I'm afraid of trees in any number. Yet there's our backyard, a rarity in Shiverton, where grand colonials and Victorians are wedged into lots the size of postage stamps. We even have a deck and Adirondack chairs, price tags still tied to the legs.

The knife slices, onion to wood, *chop, chop, chop,* a solid noise that I should like, but it flicks at my belly.

"Truth be told, I had a difficult day," Mom says. "The rhythm gets lost when the lab director goes on sabbatical. Grievances take root among the more difficult personalities. And obviously I feel guilty about being late for dinner again. Perhaps it's not the best night to strategize. I'm not thinking clearly."

"It's not like I'm going to call her back," I say.

The knife hangs in the air. "Her?" she says.

"Him. I meant him."

Mom smiles tightly at the board and starts a vigorous hand-over-hand chop. "The Berkshires are looking better every minute." She catches my alarm at my slip and misinterprets it. "Don't worry, we're not going anywhere."

I manage a fake laugh. "Speaking of difficult personalities, I saw Mrs. Lapin today. She hasn't changed."

"Still hard on Liv?"

"You could say that. Actually, she's worried the reporters are going to start up again, too. Because, you know, they might catch her off guard, when her hair isn't perfect. Or Liv's hair isn't perfect. That would be worse, I think."

Mom grimaces, slipping on quilted mitts and pulling the chicken from the oven. Its taut skin crackles. The smell fills the kitchen, and I know it's heavenly, and that I should feel hunger, but there's nothing.

"We all have different coping mechanisms," Mom says.

"Deborah is a narcissist so obsessed with her daughter's shiny image that Liv isn't *allowed* to cope." I rinse the cutting board and wash the knife. "She barely gives Liv room to breathe. Now Liv's seeing Shane Cuthbert, which is wrong on so many levels."

"Liv was always a bit fickle. Maybe her tastes have changed."

"Shane tastes like rancid meat, trust me. Or like pot. A pot-burger," I say.

"I remember him as a handsome kid. Friendships evolve, Julia. Maybe you're reacting to the fact that the Liv you've returned to junior year isn't the same Liv."

"Friendships *evolve*?"

"What Liv went through was horrific, but it wasn't half of what you experienced. Maybe she truly is okay. And you've just outgrown each other. I know that's hard to accept."

I throw the knife into the sink with a clatter. "We've outgrown each other?"

Mom's shoulders freeze. She searches for a spot to rest the pan, but the counter is cluttered with paper bags, and the table is ten steps away. She's trapped, and she has to listen to me. Because the black thing is here in the kitchen with us.

"I mean, you have an inquisitive mind. A really, really good mind. And sometimes we look for answers that aren't actually there because we don't want to face the reality that things have changed," Mom says.

"That's a load of bullshit."

"Don't be crude." Her mitts tighten on the sides of the pan, and the fat underneath the chicken lists. "This is getting heavy."

"Something's off with Liv," I insist. "You don't refuse to talk about an experience, however awful, with the only other person in the world who understands what it was like to go through it. Nor do you start dating a half Orc. Suggesting that Liv has outgrown her friendship with me is your not-so-subtle way of implanting the idea in my head because you don't want me to hang around with her."

Mom grips the edges of the pan. "That's untrue."

"You probably feel like what happened to that girl Ana shows how dangerous it was to save Liv. Like it proves some lesson," I say.

"How could you ever say such a thing? I'm not a monster!" she says.

"You never liked Liv. I did the right thing by saving her, but you hate her so much you couldn't even be proud of me."

"You think you did the right thing."

"I know I did!" I step forward and Mom jumps. The pan tips and fat splashes across her left arm. She cries out. I cover my hands with a kitchen rag and grab the pan, and she bolts to the sink, wrenching on the cold-water valve. The smell of burned flesh and butter fills the kitchen.

"Mom?"

Pain twists her mouth. She looks away.

"I'm so sorry," I say softly.

She shuts off the water and inspects the mark, blazing pink. I set the pan on the table and spread paper towels on a spray of fat congealing on the tile. She blows at the burn while digging one-handedly in the junk drawer for wound salve. When she finally climbs onto the leather counter stool, arm slathered in goo, I hold my breath, waiting for her to say something bouncy, like "At least I'm a righty!" or "If you didn't want chicken, you should have said so!"

She blows on her arm. This time, her eyes are closed. Outside, wind chimes tinkle helplessly in the bluster.

"Mom?"

"I'm always proud of you."

"I know."

"I don't hate Liv. But sometimes I do think there are better friends for you. Remember Alice next door? Whatever happened to Alice Mincus?"

"Mom," I whisper. "I haven't hung around with Alice since fifth grade."

Her eyes open and settle on me, the fine skin underneath newly crosshatched and gray. "A mother wants the best for her daughter. That is all. Can we just be quiet for a few minutes?"

Deborah wanted things for Liv, too. Different things. The pageant career she blew when she had Liv, for one. Living in the Northeast stunted that, since pageant culture is more foreign to New England than sweet tea and hush puppies. Then there was the virtuous persona that Liv resisted. When we were thirteen, Liv got the idea to meet this guy she liked and ride the T into

Boston to see a free concert. His name was Stevie Something, and he was seventeen. Which doesn't seem old now, until I think about a guy around my age dating a thirteen-year-old. Liv told Deborah she was going to my house, and I told Mom the reverse, and we took a bus to Parlee, the next town over. We met Stevie Jerkface and a friend, Nameiforget, who was supposed to be my "date" except that I don't think he was expecting a flat-chested child. Stevie Jerkface was drunk or high, and Liv giggled nonstop while we waited on the platform. Once we got on the train, the Jerky twins shared nips that smelled like pinecones. I refused, got called a word I'd never heard, and we were abandoned at the next stop—Savin Hill, or as the locals call it, Stab 'n' Kill. At which point a large homeless woman in a dress boarded the train and wandered around the car. When she bent over, we saw she wasn't wearing underwear. And that she'd been using newspapers as toilet paper, because they were still stuck there. I vomited in my mouth. Liv buried her face in my sternum. The story ended when we begged a T cop to ride the train home with us to Parlee and called Mom, throwing ourselves at her mercy.

So when Mom suggests Liv is a questionable influence, I can't deny it. But together we have history. An undeniably funny history.

Mom slides off the stool and digs through her bag for Advil, twisting the cap with her teeth and knocking back two. "I think it's important that we see Dr. Ricker together. Sort through all your questions. She thinks your obsession with the case is getting in the way of your progress."

"Actually, Dr. Ricker is on board with my approach. She even wants to hypnotize me to regain my lost memories."

Mom looks sideways at me.

"It's either that, or play with dolls," I add.

"That sounds a bit . . . regressive."

"Regressive would be hanging around with my friend from elementary school."

"Alice has always been good to you," Mom protests.

"I believe you mean good for you."

Mom pops a third Advil. I wish she would laugh.

"Let's talk about Deborah again. She's beside herself about the girl in the woods," I say. "To the extent that she could have been her mother. That would have been upsetting."

Mom chokes. I slap her back, fearing I might break every fine bone through her shirt. She waves me away. I pour her a glass of water and continue. "Also, the news will take away from her Catholic Woman of the Year announcement, which is clearly a competing local news item. I don't know how WFYT is going to decide which to cover."

"Try to cut Deborah Lapin some slack, please," Mom rasps as she pads across the kitchen and eases a glass from the hanging wine rack. "You're not being respectful."

I serve the meal that neither of us wants, tonging soggy salad onto our plates. The suction sound of Mom opening the wine fridge is the tearing off of a figurative bandage: a natural marker for a scene change.

So I go there.

"What happens if the woman in the woods has some connection to Donald Jessup?" I ask.

"Then the police will find that out. And hopefully, her family will have some closure," Mom says, filling her glass to the top with pale wine. "But that's not a story you have to follow. It doesn't have import for you."

"Kind of hypocritical, don't you think? Criticizing me, given you're someone who spends your whole life questing for knowledge."

She moves her wineglass in a slow circle. "You make my life sound like a Homeric epic."

"A scientist's mandate is to question," I say.

"Not when the question is irrelevant," she says.

"Relevance is an elusive concept. Its meaning is impossible to capture through logic."

"Something is relevant to a task if it increases the likelihood of accomplishing the goal. Your task is healing; your goal is to be well." Mom swirls the straw-colored liquid. "Trying to make connections between yourself and Ana Alvarez is not healing, and it will not make you well." The windowpane above the sink rattles in its casing.

"I take it you'll be drinking your dinner this evening?" I rise and stack her full plate on my empty one.

Mom points with her glass. "Maybe everything's not as complicated as you think it is."

"You're the one who taught me to think critically. That most stories are not black and white."

"On the color spectrum, black and white represent the highest level of contrast to the human eye. Maybe viewing a situation in black and white is seeing critically," she says, smiling as she turns it over in her mind, annoyingly mellow.

"Okay, here's black and white for you. According to the National Center for Missing and Exploited Children, there are approximately 258,000 child abductions each year. Only 115 children are abducted by strangers. That's four one-hundredths of one percent of total abductions, and fourteen one-thousandths of one percent of total children reported missing. The odds of Donald Jessup stumbling upon Liv, me, and Ana Alvarez in the woods by chance is infinitesimal. So what does that mean? It may mean nothing. You can look at it as a fluke, or you can consider the alternative. I'd think a Mac-Arthur Genius would have no trouble seeing that." I blow past her and dump the plates into the sink with a clatter. "Perhaps you can act like the mother and fill the dishwasher tonight."

Mom's smile dissolves. "Donald Jessup is dead, Julia." She sets her glass on the counter and reaches for her phone. "I need to speak with Dr. Ricker."

As she shuffles away, texting, I snatch the tinfoil wedge from the fish mug and tuck it into my jeans pocket. I throw my messenger bag over my shoulder, the hard spine of my notebook sticking out of the top at a jaunty angle, and head for the stairs.

She stops texting and suddenly looks up. "Homework?"

"Tons," I yell, charging up the stairs and slamming my bedroom door. I scoot down in my bed with the laptop against my bent knees and bring up the WFYT Web site. A new headline inside a banner blazes across the top: PAROLE BOARD CHIEF UNDER FIRE. I click it to see Paula, her dark hair brushed behind one ear, the other side in a vintage Hollywood wave. Square red fingernails pop from the cuffs of her cheetah trench coat and gleam on the microphone. Behind her are trees, stark in the camera's blazing light.

"One year after the Shiverton Abduction, WFYT wants to know why parolee and convicted sex offender Donald Jessup was not properly monitored when he attempted to kidnap two teenage girls"—wave of one lacquered hand—"from this wooded enclave on the edge of the suburb of Shiverton, last fall."

THE SHIVERTON ABDUCTION: ONE YEAR LATER materializes in front of a graphic of silhouetted pine trees. Then the Fells entrance is gone, and it's Paula, sitting in an office across a desk from a guy wearing a purple tie and a badge plate. He has a long, Roman face, sunken cheeks, and shadows under thick-lidded eyes. Across the bottom of the screen reads PAROLE BOARD CHIEF VALERIO PANTANO.

Paula scissors her legs and leans forward.

"Donald Jessup was on parole following his 2010 conviction of stalking a woman with intent to harm, before he brutally attacked two females in the Middlesex Fells Reservation in November 2013. Mr. Pantano, who is responsible for monitoring serial offenders on parole?" Paula asks.

"The governor is convening an outside committee to examine the monitoring of Mr. Jessup," Pantano says.

"Was it the psychiatrist who treated Donald Jessup following his conviction in 2010? Who said, and I quote: 'His prognosis is excellent. I do not suspect he will ever be at risk for violence'?" Paula says.

"I am not qualified to speak toward his psychiatrist's findings," Pantano responds.

"Was it the probation officer who rarely visited Jessup at his home, never talked with neighbors or local police to know if he violated his parole, and ignored complaints by coworkers at the GameStop where he worked that Mr. Jessup made them feel uncomfortable?"

"The actions of the probation officer in question are being examined internally," Pantano says.

"Or is it the seven members of the Massachusetts parole board who granted parole to this high-risk offender? The seven men and women appointed by the governor who decided Donald Jessup should be allowed back on the streets of Shiverton, so that he could strike again?" Paula presses.

Pantano runs the tip of his pinky finger over a ring on the other hand.

"The seven men and women who directly report to you?" Paula adds.

Pantano grimaces. "I cannot say that the parole board or the police did all they could to ensure public safety."

"Let me be clear: you're telling me you cannot say that the parole board or the police did all they could to ensure public safety," Paula repeats.

Pantano twists his gold ring hard.

"The governor is convening an outside committee to examine the monitoring of Mr. Jessup, who has since committed suicide while awaiting sentencing in custody at the Massachusetts Correctional Institution at Cedar Junction, as you know. I have no conclusions at this time," Pantano says.

Switch to the studio, and the pancake-faced reporter, now in the anchor chair, asks Paula if what they just heard is the department's official statement.

"You heard him, Ryan," she says. "Parole Board Chief Valerio Pantano cannot say that the parole board or the police did all they could to ensure public safety. We'll keep following this story as it develops. Live in Shiverton, I'm Paula Papademetriou. Back to you."

I whistle. "Damn, girl," I murmur.

My last thought before I fall asleep is of a severed pinky finger in a box.

I wake in the predawn dim with an anger hangover. The memories come at night now, more vivid than the daymares. So real that I'm lying here thoroughly pissed, because I remember the days after the woods, in the hospital, like it just happened. I'd been ready to cry with Liv, looked forward to a good, long, cleansing cry, one that included survivor high fives and hugs. Instead, she had observed me with an alien lack of empathy, refusing to acknowledge my busted ankle, my terror, or the fact that I took her place in hell.

Everything had looked creamy from the morphine drip, lit

from within, with glowing trails coming off the nurses' fingers as they tended to my IV and adjusted the traction ropes that held my foot. The blue fluorescent bar above my head made Liv look angelic.

"You went to heaven," I'd said, all dopey.

"I went where?" Liv asked.

"Never mind. It's the drugs. You came. How'd you get out?"

"I sprinkled a ground-up Ambien in Deborah's pinot noir and begged a ride from Boseman."

Liv's cousin Boseman was a party hanger-on who stunk of cloves and always looked me up and down with skittery eyes. He was at least twenty-four and made beer runs for the whole school, taking too much money and skimming off the top.

"I'm glad you came," I said.

"Of course I came." Liv stared at the IV taped to my hand.

"Where's my mom?"

Mom hadn't left my side. She slept in a vinyl chair under a blanket and ate leftover Jell-O off my tray. I figured Erik had finally dragged her to get something real to eat. Later, I found out she'd been in the parking lot arguing with a reporter doing a stand-up, which is when they plop themselves at the scene of the action, like town hall or a burning house. And that Liv had bumped into her on the way in.

"I have no idea," Liv said. I don't know why she lied.

"So she doesn't know you're here," I said, sulking. Even half-sedated, I wanted Mom to see what a good friend Liv was, checking up on me.

"Did you really think I was dead?" Liv asked.

"No. I get confused. Like I said, it's the pain medicine." I held up the round end of my morphine pump. It had a button in the middle that I pushed every hour. The other end was tipped with a cannula that delivered the drug into my spine. Every part of me hurt, but mostly my ankle, the one Donald Jessup snapped. Ropes and pulleys forced my body to form new bone to repair the break: an impressive contraption that you might mention if you were seeing it for the first time.

"I bet the morphine confuses things. Makes your memories unreliable. But all things considered, that's probably best. Forgetting, in order to move on," Liv said.

"There are gaps. But I remembered his face enough to ID him. And the things he said."

Liv's smile went stiff, as though she caught it before it slipped away. "Things?"

I shimmied down into my blanket a touch. Jessup's voice was still in my head: the jangly shouts and the sharp orders. The stammering when he was jonesing. The spooky calmness when he arrived at an idea. "He talked a lot."

"Did you tell the police what he said?"

Her question confused me. "They weren't interested in what he said to me. They were interested in what he did to me."

"You weren't raped. They told me you weren't raped," Liv said quickly.

There are other violations. Like forcing someone to see something in a pit that will haunt them forever.

"I wasn't raped." I said it wearily.

"See? We're both fine now." She reached for my hand, but I left it there, tethered to its needle.

"Why are you downplaying it?" I said.

She grabbed my other hand and patted it enthusiastically. "I'm simply trying to say we're okay."

"We're okay now." I sounded sour. For a second, I had wished I was her, unblemished and upbeat. Already looking ahead. Maybe I could act normal too, if I could get the fractals of my memory and how Liv was acting right then to make sense. "Can I ask you a question?" I said.

"Yes?" Liv said.

"What did you do after you got away?"

Liv asked if I was chilly and didn't wait for my answer. She pulled the sheet to my chin and perched on the bed, speaking mechanically, with measured beats and pauses. "I ran back down the trail. I had no cell—you had yours, remember?— so I had to drive all the way home before I could call the police. They went and looked for you, exactly where I told them, where the Hill crests, to the exact spot where I—"

"Left me."

She sighed like I was a child.

"Were you with them? The searchers?" I asked.

"Everyone was there. The whole town came out, it was over the top"—*Did she roll her eyes?*—"you'd just vanished."

"Were you there looking for me?" I had to force myself to be still under my blanket.

"I wanted to," she said, smoothing the blanket across my

chest. "But they wouldn't let me. I had to be examined. Make my report. Besides, they said if I went back in the woods, it would distract the volunteers."

"They wouldn't let you?" I asked.

"Of course not. I mean, he was still out there," she said.

"So was I."

Liv stared hard at the muted TV, twisting a bit of blanket between her fingers. Red, white, and blue streamers rippled across the screen and dissolved into stars that chased one another in a circle and split to re-form the number three. I'd memorized all the promos: *Trust WFYT—the Friend You Can Trust!—for the local angle on the biggest miracle-recovery story since Elizabeth Smart.* Paula Papademetriou folded her arms and nodded. I softened a little, watching Liv frown and pick at the cotton weave, and considered asking what she thought of Paula Papademetriou, just to break the tension.

"To be honest, as long as we're fine, it's really not a big deal," Liv said.

Her words hurt more than my junk ankle and my briar-shredded back and my hypothermic hands and feet. I twisted on my hip and faced the wall. After a while she left. I rolled back and felt under the sheets for my morphine pump, grabbing the TV remote in my other hand. By then the twenty-four-hour news stations had picked up the story. Every show had some version of the same opening shot—the main entrance to the woods, its trees blanched dry and pale in the camera lights. The woods I knew were wet and black. Newscasters used phrases like *plucky teen* and *heroine* and *remarkable courage*.

When one segment ended, I found another on a different station. Some channels covered my story twice in the same hour. The story became more horrific with every telling, proving that we'd been through hell, and that Liv should have been relieved that we were alive, grateful we both made it out, and shocked that it had happened. Yet she was none of these things. And I wanted to know why.

After a while, I let the morphine pump fall, and swore I'd never let anything cloud my mind again.

My alarm blasts Kiss 108. I roll over and hammer the top with my fist, then feel for the thick glasses I abandoned for contacts in sixth grade. My notebook lies, propped on its fanned pages, spine-up on the floor next to my bed. The memory trails off like the ends of clouds. I grab a pen and scribble in the growing light:

Things I Know About Liv:
- Drove home before calling the police
- Said my memory is unreliable
- Lied

FOUR

355 Days After the Woods

Principal Ligand splits his pants as he mounts the brick wall, unsteady in wingtips. He yanks down the back of his tweed jacket. Someone hands him an electronic bullhorn.

"All students must now report to their homerooms!" He turns side to side like he has a rod in his back. "If you do not enter the school now, you will be marked tardy."

A line of male teachers stand with their arms crossed like undersized bouncers. We huddle in clumps, the bus kids and the kids whose parents drop them off, and the ones who drive, like me, all standing outside in the bright, cold morning ignoring Ligand and his visible boxers along with the first bell. We shift and shiver and steal looks at the white vans with their curlicue cables and satellite dishes parked in a wagon circle around the WELCOME TO SHIVERTON HIGH SCHOOL! HOME OF THE CHIEFTAINS! sign. The WFYT van has driven up on the grass, its wheels sinking in the mud. The crowd of students gives off a dangerous, honing energy looking for a place to land. A pack forms around a boy named Ari, the son of a wealthy computer executive and a leader because of his brutal sarcasm and contempt for authority. He dashes across the driveway and a patch of butterscotch grass, circling the vans and disappearing behind the welcome sign. Two boys shove each other until one, then the other, follows Ari across the grass.

The kids near the wall dissolve, and there is Liv near the curb. She stands stiffly, feet together, wearing a cropped puffer jacket and pencil jeans, an arc of space between her legs. She spots me and holds my eye, her mouth a line of fear. I close my eyes for a second and try to shed the anger from last night's stupid dream. I start toward her. At the same moment, the crowd follows the boys and Ari, and I am swept onto the lawn, pressed in among morning smells of body spray and clean hair. Everyone ignores the drunken sounds of Ligand garbling into his megaphone. Ari scales the back of the sign and pokes his head over the top, balancing on his stomach and waving his hands over a reporter's head. When the camera light trained on him dies, the reporter shoves up the sleeves of his logoed half-zip and charges behind the sign. Ari and the two boys fly back across the lawn to cheers.

A black SUV pulls up on the grass. Everyone buzzes and cranes to see if it's really her, because everyone in Shiverton claims to be six degrees from Paula Papademetriou. The thrill of seeing Paula in her official capacity is infectious. They speculate that she's in her own car because she probably came straight here, maybe from Starbucks, because someone saw her there in her tennis skirt last week. And in the long line for the pharmacy at CVS. Buying kale at the farmers' market on the town common. A lot of TV people are tiny in real life, but Paula is tall—not Madonna-sized, not fun-sized, they say. Serious and real.

Her hair is the color of espresso and brushed straight back from her face, which is made of angles and hard planes. We jam our hands in our pockets and huddle against the brisk November morning air, but she looks at ease, coatless in a pantsuit. She holds notes that she passes to a man crouching nearby as the camera starts to roll. Her camera voice is lower than in real life; I know this because I've heard her at the organic pizza place, holding a glass of chardonnay at a tall table. Mom and I were on the other side of a hedge of plastic plants. That night, her voice matched the high, shrieky voices of the other mothers. This voice is much better.

"A real-life horror story is unfolding here in Shiverton, now that police have identified the body of eighteen-year-old Ana Alvarez, who went missing while jogging in a remote section of the Middlesex Fells Reservation in August 2013. The police will not say exactly where she was found, only that her death is suspicious. Alvarez was a freshman at Tufts University School of Veterinary Medicine, and sources tell me that officials have seized her computer and smartphone in their investigations into whether or not she knew her killer. I'm here at Shiverton High School, where the two students who were attacked last November by the man many believe is the prime suspect in Alvarez's murder are enrolled as juniors. That man, Donald Jessup, committed suicide in jail while awaiting trial. This latest development only intensifies the scrutiny local law enforcement faces, as new questions are raised about this predator who many say should have been under the strict surveillance of the police."

The light dims and Paula crouches, shuffling papers. She holds a phone to her ear and looks up at the cameraman, wrinkles layering her forehead.

Liv appears before me. Up close, I can see that her pupils are a shade too large, and her hair hangs in matte clumps.

"What do we do?" she asks, her voice pitchy.

"We stay together," I say.

My phone vibrates in my back jeans pocket. I wonder if it's Mom, mobilized and ready to dismiss me from school. My hand drifts to my phone. Paula pops up and peers into the student mass. The cameraman follows her gaze and rips off his baseball cap. The mob swells as Ligand's voice grows hoarse. I step back and get shoved from behind, taking Liv with me. A circle widens around us. A pug-faced senior named Seamus points at me.

"She's over here! They're both over here!" Seamus yells toward the vans.

"Oh my God," murmurs Liv.

Paula charges toward us holding her mike like a torch trailed by the man balancing his camera on his shoulder. The reporter in the half-zip follows behind. To my right, I feel the sounds of a scuffle, *thump-thump-oomph*, less a noise than a vibration, someone shoving and someone shoving back. I turn to see Seamus bouncing on his toes and snapping his head to his shoulder like a boxer. Strings of spit fly from his mouth as he curls his fingers, beckoning a boy with his back to us, hair curled around the edges of a purple hoodie.

I know that back.

Kellan MacDougall aims a roundhouse punch at Seamus's skull, and Seamus ducks just in time, covering his head with his arms. Girls scream. Seamus sends a hook to Kellan's sternum while he's off-balance. Kellan staggers for a second, then lunges for Seamus. They lock arms and teeter like drunks. The circle around them widens, and I step back numbly along with them. Kellan bear-hugs Seamus, whose face turns white as Kellan draws his knee into his gut and leaves Seamus crumpled on the grass.

Liv shrieks. The reporters are almost upon us.

A hand grabs me by the waist. I grasp the inside of Liv's arm and squeeze, thumb to bone. We follow the back of Kellan's head, past bookish types clutching books to their chests and musical types holding their instruments in front of them like shields and more boys, intoxicated by Seamus's blood, swinging wildly at anyone who will swing back at them. Kids scatter to the student parking lot, taking advantage of the distraction to hit Starbucks. When we reach Kellan's dented Jeep Cherokee, I rest my arm on the car to catch my breath, but Kellan pushes my head down cop-and-perp-style and shoves me into the backseat.

"We can't leave," I say.

"You want to pick your way back through that mob and get crushed?" Kellan says. "Make room, incoming!"

Liv lands in my lap. Kellan jumps into the driver's seat and peels out. Liv springs upright and yells, "Let me out!"

"You hear that siren? Ligand called the cops. If I stop now, I'll need to explain why I slugged Ligand's nephew. I'm thinking for now I'd like to remain Anonymous Hooded Student, even if that nephew is the biggest drug dealer at Shiverton. Then there's what my father's going to think about this."

Liv digs in her backpack and pulls out a pack of cigarettes. Her fingertips are blue and shaky. She tries to light one skinny stick.

My eyes pop. "You *smoke* now?" I ask her.

Kellan eyes her in the rearview mirror, and calls back, "Not in my truck!"

Liv jams the cigarette into the pack until it snaps. Swearing, she fights to roll down the sticky window and tosses the broken butt into the wind.

"Couldn't spring for electric windows?" Liv asks.

"Wow, you're welcome," Kellan says.

"Thank you for saving us," I say, embarrassed for Liv. Apparently her one-time hook-up with Kellan left things awkward. Kellan is hot, beyond hot, and beyond me. He's also smart, and nice to everyone. Thus everyone loves him. I love him. Whereas I'd been over the moon after Liv's conquest, the day after, she barely said "meh." Liv could get anyone, but she never truly crushes on any one guy. When she does hook

70

up, she does it grudgingly, as a response to the attention the guy is giving her, the equivalent of petting a puppy. I always figure she's picky, but in the back of my mind I wonder if Deborah screwed her up in some related way, that all her crazy axioms—"The worst lies are the lies women tell to themselves. That a man will love them if they let themselves slip, even the tiniest bit" or, "You stole my figure. Now you'd better take care of it" And the worst, "You can be very difficult to love"— left something dead inside Liv. Accepted truths that made her unable to care about anybody. Guys were too much work, especially if the odds of being loved were so slim.

I feel for nonexistent seat belts.

"So where are we going?" Liv says, her temple pressed against the glass, her hand limp on the seat between us. Her sleeve is hiked up, exposing an odd new thatch of golden down on her forearm.

"I hadn't thought past smacking down a stoner and taking a hit in the gut," Kellan says, flexing his knuckles on the steering wheel, examining his cuts.

"Are you hurt?" I ask.

"I usually wear hockey gloves when I throw punches," he says, smiling back at me.

Liv pulls out a white plastic bottle. The label screams, *Now with caffeine!* She shakes out two horse-sized pills that smell like licorice and tosses them to the back of her throat.

"What are those?" I ask.

"Herbal energy supplement. Yo, up front!" Liv yells. "Can you drive a little more smoothly?"

71

"Sorry, my truck doesn't have shocks," Kellan explains.

Liv presses the heel of her hand to her skull. "Well, you're hurting my head immeasurably, MacDickwad."

Kellan does a double take past his headrest. "Excuse me?"

"You heard me," Liv says.

"Did you just call me a dickwad?" he says.

"MacDickwad," she replies.

I rush to speak. "Liv gets mean when she's nervous."

Liv narrows her eyes at me.

"But it's true. You get snappish when you're frightened," I say.

"Who said I was frightened?"

"Listen. I get that you two went through something," Kellan says. "I'm sure it was terrible. But that's no excuse to be so rude."

"You didn't have to rescue me, MacDickwad," Liv says.

"I'm sorry. You would have preferred getting trampled and/ or totally exploited by some slimy reporter?" Kellan says.

"You're just pissed at Paula Papademetriou because she's exposing the police for the lame job they did keeping a paroled predator off the streets. Your daddy doesn't look so good anymore, does he?" Liv taunts.

My hand reaches for the notebook inside my bag. I need to make notes while they're fresh, stare at the page until it means something.

veterinary, computer, smartphone, killer
cantaloupe rinds, silver wrappers, water bottles, sneakers

I feel kidnapped and anxious. The connections between what I heard Paula say at the schoolyard and what I saw in the pit want to be made now, and all this driving and arguing is a waste of precious time.

Kellan takes the winding border road that leads to the highway and merges into the rotary, looping and exiting again in the same spot. "You ladies have any particular destination in mind? Because I'm feeling really good about chauffeuring you two right about now."

"No one asked you to," Liv says.

It becomes clear. I must see exactly where Ana was found.

Kellan grips the wheel and sits back. "I'm starting to get why you hang around with a lowlife like Shane Cuthbert. Two peas," he tells Liv.

They're wasting time.

"Oh please. What about that preppy—check that, *aggressively* preppy—blonde? Granted, she doesn't have a brain in her head, so she can't threaten your manliness," Liv retorts.

"Nice. Real nice," Kellan spits.

In my belly, the black thing opens one scaly eye.

"I mean, why not a real girl?" Liv says. "Like Julia, for example. Julia's a certified heroine, not some flaky puck-f—"

"Take us to the woods!" I shout.

Kellan's eyes flash at me in the mirror.

Liv's head snaps around. "We are not going to the woods."

Kellan pulls over hard into a drainage ditch and twists in his seat. "Why would you want to go back to the woods?"

"To see where they found the dead girl."

"That is the absolute last place I would think you would ever want to be," Kellan says incredulously.

"It is," Liv says, blinking madly. "We are not going."

"I hate to admit it, but Liv's right," Kellan says. "There's an extremely good chance my dad could show up there. And the Fells is probably Paula Papademetriou's next stop."

"We are absolutely, positively not going," Liv murmurs, shaking her head.

"You're talking about nosing around a crime scene where the police dug up a body. Maybe a *murdered* body," Kellan says.

"No one said anything about digging," I point out. "Based on my research, the elements would have exposed her."

"Aren't you afraid of what you'll see? There could still be remnants. Hair. Blood," Kellan continues, as though he's thinking of these possibilities for the first time and starting to freak out.

"Doubtful," I say. "The rain would have washed them away."

"Seriously, what's wrong with you?" Liv says. "Do you have to be so macabre?"

I shoot Liv an insulted glare. But Kellan ignores us, earnest as all heck, determined to offer some special wisdom gleaned from being the son of a cop. "You have no idea what's up there. And seeing disturbing stuff can really affect you. There's no unseeing it. My dad knows cops who have this condition called PTSD from the bad stuff they've seen—"

"You might say I know something about it," I interrupt flatly.

"Right. I'm sorry." His eyebrows gather, pained. "That was out of line."

That's when I notice his eyes are clear green glass, eyes GIRLS titter about, and there is empathy there, but not pity. I know pity, it repels me, and his eyes do not repel me. I could get lost in them, but I won't. I sort of wish he would turn around, because it's easier to look at the back of Kellan's head than his eyes.

"I just don't get how seeing a grave can be a good thing," he continues, his voice softer, the edges of his words rounder. "Given what you've been through."

Green glass. Rare. An eye color no one else has.

"That body has nothing to do with what happened to us," Liv says firmly. "It's irrelevant."

I pull my eyes away from Kellan. "Relevance is elusive," I tell her.

"What does 'relevance is elusive' mean? Can you ever talk like a normal person?" Liv replies.

"It's interfering with a crime scene. And that's what we'll get punished with: under federal law we could get twenty years," Kellan says.

"We'd get off," I say. "Any lawyer would argue lack of knowledge and lack of intent."

"How can you possibly know that?" Kellan asks.

"I researched it," I say.

"Of course. Let me try a different tack," Kellan says. "I know I can't possibly understand what you went through—"

"Well, *I* understand what she went through," Liv interjects. "And there is no reason for us to go into the woods. Period."

"No, you do not understand. Because you weren't with me. You. Left. Me." I bite off every word.

Liv throws up her hands. "Oh fine! The whole world knows: you went through hell and I didn't. You screwed up your ankle. You got hypothermia. But you didn't get raped. The doctors said you weren't raped."

Kellan turns forward, the tips of his ears turning red. "We should head back."

"You got away, Julia. He couldn't catch you. You won!" Liv says.

"What do you mean, I won?"

"I mean, we're here and he's dead! We're putting this behind us, like we've had a thousand conversations about, like you *said* you were going to do." She looks from me to Kellan, desperate. "The whole idea of hiking up there is stupid. Kellan, tell her."

Kellan lets out a hard puff of air. "Is this some kind of closure thing?"

"If closure implies a need for information and an aversion to ambiguity, then that sounds about right," I reply.

"What if I have an aversion to your sick fetishization of things ghastly and *irrelevant*?" Liv says.

Kellan meets my eyes in the mirror. "Is this what you want to do?" he asks.

I nod.

"What if they assume we're kids who skip school to smoke in the woods, and they chase us off?" he says.

"We'll leave if they make us," I say.

Kellan falls back into his seat and is still for a minute. Liv sits erect, holding her breath. He checks his side mirror and pulls out, tires squealing in the mud, and makes a sudden turn in the opposite direction. My bag spills onto the floor. Liv tumbles across the seat into me.

I look down at my lap and soften my voice. "Donald Jessup is dead. There's nothing in the woods to be afraid of anymore." She scrambles off my lap as though it's on fire. Smoothing her hair behind her ears, she settles in her seat, her eyes sharp as she works her jaw, tight and angry.

Kellan guns the gas with a low growl. "If this thing will get above forty miles an hour without falling apart, we might actually beat the reporters there."

We roll up to the main entrance in our truck plastered in Chieftains Hockey stickers. Police cars and detective sedans overload the parking lot. Kellan creeps a quarter mile down the main drag and pulls over.

"This is smarter than parking in the lot," he mutters to himself, jumping down from the truck and stuffing his hands into his front pockets. "We say we just happened to stumble upon the scene."

It's like a sick-humored Mother Nature served up a

diametrically different tableau for my first visit back. That day, everything felt alive with possibility. Today, everything feels dead. The hard rains have washed away the scents of living things, along with the debris that hid Ana Alvarez. Cops talk into headsets and phones and two-way radios. The news vans haven't arrived. Liv walks a step behind Kellan and me, her pale hair knotted in the back now, jamming on oversized sunglasses. We come to the entrance gate where my sneaker slipped before our run almost a year ago. Electricity thrums my spine as I realize that some of these guys may recognize me, never mind Kellan. I calm myself by remembering Mom was strict about not letting the cops near me more than necessary. If they recognize Kellan, well, the jig's up.

A husky detective approaches, tucking his shirt into chinos cinched by a belt with three weathered holes. I angle to read the ID trailing over his belly bump, but it's impossible. Kellan does the same. The detective points to a strip of yellow tape stretched between two trees at the top of the stairs, the ones Liv sprinted up first. I look to Liv, wondering if she's remembering the same thing. She catches my eye and looks away, hugging her elbows.

The detective holds up his palm. "Can't go into the woods today. Police business."

"What's going on, detective?" Kellan says.

"Nothing for you kids to worry about." The man dips his head to read the embroidered arm of Kellan's sweatshirt, hairs combed over his scalp. "You a Chieftain? What position you play?"

Kellan runs his hand over his mouth. Finally, he says, "I'm Joe Mac—"

"Offense, sir!" I blurt. "Right wing, mostly." Kellan sneaks me a look of surprise that I should know this.

"Nice! I played defense myself, back in the day. Kept going in an old men's league." He holds his back and twists at the waist. "Before sciatica started giving me trouble."

Liv steps forward. "Did they take it out yet?" she asks.

The detective lifts his chin at Liv, wary.

"The body. Did they take it out yet?" she says.

"Now, I can't comment on a crime scene. They're still working up there. It's going to be a while. The woods is no place for you kids today." He leans close to Liv and sniffs; she pulls away from his attempt to smell weed.

A second detective, stern-faced with a brush cut, approaches, and they leave together, knuckles on hips. I strain to hear over the workmanlike buzz among the other cops and the traffic hum on the border road.

"Not . . . a print?" the first detective says.

". . . even a fiber," the second detective says.

The first detective shakes his head. ". . . miss a hole in the ground?"

The second detective raises his voice defensively. "You ever been up there? The trails only circle the perimeter. Deep inside, it's like it was back in the Indian days. Twenty-five hundred acres of nothing but trees and swamp. So unless she got dragged up there, she was running off trail."

"Wasn't saying anyone's at fault. They gonna put out a statement?"

"No way. Too gruesome."

"Let's hope the news doesn't get it."

Liv is at my side, dragging her nails down her cheeks. "What did they say? You heard, I can tell."

"It sounds like they didn't get any evidence off the body."

"That means Donald Jessup might not have done it," she says.

"Or that more than a year has gone by and weather has advanced decomposition and erased evidence," I say.

The second detective yells over: "You kids should stay out of these woods anyway. S'not safe to begin with. Never has been. You're asking for trouble, going in there. Hey, shouldn't you be in school?"

"Thank you, detective." Liv spins on her heel and charges toward the car, head down, as though counting steps.

Kellan lets me go first. Once we're out of the detectives' earshot, I say, "We can still hike up to the Sheepfold. We'll park at the back entrance in Parlee and walk east toward the fire watchtower. It's overgrown, but you'll be okay in sneakers."

Kellan stops short. "You mean that. You're serious."

"I always am." If I was the kind of GIRL who cared about making myself attractive to Kellan MacDougall, this would be an epic fail moment.

He smiles, warm and wide. I was wrong about his eyes; they

aren't sea glass at all. They're darker, with depth behind, and a glow, maybe. What does admiration look like?

He takes my arm and gently moves me toward the car. "Dumb and Dumber haven't figured out who we are. Let's not push our luck."

Ahead, Liv slams the car door shut.

I pull away and face him. "Come with me." My voice sounds breathy and passionate, and I startle myself.

"Listen, I would really like to help you. But do you know how much trouble I'd be in if any of those guys were from Shiverton? We're lucky that detective happened to be a Parlee guy. Word still might get back to my dad," Kellan says.

"No offense, but if they didn't know who Liv and I are, they're not going to piece together who you are. See, we're kind of famous around here," I say as I smile, despite myself.

"Okay, then, reality check: those cops will never let us get near the Sheepfold. If we sneak in, we get arrested for disturbing the scene of a crime." He steals a look back at the Jeep. "Can I say something that might be completely out of line?"

"Something along the lines of how I could get PTSD?"

He laughs. "Here's what I'm wondering. You're the one who got caught by the dude. You're the one who spent a night in the woods escaping him. So how come Liv's the one acting like a nutjob?"

I turn and face the trails. It's midmorning now. A light mist rises from the forest floor. Sunbeams pierce through trees, highlighting their jigsaw edges. It seems that some trees are meant to fit with other trees. Liv, me. Donald, Ana. Parts of the same picture. What happened in the woods is a vast puzzle for me to solve, or walk away from. Solve it, or leave it.

Sneakers in leaves. Kellan's mouth near the back of my neck. "Julia?"

"Liv wants to leave the woods," I murmur, my head thrown back, tracing the jagged lines in the canopy.

"Most people wouldn't blame her," Kellan says.

From the Jeep, Liv yells at us to hurry up.

I'm not like most people.

I stoop to pick up an oak leaf, twirling its stem between my thumb and forefinger. Veins radiate out, starting and ending at the midrib, the leaf's spine. I close my eyes and run my finger over the midrib, a distinct indent on the front, an unmistakable ridge on the back. Starting and ending at the same place. Imminently traceable.

"I'm not ready to leave yet," I say, heading to the truck.

Mom chews and swallows and dabs a napkin at the corners of her downturned mouth. Erik has overstepped again, welcoming my questions about the latest news on Ana Alvarez. The fact that he's required to wear a parent filter when he's not allowed to act like my parent would, on a normal day, be the elephant in the room. But today, the elephant is Ana Alvarez, and I'm outing her, right here in our kitchen.

"I just wish they would stop the generalities and report exactly where they found the body," I say.

Erik scrapes the last bit of basmati rice from the takeout tin. "They found her near the fire watchtower."

"Erik! Really?" Mom refills her glass with cabernet. The frenzy at school this morning has her on edge. I had hoped the wine would relax her instead of making her sullen. Usually one glass of wine and she jokes about her colleagues' hygiene; three and we're besties, and does her long hair age her, and should she cut it?

"She needs information to process, Gwen. It's healthy," Erik says.

"That rice is healthy too. I didn't want more or anything," I say.

Erik scoot-bumps me across the bench. I scoot-bump him back.

Even over Indian takeout, Erik smells good, like grapefruit and glass. I wonder if he rode his bike here from Cambridge.

"Where near the watchtower?" I continue.

"They didn't say." Erik steals a look at my mother, who frowns. "But I doubt they'll get that specific. At least not on the news. Certainly not on public radio."

Mom sets down her fork. "Can we speak in the dining room?" she asks him.

Erik drags his napkin over his mouth and unfolds his long body from the bench. I shrug at him, and he winks. Once his back disappears, I tiptoe after them to eavesdrop.

"You crossed a line. You shouldn't have told her about the

forensics. Sometimes I think you forget she's a child, let alone that she was attacked less than a year ago," Mom whispers.

"Repeating what I heard on the news is hardly telling her forensics," he says.

"She's still at risk of retraumatization. Elaine Ricker says she presents as classic post-traumatic stress disorder."

"You know Julia. She needs information. You told me she spent months researching like mad: kidnapping statistics, sociopathic tendencies, martyr complexes. Trying to apply *game theory* to her own abduction, for God's sake. The girl is starving for information to make sense of what happened to her. If knowing more about the psychopath who stole her sense of security helps her in some way, I say go for it."

"Then it's a good thing we decided a long time ago that you don't have a say. Or have you forgotten?"

Ding-dong!

Damn it, doorbell! The conversation pauses. Mom calls out, "Julia, do not get that!" She shifts to a rapid-fire whisper: "Parents from Brazil . . . decomposition hastened by so much rain . . . veterinary student, very promising . . . tasteless gossip about leading a double life . . . important to determine there isn't another criminal wandering the woods."

The doorbell rings again.

Erik must be making to answer, because Mom shouts, "No! I'm calling Elaine Ricker."

Ding-dong!

I run for the door, swinging it open. A blast of air rushes in. The streetlights are out and the night is starless. Against a lacy backdrop of trees, a figure is making for a truck at the curb.

"Julia! Did you just open the door?" Mom calls.

Kellan turns and grins, warm and wide. As he lopes back toward me, I spy something in his hand. "Hope you don't mind me dropping by without calling. I found this under the backseat of my car," he says.

Even in the dark I recognize the squiggly black design on the cover of my notebook. Cold horror falls over me. Another half hour and I would've tried to download Erik's intel onto its pages and found it missing.

"Julia?" Mom calls, urgently now.

I snatch the notebook from his hand and smile tightly. "My French. Thanks. Test tomorrow. I would've been screwed."

"Tomorrow's a teachers' professional day. No school, remember?" he says.

I laugh, but it goes on way too long until it dwindles to a pitchy sigh. "You're correct!" I shake my finger at him, like he's a rascal. "Friday. I meant Friday."

"Right. Glad I caught you at home." Kellan turns and strolls down the walk. The door is halfway shut when he stops and turns.

"You're some overachiever," he calls.

I ease the door open. "Sorry?"

"Taking French, too. Because we're in Spanish together."

"Did I say French?" I bring the notebook to my nose, examining it as if I've uncovered some important missed detail. "This is my stats notebook."

He half smiles, coming up the walk. "I take stats. Most of the coursework's online. But you use a comp notebook. Old school. Nice."

"I like to figure things out on the page, you know?"

"I do know."

I frown.

"Julia!" Mom comes running into the front hall. Not being athletic and maybe because of the wine, she flails and skids. Erik races behind, his arms outstretched, like he's trying to contain her. It's a scene.

"Oh, wow. Okay. Mom, Erik, this is Kellan."

"Hello." Mom stuffs her hair behind her ears, composing herself. "Gwen Spunk. Nice to meet you."

"I left my notebook in his car today. He came by to give it to me. In case I needed it tomorrow—I mean Friday—for school."

Mom cocks her head. "In his car?"

"When the reporters came. He let me wait in his car until the crazy died down."

Erik jabs his hand in front of Mom. "Erik Meijer. I work with Julia's mom. It was exceptional of you to save Julia like that."

"Yes, thank you, Kieran," Mom says.

"It's Kellan," I say, turning to Kellan. "When you rang the doorbell Mom thought you were a reporter. She was about to rip you a new one."

"Julia!" Mom says.

"I can understand, after this morning," Kellan says. "I'm not a fan of reporters either."

"Kellan's dad is Detective Joe MacDougall."

Mom's face turns positively purple, like she doesn't know whether to hug him or slam the door in his face. Joe Mac-Dougall may have put Donald Jessup in jail, but according to Paula Papademetriou, he's high up in the same police department that blew off babysitting Jessup. Also, his rough bedside manner when they first brought me into the hospital has to be on her mind. He came inside the exam room when the nurse was helping tie my johnny, asking for my version of what happened. The nurse blocked him with her body while she swabbed the cuts on my back with bacitracin. He took my clothes in a bag. They argued. Mom stood by, silent and straining against the awfulness of it all, squeezing my hand.

Erik cups Mom's shoulders. "Would you like to come in, Kellan?"

"I should just go," Kellan says.

"Wait!" Mom shouts, roused from her trance. "We have Indian. Do you like Indian?"

"There's plenty to go around," Erik says as he smiles approvingly at Mom.

"Just not rice," I say. Because it's important to make that clear. Seriously, what's wrong with me? Maybe I need an Erik to finesse my social gaffes too.

Erik moves past me gently and takes Kellan by the upper arm. "Do you like naan?"

"I love naan," Kellan says.

"We have naan!" Erik slaps Kellan on the back. Kellan was ready to bail, twice. Now they're forcing him to come in. Suddenly I feel like the friendless kid whose parents socially engineer her life so she's not lonely. My ears begin to burn. Kellan looks back at me and smiles mischievously, like he just got away with something. I decide his staying means nothing, since most guys like to get fed.

The food is cold, but Mom and Erik are warm with wine, more than I realized, and Kellan keeps commenting on how great the food is, and how he's embarrassed because he's acting like he hasn't seen food in days. It feels like a downer to point out that I have experience in that area. Erik peppers Kellan with questions about hockey, which Kellan answers behind a balled-up fist, because he's shoveling in tikka masala piled on torn corners of naan. Mom can't follow the hockey talk, but she makes a lot of affirmative noises, too many, and refills her wine glass twice.

I ponder what Liv would make of Kellan MacDougall in my breakfast nook.

Mom folds an arm over her chest and sits back. "So Julia and I were remembering all the good times she had with Alice Mincus last night over dinner. Do you remember Alice, Erik?"

"Of course I remember Alice." Erik looks to Kellan, as if he needs to explain remembering Alice, and says, "I've been around these ladies for a while."

"What Erik means is, I haven't hung around with Alice since I was ten," I say, turning to Mom. "Your parental machinations aren't really interesting to Kellan. Or Erik, for that matter."

Erik tosses back his wine. "Anyone ready for dessert? The kheer's not ready yet, but I brought ice cream."

"How does the song go? *Make new friends, but keep the old. One is silver, and the other gold,*" Mom sings off pitch.

Kellan's eyebrows climb. Erik stands at the freezer, wedging displaced Boca Burgers back into their packed towers. "How is your father these days?" he calls to Kellan.

Kellan puts down his Coke. "He's good. Had to stop coaching this year. Things got busy at work," he says.

If I were him, I'd be wondering if in this household, I'm considered guilty by association. But he's either stupid or really good at acting blasé.

Mom drags her glass in a circle. "Tell me, does the press pester him?"

"I'd use a different word," he says.

"Piss him off?" I say.

Mom wrinkles her nose at me. "Julia."

"The press isn't exactly making the police look good these days," I say.

"It's really just one station." Kellan swigs his Coke. "Paula Papademetriou is trying to say the police were at fault for what happened to you." He turns to me. "Is that what you think?"

"I'm still sorting things out," I answer. Understatement of the Year.

"That's what I figured," Kellan says.

"That's what you figured?"

"You just seem to be someone who thinks through stuff a lot," Kellan explains.

"As opposed to someone who thinks through things a little? Someone who doesn't think at all?" I say, when what I really want to say is, *As opposed to someone who works things out in the pages of a comp notebook?*

"As opposed to someone who just wants to forget," Kellan says.

Did he read my notebook or not? I fidget in my chair as the black in my gut burrows down.

"No one wants ice cream, really? Just me?" Erik says, head in the freezer.

I stand abruptly. "Can we talk in the dining room?" I ask Kellan.

Mom coughs.

Erik returns with four bowls and an undersized tub of Karamel Sutra.

"I'd like some ice cream," Kellan says.

"They'll save you some," I say.

Erik looks at the tiny tub sadly.

I charge out of the room and position myself behind the back of a dining room chair. Kellan appears in the doorway.

"You have a lot of opinions about me for someone who barely knows me," I say.

"I said that you seem like a person who thinks."

"I'm going to ask you straight out: Did you read my notebook?"

"Because when I'm looking for a good read, I think: stats?"

I squint at him.

"You're hostile considering I recovered said notebook," Kellan says.

"Maybe I do have a problem with your father for letting Donald Jessup out on the streets."

"If that was true, I'd say you have a right to be pissed. But it's obvious that reporter is trying to revive her career. The story might be hot today, but tomorrow, no one will care, and she'll be on to her next conquest."

"Kind of like hooking up at a woods party and blowing someone off the next day?" I spit.

Silence.

"You're talking about Liv Lapin," he says.

"I am indeed."

"Liv was basically using me, because I was there," Kellan says.

"Oh, that's rich. The classic story: girl uses guy."

"Did Liv say she was pissed that I never called her?"

"Well, no," I answer.

"Then why do you care?"

"She's my friend."

He smiles slyly. "Sounds like your mom would prefer you hang with Alice."

I hold the sides of my head. "Oh my God. I was friends with Alice in fifth grade! Liv is my best friend!"

"You sound like you're trying to convince me. But I don't need convincing: you risked your life to save her. Maybe you're trying to convince yourself."

"Where do you get off saying that?" I ask him.

"All I know is that there's a pattern. I blow off Liv. Liv couldn't care less, but you want to raise an army against me. Some chick gets killed in the woods, the same way you could've got killed in the woods, which should freak you out. Yet it's Liv who hides while you want to go examine the body."

"You're saying I have a pattern of overreacting while Liv underreacts?"

"I'm saying you and Liv together are a hot mess."

"You think I'm a mess?"

"Together you're a mess. Alone, I think you're fascinating. And a little bit of a mess. But mostly fascinating," Kellan says.

I shoot him my best dirty look from under my eyelashes, which I hope is at once meaningful and alluring. He smiles wider. But I'm just getting started.

"You mean morbidly fascinating. I get it. You can't look away. I'm the girl who had interactions with a sociopath. Extended, day-long, night-long interactions. We hung out together. He fed me. Offered me hits off his joint. And everyone wonders: Did he touch her?"

Kellan drags a knuckle across his forehead. *Didn't think I was going there so soon, did ya, buddy?*

"The supposition makes me automatically creepy," I continue. "And there's the automatic next question: What did I have to give away to escape?"

"You don't have to go there . . ." Kellan says, trailing off.

I circle the table. "Donald Jessup was a paroled assailant of women. He played a soft-porn video game that involved

92

hunting women in the woods. He lived with his shut-in mother and barely left the house, except for that one day, when he happened to get some kind of stirring that involved dressing in camo and packing a hunting knife. So how could I possibly have escaped untouched in that most carnal of ways?"

"But you did."

"I did." I sit on the table's edge and slap my thighs. "And now, no one really knows what to do with me. Every time I ask too many questions, they shut me down, or redirect me, or tell me to move on. It's like I'm this oddity. In 88.5% of all abductions, the girl is killed within the first two hours. What do you do with the girl who comes back?"

He sits near me. "What happened in the woods?"

"You really want to know?"

"I've always wanted to know."

I pull back. "What do you mean, always?"

"I've lived with your story for the last year. It's where my dad was, in his head, all the time. With you, I mean."

"Your father found and arrested Donald Jessup within forty-eight hours. What was he preoccupied with for the last year?"

He looks down for a moment. "Maybe I'm not supposed to talk about this."

"You're the one who wanted to go there."

He meets my eyes. "Once my father realized there were lapses, he felt sure you and Liv weren't Donald Jessup's only victims."

"Oh."

93

We're quiet for a moment. Laughter booms from the kitchen. Erik swears he's telling the truth about something, and Mom is flirtatiously dubious. In a flash, I realize that it's a relief for my mother when I'm not around. She sounds young and happy and maybe drunk, but still, young and happy. Happy to have the attention of a gorgeous guy; happy to be brilliant and pretty. Light. Free of slithering black things in your belly.

Kellan slides closer. "You don't have to tell me what happened. Just tell me what it was like."

"When I was alone? Or with him?"

"Both."

I drop my head. "Moments were splintered, in the woods. I have no way of knowing how many pieces there are, or if I have them all."

"I can imagine. I mean, I can't imagine."

"You can't. See, absolute darkness isn't absolute. You can still make out shapes, ripples of movement. Branches buckled. Things flapped and scuttled. After a while, it started to rain. Your skin feels spongy, like it doesn't belong to you. Water fills your ears. It slips between your lips, even when you jam them tight. You don't bother brushing it from your eyes. Soon you stop feeling it. Sometimes, I think Donald Jessup isn't what changed me. It's the woods that changed me. It's where I learned to live inside my head."

Kellan swallows hard.

"Hunger. Cold. Your lacerated hands. The need to piss and sleep. All those things vanish. You turn off a switch, rid yourself of the burden of bodily pangs. The only thing left working is your rational mind trying to calculate a way out," I say.

From the kitchen comes a shout and a cackle. Kellan puts his hand over mine, as if to say *Mute that boozy interruption. Go on.* His hand is warm, but not yuck-warm.

I keep my hand still.

"A lot of people would have curled into a ball and waited to die," he says.

"It was pure survival instinct. I had no choice."

"It was a choice," he says. "You chose not to die."

"I guess. But here's the thing: sometimes, I think I got stuck in that mode. I can't turn the switch back on. I can't stop calculating and start feeling again."

"Maybe you're still trying to survive," he says. His eyes dance as he moves my hair off my shoulder. It would be natural to slip my hands around his neck, breathe in his boy smell.

"I should check on Mom," I mumble, staggering away and into the kitchen.

Mom and Erik are three-quarters into a new bottle of cabernet. Erik perches on a counter stool, knees pointed, bopping his head to the Sirius grunge station and smiling at Mom, who's decided this is the right moment to belatedly carve our Halloween pumpkin, which smells rotten. She's got the top off, and is digging the guts out with bare hands, sleeves up to her elbows. They both look snockered. Someone has lit votive candles and set them on the counter and the breakfast table. The timer dings, and Mom rushes to pull some kind of Indian rice pudding off the stove. I block her way. "You wash your hands and let me get that," I say, slipping on potholders and lifting the pan. The aroma of cardamom and raisins grows, nearly eclipsing the pumpkin funk. My stomach growls. Mom and Erik take forks to the pudding and hash out whether or not some professor's article was worthy of having been published in the *Lancet*, and how they are sooo bad to be gossiping about it, never mind having double dessert, shame on them, giggle-giggle.

Kellan and I stand back, gawking. "Should Erik ride his bike home?" I whisper, flustered. If there's anything more paralyzing than seeing a parent drunk, it's seeing your parent's friend drunk and scarfing down rice pudding.

"I'll offer to drive him home." Kellan tilts his head until our temples nearly touch. "But I think he might stay."

"Should I throw a sheet and some pillows on the couch?" I ask.

"They'll sleep together, dummy," he says.

"Oh no. They're research partners. It's not like that," I say. *But I can't tell you what it is like, either.*

"Oh really? I guess you weren't picking up the signals I was picking up. There's major history there."

I nearly yell "Ha!" Instead, I deflect. "It's . . . complicated. They're kind of codependent. Like, Erik completes my mother when it comes to things like social skills. She doesn't have the greatest EQ. After the woods, she dragged me out of Shiverton, supposedly to get away from the nosy reporters and bad

96

memories. So where does she take me? To the Berkshires. Home to the largest state forest in Massachusetts. This at a time when I'm avoiding trees in any number."

"I maintain anything in large numbers is scary. Take kittens. One kitten is cute. Five hundred kittens in one place? Terrifying. The principle applies to anything. Birds. Ladybugs. Babies."

"It's not a joke," I say, trying to scowl, though I want to laugh. Because an argument right now would make it easier to keep things on the right plane, with this guy who not only hooked up with Liv, but is involved with an aggressively preppy puck—

"I know. You were traumatized. And half the time you feel like you're being punked, because of the wildly inappropriate things people do and say in front of you. Like trying to make you feel better by sending you to a vacation home surrounded by woods," Kellan says.

"Or worrying I might get PTSD from seeing Ana Alvarez's dead body, because it's not like I might already have it from, say, getting abducted."

"Or saying they're acting like they haven't seen food in days, when you went two days eating, what?" he says.

"Basically nothing." I smile a bit. "You caught that."

"And I'm sorry for saying it." He leans against the wall, thumbs hooked in his pocket, his signature slouch. "It must be hard to feel like the world is periodically surreal. Like you're being punked all the time, or on *Candid Camera*. Don't you feel like looking into the camera sometimes and saying, 'Seriously?'"

My jaw drops. How does he know?

"But I've figured something out about you. You think it's kind of funny when people make those gaffes," he says.

"I think it's funny when someone offends me?"

"I know you do. You'd be looking straight into that camera, your eyes wide with disbelief, getting a laugh. You know what else? If I was in the audience, I'd be laughing with you."

The show of my life. Who gave him a seat in the audience?

Kellan points at a votive on the counter dissolving into a molten mess. "That's going to leave a stain."

I yelp and blow it out.

He lifts his back off the wall. "Oh, and the fact remains that your mom and Erik are totally a couple. You might be a brainiac, but you're the least aware person I've ever met."

"Now I'm truly offended," I say, frowning energetically. He smiles, mocking and irresistible. We stand like that, me scowling, him smiling, until he wears me down and I laugh.

Suddenly Erik lurches across the room to us. "Did you kids see my bike helmet in the dining room?" he slurs.

Mom insists he's in no condition to ride, and besides, they're expecting torrential downpours. Perhaps Kellan could give him a lift?

Kellan's eyes bore into me. My face gets hot. He doesn't want to leave. Do I want him to leave?

I shake my head. "Go."

Kellan disappears into the front hall looking for his coat. I pace, trying to pull myself together. Erik staggers in first, jacket over his shoulder. Kellan follows behind and Mom chases after them, forcing the pumpkin onto Erik, saying he needs fall decorations because his condo is as spartan as a monk's. I don't ask how she knows what the inside of his condo looks like. They climb into Kellan's truck as I stand in the doorway waving. Mom sprawls on the couch, minutes from sleep. Smoke from a neighbor's coal stove laces the air, and I breathe deeply as I walk down the driveway to move Erik's bike into the garage. Back inside, Mom snores. I tuck a blanket under her chin and walk around blowing out votives, greasy wax puddled on countertops. *We can chip at it with butter knives tomorrow*, I think, shutting off the nineties grunge music and dragging myself upstairs.

I reach for the picture tucked into my mirror. It's the same picture Liv has of middle school graduation. It's a gorgeous shot of her, her rosy cheek squished against my pale one. Easier times. It was never really the same after that, when Deborah began focusing on every thing about Liv: a gradual shaping of the way she looked, the friends she made, the clubs she joined.

From the top of the stairs I listen to Mom's woolly snores. In her empty room, the coat she wore to work still lies across her bed. I feel a finger-flick at my thawed heart: single mom, lonely mom, only able to laugh when I leave the room and after two and a half bottles of cabernet. I really am a drag.

But fascinating. Mostly, morbidly fascinating. Any girl can have an apple face, or boobs since fifth grade. But she can't be an ironic heroine survivalist.

I grab my notebook and flop onto my bed.

Things I Know About Kellan MacDougall:
- Loves to be fed
- Wants to know what it was like in the woods
- Would laugh with me

My notebook falls to the floor with a satisfying flutter. I lie back and drift off, Kellan's voice curling around me, until I'm distracted by the feel of something solid underneath my butt. My fingers graze the sharp point of the little tinfoil wedge. I unpeel it carefully, and the numbers are faded, but I grab my phone and type them as best as I can make out, giggling.

Hi I type.

Immediately, the telling ellipses appear on my iPhone screen. Three little circles, three little hooks to keep me tuned in. My breath hitches. Three words appear.

Is this Julia?

FIVE

356 Days After the Woods

It's nearly eleven a.m., and Mom is home sick, scraping candle wax off the counter with a butter knife. "Remind me never to order from the new Indian place again," she groans, picking at the fossilized mass. "Clearly the tikka masala was bad."

I murmur in agreement, reminding myself that I should be relieved. She wasn't supposed to be home on my day off, but her debilitated state will make ducking out easier. Still, seeing her vulnerable makes me feel worse about where I'm going.

The knife crashes to the floor as she cups her mouth with both hands.

"Do not puke!" I yell.

Her hands fall slowly. Her face is green. "I'll be okay," she whispers faintly.

"I beg you to go back to the family room and lie down. I'll

scrape the wax and put away the dishes. I can't clean around you. Puke, and there will be more to clean."

Mom touches her fingertips together and bows to me, wincing from the pain of gravity. A *whoosh* as she collapses onto the couch. "Tell me again where you're going?" she calls weakly.

"Starbucks. With Petra. Nice girl, you don't know her," I call back. I consider telling her that Alice might join us for extra insurance, but I can't afford tripping her antennae right now. "We're going over biology for the exam this week. It's on the nervous system of a hare."

"Fun. Fix yourself lunch, please. I won't be eating."

Neither will I, I think, stomach tight. I throw myself into flaking wax off the granite counter. Next, I attack chunks of pumpkin innards, a nasty mess of threads and dangling seeds. I pry them from their sticking places and dump them into a large wooden bowl. I think of bits of melon rind I saw once, in the woods, in the pit, along with other things. I grab the edge of the counter, which is smooth and gloriously man-made, reminding myself I am not in the woods, and that pumpkin is not melon. I shake my head loosely and notice Mom's phone, lit with messages. Six from postdocs, none from Erik, which feels like a bad sign, as far as the evolution of their unrelationship goes. I wonder if he's still hungover too. In the distance, Mom snores. I snatch a pen to write a sticky note, then stop. Promising a return time will only complicate things. I crumple the first piece of paper, peel off a new one, and stick it on the fridge. I write "Feel better!" with a smiley face for good measure.

But for a shiny black SUV, my car is conspicuous among the beat-up numbers parked in the Parlee entrance lot. My brand-new Dodge Dart SXT is one of the many new things Mom threw at me for coming out of the Fells alive. If she couldn't protect me, paying for ten standard air bags, front crash prevention, and a body that weighs 2,750 pounds might. The car feels downright sparkly, and since break-ins along with roaming sociopaths are not uncommon in the Fells, I tuck my car next to a Parks Department truck.

Yellow caution tape flaps between saplings at the trailhead, sending a trill through my nerves. There's a fresh memorial pile on the bottom of the steps. Stuffed puppies and kittens. A light blue T-shirt that says Real Doctors Treat More Than One Species. A Brazilian flag. Flowers trapped in cellophane. It's a smaller pile, I imagine, than the one that's cropped up at the main entrance by now. But the main entrance is too main for my purposes.

My stomach hardens. Get down to business.

I slide my backpack off my shoulder and bend on one knee, checking my notebook against my watch. The sun sets at 4:25 p.m. The hike to the fire watchtower is 4.3 miles. Walking on a flat trail at an average pace, I can expect to walk three to four miles in an hour without stopping. Since the half mile before the tower is rocky and steep, I figure about a half to one hour just for that section. The entire trip should take no longer than two and a half hours. I could figure more, but this isn't intended to be a sightseeing stroll.

"Your answers aren't in there. Trust me. I've already been."

Paula Papademetriou appears at the trailhead. I check past my shoulder like she's talking to someone else, but we are alone.

"Did you follow me here?" I ask, startled.

She steps over the yellow tape in hiking boots, jeans, and a short quilted jacket with buckles. Her ponytailed hair is damp at the temples. Her face is bare, with pointed cheekbones and a square jaw. It's a face to apply makeup to, slip glasses onto, try any hairstyle. Strong bones under her clothes too. If I put my thumb and index finger around her wrist, there would be a half finger's length between them before they met. It's a weird thing to think of, Paula Papademetriou's thick bones.

Even her bright teeth look powerful. "I came out of the woods, remember?" she says, looking at me sideways, teasing. "I was here first?"

"Right." I shrug awkwardly. "Obviously."

"That doesn't mean I didn't have a feeling you'd be here." She holds out her hand, tanned, with squared, French-tipped nails. A thin diamond bracelet flashes on her wrist. "It's really nice to meet you in person. I'm Paula."

Her voice isn't the high one I heard gossiping in the tavern. It's low and throaty, the kind of voice owned by a dame in a dime-store detective novel. Closer to her TV voice, but not that, either. I wonder how many voices she has.

I tug off my thin glove to shake her hand. "I'm Julia."

She laughs, and it's kind of musical. "I know who you are." She brushes her hand against her thigh. "Sorry I'm a little sweaty. The hike was longer than I estimated."

"It's 4.3 miles to the fire watchtower. If that's where you were going."

Paula's eyes narrow slightly. "You have my number," she says, then seizes the opportunity to get literal. "And now I have yours. You sent me a text last night. You're a woman of few words."

I blush. My "hi" text was the equivalent of a giddy prank. "I wasn't sure if I had the right number."

"Well," she says, digging through a slouchy bag slung over her shoulder, "now you do." She hands me a business card with raised lettering and her phone number. "My business card, with my private cell. It's old-fashioned, I know."

It says:

PAULA PAPADEMETRIOU
News Anchor and Investigative Journalist,
3 News Boston WFYT-TV
If your mother tells you she loves you,
check it out.
781-555-9698

"That saying is pretty funny."

"Words to live by. It's an old journalism maxim my first producer used to say. It means familiarity and history do not excuse you from checking and double-checking your sources. Never be content with what you're told. Always dig."

I tilt the card in my hand. When she leaves, I will tape it to a page inside my notebook. "Even when everyone's telling you to be content?" I ask.

"Especially when everyone's telling you to be content."

I look toward the sun. "I should really hit the trail. I want to get in and out before dark."

"I imagine you would. Pardon me for saying this, and I'm sure you've heard it ad nauseam, but you are a remarkably brave person. Most people in your circumstances would never want to see the woods again, never mind a crime scene that could have been their own."

Person instead of GIRL. And she called me a *woman*, too, before. It's like she knows I'm not a GIRL anymore.

Paula's face softens. "I've angered you. Forgive me for being so direct. It's an occupational hazard," she says.

"I was just thinking. I space out like that sometimes. Actually, I'm okay with directness." I get quiet again, not sure what else to say. Paula looks at me searchingly for so long, I feel compelled to fill the silence.

"What I mean is, it's a nice change. Pretty much everyone treats me like I'm a porcelain doll," I explain.

"That must be unbearable," Paula says, sympathetic but not patronizing. Which is nice.

I shrug. "I can't blame them. What happened to me was scary. And it scares them. So they act weird."

"You deserve to be treated like a normal person."

I gaze at the trail, thinking about that. Mom would have me banished to the countryside. Ricker wants to shape me to fit the textbook trauma victim. But Paula thinks I should be treated like a normal person.

Wind stirs the few stubborn beech leaves clinging to branches.

"Part of it, I think, is that they're afraid I'm going to spill lurid details of what happened to me. When mostly, I just ran and hid and ran," I say.

Paula eases backward to sit on the entrance step, resting her forearm on one folded leg, the other extended luxuriously. Like me, she takes up a lot of space. "You must get angry," she says.

"Technically, I no longer have an object to be mad at. Donald Jessup is dead. His mother is an old hoarder who lives in a house with petrified dog poop covering the front lawn. I can't exactly take out my anger on her, even if she did spawn Satan. There's really no one else."

"No?"

I work my mouth into a corkscrew.

"Sit," she says as she pats the stone stair next to her. "You were saying?"

I sit. "The only other person is Liv. And I can't blame her. She's the other girl who was with me, in the woods," I tell her.

Paula smiles. "I know who Liv is."

I laugh a little. "Yeah, you do. You probably know more about her than I do."

"The girl who got away," she says slowly, resonant.

"She *ran* away. Anyone would have."

"And you're the girl who got caught."

I smile ruefully. "For a while."

We stay this way for seconds, then minutes. The distant roar of Route 93 is cotton to my nerves. Paula smells like vanilla and lemon. It doesn't feel like I'm sitting next to someone you can see on TV any given night. It feels like I'm sitting next to an aunt, if I had one. Or a girlfriend of my mother's, if she had one.

"Can I be honest?" she finally says.

My heart trips a little.

"If I were Liv, I would have run too. I could never do what you did."

"But you get why I did it?" I ask.

"I totally get it. I might seem old to you, but I remember what it was like, being young and having a best friend." She moves a bit of hair behind my ear. It's a little weird, and a lot like what Kellan did last night. Again, I don't dislike it. "You're probably closer than sisters. I imagine an experience like this, horrific as it was, bonds you for life."

I stand and throw my pack over my shoulder. "I don't mean to be rude. But I really need to get going."

"I'll walk with you. You shouldn't be alone anyway." Paula scrambles up, limber and quick. "Do you mind if I walk with you?" she asks.

"Guess not," I mumble. We ignore the caution tape and take the trail fast, walking wide over roots and loose rock. This section of the Fells is intentionally less groomed than the main loop, to keep partiers away from the watchtower, and is illegal to enter after four p.m. for the same reason. Glass bottles and cans litter the brush, along with plastic dog-waste bags and cigarette butts. It's the way I came out on my stretcher, holding the hand of the biker who rescued me after I almost killed him when my screams made him crash. He had the gaunt cheeks and prominent eyes of an adrenaline junkie; he was, I believe, more frightened than I was. We must have talked, or we didn't. He stayed with me until the paramedics and the police came, and they say I wouldn't release his hand, even in the ambulance, but I don't remember that. I do remember being flat on my stretcher, the sun glittering painfully through the lacy treetops, hurting my eyes, but I kept them open. I would keep my eyes open when they set my ankle. I would keep my eyes open when the sad-mouthed nurse swabbed me for evidence of Donald Jessup.

"I understand why you want to come out here," Paula says suddenly.

"You do?"

"You believe your cases are linked. You need to see what happened to Ana Alvarez to understand the fate you escaped."

"Some people call that macabre."

"I call it necessary. Otherwise the entire episode has a randomness that doesn't sit with you. If Ana Alvarez was your corollary, Donald Jessup had a plan. And if Ana Alvarez was his trial run, at least knowing that would put order to chaos."

I scowl at the ground, my quads itching to run.

"You think if you go to the spot where they found her, you'll know. You'll know if he did it, because you'll know what his plan was."

I pump my arms hard. I can't decide if I'm mad that Paula's making me sound like an awful person, or that she's cutting too close to the truth. Either way, the black in my belly is on high alert. "You think I want Ana Alvarez dead?" I ask. "You think her murder is useful to my recovery? What kind of a person do you think I am?"

"I think you're the kind of person who's never content with what they're told," she says.

"Who checks out their own mother. That's pretty sad."

"If it makes you feel better, it's not sad."

"You know what would make me feel better?" I huff. "If reporters didn't pop out of the bushes or the trailhead or vans at Shiverton High School, and I could get on with my life." I pick up my pace to a jog.

"There's a place to put your anger, you know," Paula says, struggling for breath.

"Besides on you and your compadres? Because that feels right, right about now."

"When the police caught Donald Jessup he was wearing an ankle monitor." She pants mightily. "Do you know what that is? It's an electronic device that recorded his location. Donald Jessup was required to wear it—it looks like a thick, black, rubber bracelet around his ankle—as a condition of his parole. The monitor sends a radio frequency signal, a ping containing the offender's location to a receiver. If the offender moves outside of the allowed range, the police are notified. The allowed range did not include any area within twenty feet of a place that children congregate."

I start to sprint, calling back, "Like a playground?"

"Like a high school!" She stops and plants her hands on her

thighs, leaning over. "Donald Jessup violated his parole by parking at Shiverton High School more than ten times during October and November of last year!" she calls, straining.

I know she's making a point, but my thoughts migrate as I gain speed. What kind of car did Donald Jessup drive? A beat-up truck? A geriatric Cadillac with handicapped plates? His mother's? A Lester-the-Molester white van with tinted windows? Did he park in the student parking lot? Why did no one notice?

I trip over a root and sprawl on my hands and knees. Paula catches up and grabs my elbow to lift me. I pull away, swiping at a tear, embarrassed. "How is the tracking even accurate?" I ask. "Couldn't Jessup just take off the bracelet if he wanted to go somewhere he wasn't allowed?"

"Ankle monitors are tamper-resistant. It alerts the police if the wearer tries to remove it," she explains.

"So Donald Jessup was stalking us. What does that prove? We already know he was a pervert."

"It proves the police failed you. You didn't know Donald Jessup was wearing an ankle monitor because the police hid it from you, your mother, and the media."

"Why would they do that?" I ask.

"Julia," Paula says, trying to touch my arm. I dodge her grasp. "When the offender moves outside of the allowed range, the police are notified. What's more, Jessup's parole officer was required to check in with the police weekly to make sure that he wasn't violating his parole. It was a double oversight."

"So they were lazy."

"That's not all. The pings indicated Donald Jessup was walking here, in the Middlesex Fells Reservation, nearly weekly from September to November. At minimum, that kind of suspicious behavior warranted checking up on him, seeing as his prior took place where women jogged or walked."

The sun goes behind a cloud, or the tree canopy grows thick. Either way, I don't like it. "Where did he walk?"

"Between the Sheepfold and the fire watchtower. Where we're headed at this exact moment," Paula tells me.

"Right," I whisper, unsure if I said it to her or to myself.

"There's more if you want it."

I stare out in the direction of the tower.

"He drove down Wildwood Road, parking for ten to fifteen minutes at a time, multiple times."

"Liv's house." I turn to face her. "So he was stalking us."

"It appears that way. But if that's what he was trying to do, he wasn't successful. I've traced his movements on a timeline with Liv's and yours, and they don't match up."

I make a face. "You know where Liv and I were every day last fall?"

"For the most part," she says plainly, like it's not unusual. "But here's the thing. On the days Donald Jessup was hanging around Shiverton High, you and Liv were on a field trip, out sick, or it was a Jewish holiday and there was no school. Donald Jessup was at Shiverton High *only* on the days you and Liv were not."

Far away, an owl screeches, or a person screams. I take off again, yelling over my shoulder, "So he had bad luck!"

She lets out a theatrical groan, then resumes her chase. "Cross-country training in the off-season," she calls from a few feet behind. "You train differently on different days, is that right?"

"Hard and easy. Hills some days, speed work on others. Hard is hills, easy is flat, like grass and cement. We use the track, too, but not last November, with the Aberjona rising and the floods." I glance backward; she's really struggling. "Why?"

"Different routes on different days, correct?" she pants.

"Yep!" I call.

"Hill work was in the Fells, speed work was in a loop from the high school to downtown. Always the same?"

"For group practices, yeah, pretty much. What are you saying?"

"Donald Jessup's monitor showed him at various points"—she pauses for breath—"on both of those routes"—she sniffs juicily—"but never on the days that the team was running them." She yells in defeat, "Uncle!"

I jog back and around her in circles.

"Julia," she says, her face pinched.

I keep circling her.

"Julia!" she repeats, clearly pissed.

I halt. "Whaaat?"

She says, "What are the odds he'd get it wrong every time?"

I rake my hand over my face. "Maybe he was staking the places out. Maybe he was working up his courage." I should want this information. I need this information. Yet the urge to deflect is overwhelming. I pull out my phone. "I need to check in with my mom." The phone goes to voice mail, and I hang up.

For a while the only sound is Paula breathing. She sits on a log and unlaces her boot, yanking it off to reveal blood seeping through her sock toe. "Ouch."

"No one answering at her work?" she asks, looking up at me sideways.

"She didn't go in to work today," I reply. "I guess she's still asleep."

Paula pulls at the tip of her sock gingerly. "Asleep? It's past noon."

"She had too much wine last night. Company came over. A couple of guys. Guy *friends*. Both of ours," I stammer. Somehow it all sounds so wrong.

She winces, in pain, or possibly at what I said.

"It's not typical that she's asleep. Usually she goes in to the lab on days when there's no school."

"Of course. You're sixteen. Still, I'm sure your mother resents putting in so much time at the lab, away from you." She shakes out her boot, whacking it on a rock before jamming it back on.

I smirk, which she interprets as psychological pain over my domestic situation, because Paula stands and places her hand on my shoulder. "You have every right to be angry at all the people who failed you," she tells me.

I close my eyes against a second wave of unwelcome thoughts. Donald Jessup's knob of a head behind a steering wheel in downtown Shiverton, buckles on his camouflage jacket clinking as he eases down on the brake, watching the backs of girls' heads as they run. Maybe one head is blond, the other, brunette. I ought to be recording the facts Paula has spread before me. Yet it's all too close. A dull throb starts at the top of my head.

"Julia, you don't look well."

Paula places her hand on my other shoulder. As her jacket swings open, the buckles shake and clink the way his buckles did. Snowy fuzz creeps into the corners of my eyes. Not a daymare, not here, not with her. A knot hardens at the base of my throat and my hand rises, filled with air, untethered.

No!

I yank down my hand and grab the hem of her jacket blindly. It is smooth and finished and tailored, and that is good. The buckles are on her jacket, a woman's jacket, this jacket. Good.

"Julia!"

I wrench myself away and stagger, sweating, plucking at the armpits of my coat and swallowing air.

"You're not well. I have a granola bar you can eat." She forces me to sit on a fallen tree, unwraps the bar, and hands it to me. "When you're feeling better, we're turning around."

I devour it, noisy and uncaring. When I'm done, I feel steady enough to look her in the eye. "Liv and me. He was looking for us, that day in the woods."

She nods solemnly and helps me rise, linking her arm in mine, and we walk, her limping, me with my head down, the mile back to our cars in silence. The sun drops lower. At one point, a biker comes out of nowhere and whooshes past.

I let loose a little yelp. Paula swears at him, and we both laugh.

It's ages before I convince Paula that I'm all right to drive. To do so, I have to give her something, a benign bit of me that I wasn't wanting to share. I tell her about the notebook, not specifically, but that I like to organize my thoughts in writing, like her, I bet. She is jazzed, says we are connected in so many ways, and that even though she knows I have the bloodline to be a famous scientist one day, she recognizes a future journalist when she sees one.

For the second time, I find myself liking someone I don't want to like. Someone with capable hands. I wonder if it's too late to set the boundaries, and if not, what will they look like?

When Paula finally drives away, I lock my car door and prop my notebook up on the steering wheel, wondering how to represent all of Donald Jessup's missed connections with Liv and me. How a stalker even chooses his next victim. Did he pick us out of the pack running through town that rainy fall? Shouldn't a sociopath who already killed once be better at stalking his victims such that he doesn't miss every opportunity to stalk them? I draw a whorl, one line never meeting itself. Eventually my mind moves to easier thoughts.

I write:

Things I Know About Paula Papademetriou:
- Had a best friend
- Isn't content with what she's told
- Thinks I'm not content with what I'm told

A blast of music draws my attention back to the woods. I check the rearview mirror in time to see Shane's ancient matte black GTO pull in across the small lot and park, its windows open halfway. I spin fast to see a head in the passenger seat. Blonde, heart-shaped face: unmistakably Liv. I know why they're here. The parking lot at the Fells' fire watchtower entrance is famous for smoking, hooking up, and perverts alone with newspapers in their laps. The cracked window suggests the first. I stash my notebook in the wedge next to my seat and climb over the console to the backseat. If the car looks empty, it will draw less interest, in case Shane gives the lot a stoned-and-paranoid once-over.

"I'm stretching my legs," Liv says over a rusty creak—the GTO's door opening.

I slide to the backseat floor and fold into a tight ball, as if my perfect stillness will render my car invisible. I'm not a praying sort, but I mutter a short prayer anyway, that Liv has chosen this one time to partake in what Shane is offering, and her fugue state will cause her to miss my car. I add a quick thank-you prayer, too, that Mom choked when the dealer suggested the SPUNK vanity plate.

A second car door slam. I hitch my breath.

"What you really mean is you want to shake off the smoke so Lady Deborah doesn't smell it," says Shane.

"I'm not the one smoking," Liv replies, her voice thinner, moving away. I scramble to peek through the rear window in time to see Liv heading for the trailhead.

"Fine. You don't want Mama to know you consort with

delinquents. That's cool. Except you'd think you were the one stoned, all paranoid, ducking down like you got shot when we drove by Paula Pappa-dem-meaty-o's in that SUV. Do you know she lives in Shiv—?"

"I'm aware," Liv interrupts.

"Have you ever seen her in person?" Shane says.

"Yes, Shane. She was just at our school," Liv says.

"Man, she's tight. Who would think she has a kid our age?"

"My age," Liv says, reminding me that Shane's real age is up for debate, a question related to the accuracy of his adoption records that emerged around fourth grade after he grew a full mustache.

Shane walks toward Liv, the cuffs of his thin jacket rising as he twists pale wrists back and forth. He sprawls on the stairs where Paula asked me to sit hours ago.

Liv glances back. "Don't get too comfortable. You know I hate it here. There are so many other places to smoke."

"I won't be but a moment, milady." He reaches around to his back pocket and pulls out a plastic bag.

"You should save that. You owe Boseman," she says.

He drops the bag in his lap and reaches into his coat. "Just a pinch. Your knuckle-job cousin won't know the difference." His head hangs down, twisting the joint, flicking away seeds with fingernails that I know are dirty. Liv ignores him, gazing into the woods, not unlike the way she did that morning last November. I wonder what she's thinking about. Is she imagining what I went through? Remembering what she went through? Shane lights the joint and sucks, then exhales through pursed lips.

"Harsh," he gasps, but it doesn't stop him from taking a second drag, then a third. After a while he notices Liv. "What are you staring at, girl?"

"Nothing."

Shane stubs out the roach on the stair and considers it, then flicks it into the woods. "Wait. I know. You're thinking about the boogeyman in the woods. Your personal boogeyman. Look out, hot runner girl! I'm going to hunt down you and your friend!" He lets loose a grating cackle.

"Not funny."

"He's dead, babe! He can't get you now!" Shane stands, his legs and arms rangy. "Unless you're afraid of his fat ghost?" he asks, tickling her roughly.

"Stop." She tries to slap him, but he dodges her, laughing. He catches her by the waist and holds her. They rock for a second, Shane nuzzling the back of her neck, Liv still staring down the trail. She breaks free and spins round. Her face is different, flushed and excited.

"You know what I just realized?" she says. "We never talk. Just, talk."

Shane drags his hand down his mouth and laughs, unsure. "You want to talk? With me?"

Liv takes his wrist and pulls him down until they are seated on the railroad ties. His head bobs slightly.

"Like, what's your favorite food? Or, what's the best concert you've ever been to?" she says, downright bubbly.

Shane leans in, about to speak, but Liv puts her finger against his lip. "Shh! I know a topic. You've never told me about your birth mother."

He backs away from her finger. "I don't know my birth mother. Dang, Liv. Why are you bringing that up?"

"She was a prostitute, right?" Liv says, smiling brightly. It's so bizarre, I crawl up an inch more to see better.

Shane makes a *pshaw* noise and turns away, his leg bouncing.

"I mean, it must be a Russian thing, because all those girls who get brought over here for prostitution rings are Russian. Or Eastern European, anyway," Liv says.

"A Russian thing, huh?" He takes the bag from his pocket and removes a package of rolling papers, slipping out one and tossing the pack to the ground. He folds the paper and drops in a pinch of weed, licking the paper sideways and twisting it over itself.

"Generally they're total skanks. Not remotely attractive, just young, with faces like sheep. Except, have you ever heard of the Russian Barbie? She's this woman who's had a ton of plastic surgery to look just like a Barbie doll. Her name is Valeria something. Her skin is matte—matte means not shiny. In this case, plastic-looking. And her waist is the size of your wrist. Oh, oh: and her blue eyes are opaque! They say she does that with contacts—"

He blows the joint dry, his eyes slanting at Liv above it.

"It must be a DNA thing, the way all these Russian people are desperate and oversexed."

"Oversexed, huh?" Pocketing the joint, he cocks his head, smiling, and gets close to her nose. Sinister. "Maybe you can help me with my genetic defect."

Liv doesn't blink. "My mother's no picnic, don't get me wrong. And she'd be the last person to turn her nose up at going under the knife. In fact, I'm pretty sure she'll try to use my college fund for a complete overhaul when she turns fifty. But at least she's not a whore for hire. I don't know if I could deal with that."

What is Liv thinking, saying this stuff?

"You're lucky she didn't pass chlamydia on to you," she continues. "Newborns exposed to chlamydia get terrible eye infections. I'm thinking about this because your eyes are super-red right now. Or syphilis. Syphilis is easily transmitted from mother to child. The mothers go crazy, like Al Capone and Hitler, and the babies end up with problems with their brains, skin, and teeth. They're often premature. Wait: you were a preemie, right?"

"Shut the hell up."

"Surely she had HPV. I mean, everybody has HPV, so a hooker definitely had to have it. Sometimes the hormones from pregnancy can make the genital warts grow big enough that they block the birth canal. Then the baby has to be delivered by cesarean section. Were you a C-section?"

Shane glares, baring his teeth. "Enough!"

My fingers float to the lip of the window and do a nervous dance.

"I'm just saying"—Liv lifts a flop of hair from his eyes delicately—"I wouldn't feel bad about your mother. It's not like you can help that she was a whore."

Shane grabs Liv's wrist hard and twists it. Liv yelps. He shoves her wrist forward, sending her flying backward off the stair and onto the hard ground. I scream—a gargle that I swallow—tuck my head, and bite the flesh triangle between my thumb and finger. Then I rise to see again, because he might do something more. I need to stop him, but he's crawling over to her, weeping like a baby, and she is already on her knees consoling him.

"What the hell? You made me do it. Why'd you start talking like that? I shouldn't have shoved you, you just made me so mad. I'm sorry." He drops his face into his hands and bawls.

"Shane!" Liv peels his hands away from his face. "Shane, listen to me: I crossed the line."

He buries his face in her chest.

"Look at me!" She lifts his pocked, gleaming cheeks and forces him to look in her eyes. "What you did was right. I said something horrible about your mother. I deserved it." Liv's voice is different. Commanding.

"I won't let it happen again," he blubbers.

"Shh. Your love for me is just so strong, sometimes you can't control it. It's okay. I get it. I'm flattered. It means you must really love me."

His head rises slowly. "So much."

She pulls his head against the middle of her chest. "I'm counting on it."

*   *   *

I lie in a fetal position on my backseat, past when they stumble back to the car, arms entwined, past when I hear them finish making out, past when Shane revs the engine of his muscle car and does two hard skids then a long, slow burnout, past when the sky blazes orange just before the sun dives below the horizon. Only then do I open my car door, lean into the crisp air, and vomit.

SIX

357 Days After the Woods

"Here we are, you and me. Not what I expected. But something."

I squeeze the tiny sharp stick I conceal in my palm, barely a stick at all, but I will jam it in his eye if he tries to touch me. My body tingles, ready to fight.

"But something," I repeat.

He scowls. It was nervy to remind him I am human. I cower inside the polyester sleeping bag. Two sleeping bags, tucked inside a hollow log, in this spot. Premeditation. My bowels rumble, loose and spastic, reminding me of my second-biggest fear at this moment.

He stamps over and looms, night vision goggles perched on his fore-head. I inch my stick nearer to the opening of the bag. He sways, reek-ing of smoke and wet wool. In another world, he is the guy in short sleeves and wrinkled khakis working at Best Buy. Here, the fire makes sinister shadows across his face. He shakes his finger in front of my nose.

"Not. Her."

He giggles and falls back onto his sleeping bag, feet flying up in the air like a baby. He plants his boots and reaches up his pant leg, flourishing the knife. "Just in case you get any stupid ideas."

A stick is no match for a knife.

He props his back against a tree to stay awake. His movements become twitches until he slumps. I slip one hand from the bag and wave it in the air.

One minute, then two.

Clouds pass in front of the moon and shadows fall over his slumped form. I am colder than I ever thought possible. But my body is still mine. After hours of this creature dragging me to wherever in this woods he is taking me to, my body is still mine, in that way.

My eyes sweep over our crude campsite with its fire that has attracted no rescuers. I trace every shadowy outline beyond it for some clue. If I'm right, we're in the exact place where Liv and I aren't supposed to go, but do. Ten feet behind me should be the north edge of the Sheepfold, a steep slope camouflaged when the ground is covered in leaves. But in early winter, when the ground is bare, you can see it's a yawning gorge. I roll over in my bag and squint into the darkness, until I detect the barely perceptible demarcation, where violet turns to the absolute absence of light. The drop.

I wonder if he knows these woods as well as I do. The pain in my ballooning ankle has gone from sharp to fuzzy. Even if I manage to hop-drag past without waking him, it will take hours to reach the groomed trail. He knows this; it is the only reason my legs are not bound. If he wakes, I will never outrun him.

There's only one thing to do. Don't use my feet.

I shimmy into my bag, sneakers pushing against the bottom seam. Raise my bound hands above my head to protect it. Close my eyes. And roll.

I careen over jagged rocks, roots, stumps. Don't think tuck head don't think tuck head. The bag shreds until parts of me are exposed. Sometimes I'm feet first, sometimes head. I coil my body tighter, my back into a hard shell. Leaf and rock enter the open top and fill the bag. Twice I am ensnared, twice I jam my elbows and knees into the earth, hurtling myself over obstacles. With every gyration I am farther away from him.

I've been falling forever when the mud slows me to a halt. Loam and grit blur my vision, but moonlight throws the ledge into relief. I've dropped at least eighty feet, and my body, thickened ankle and all, is bruised horrendously, but intact. I am covered in warm blood and mud. My hands are free. The bag hangs off me in shreds.

I'm not dead.

Even if the noise of me hurtling down the chasm woke him up, I just put eighty feet between us. For the first time, I feel like I might get home.

"Julia, I'm going to count from one to five, and at the count of five you're going to feel wide awake, fully alert, and completely refreshed. One, two . . ." Ricker counts.

"I'm awake," I say.

"Three, four, five."

"I said, I'm awake."

"How do you feel?" Ricker asks.

I prop myself on my elbow. "Better than I usually feel, because I'm here and not in the middle of class, for example.

There's nothing worse than the stares you get when you're standing there gaping at a wall, with no clue if you've been doing it for five seconds or fifteen minutes."

Ricker's pen freezes midair. "You're saying this isn't the first time you've had a regressive memory?"

"It's the first time I've made one start." I swing my legs off the couch and sit up. "Though yesterday, I made one stop."

Ricker breathes hard through her nose. "I require total honesty in this room. Is there a reason you never mentioned your memories before?"

"They've really just revved up since I've been back at school. I'm not the one with the diplomas, but I'd say that makes sense."

Ricker's eyes flick to the diplomas on the wall. She catches me catch her, and frowns. "Triggers most certainly cause memories to emerge. And now, triggers are all around you. So yes: it makes *sense*, as you say." She ducks her head and starts scribbling; I lean forward slightly to peek at the page, because it feels like a power move. Get things back on the right track and such. Boundaries.

I really do like her.

"So we're on the same page," I say. "I mean, think about it. The Berkshires were basically sensory deprivation. Besides the trees—which for a while were not my thing, but I'm warming to perennials—there was nothing to do. All I had were my weekly e-mails from Liv. And my appointments with Patty Petty. She was whacked. Did you know she tried to make me dance?"

Ricker refolds her legs, flashing a brilliant smile over her pad. She's openly, undisguisedly, blatantly not listening.

"You're smiling. Why are you smiling?"

Ricker looks up. "If memories emerge, it's a sign that the survivor has found a safe environment and has reduced the level and frequency of her daily dissociation. Now her repressed memories may be brought to her conscious mind."

"As far as signs go, that sounds like a good one to me."

"It's a sign your mind is working toward something."

"It's an almost-anniversary present to myself." I say this, hoping she'll say something about the fact that we are nearing the one-year mark of the Shiverton Abduction, in news-speak. But I'm thinking Ricker's the type to forget to buy a card.

She touches my knee. "It is a good sign. Tell me again. You began to have a memory?"

"My friend's jacket had buckles on it. When they clinked, they reminded me of the sounds Donald Jessup's jacket made."

She rises and walks to the bookshelf. "But you were able to draw back, realize you were in the present, and stop it?"

"Right. I stepped outside of myself, sort of. Told myself it was her jacket, not his."

"Her?" She pulls down a gold-embossed book.

"My friend. Alice," I lie. "What, is that weird?"

She flips through the book. "It's unusual. Not unprecedented, but unusual."

Nervous she's going to ask about Alice, I count cracks in the leather couch. There are seventeen. She runs her finger along a page. I clear my throat. "When do we get to talk about what I remembered?"

"Regression therapy can be an intense experience."

"Trust me, I'm familiar. Imagine being thrown from an airlock. It's like being on the receiving end of a mighty suck," I say.

"Because of their intensity, I generally don't like to examine sessions right away. There should be a benefit from hypnosis, a sense of relaxation and wellness that you spend some time enjoying. We'll discuss it at our next appointment."

"Wait, what? We're not going to talk about it? Don't you think some of the stuff Jessup said was weird?" I ask.

"I need time to listen to my recording. I can't really say."

"I get that we're not evidence-gathering here. And I'm not saying I want to start talking to the police again. But I thought maybe we could talk about it—"

"Julia," Ricker interrupts me.

"Hang on. So that means I'm only getting hypnotized once every two weeks? That's not enough!"

"It's rather aggressive, all things considered. You need to understand something. We're not trying to reimagine Donald Jessup's intentions. Those don't matter. What you remember, those things may not have actually happened. And whether they did or not, it's letting out the emotion that's important."

"May not have actually happened?" I stick my middle finger into a crack and scrape a loose staple. The warm blood comes fast, but I force myself to leave my finger there, bleeding into her couch. Stain on you, Ricker.

"Memory is fragile. Everything you recall is not likely to be correct. Under hypnosis, a person will elaborate, fill in incomplete bits to make a full story. Memory is not like a tape recorder or a video. That said, the reality as perceived by you is what we should concentrate on."

"The reality as perceived by me. Wow," I repeat.

"As a rule, the deeper the hypnosis, the less reliable the memory."

"You remember me waking up on the count of 'two,' right?" I yank my finger from the couch and grab my bag. "This was fun. But really, I don't see the point. If I can go back to the woods any time I feel like it, why do I need you? If my memories are all made up—or partly made up—why bother? I'm going to go enjoy my relaxation now. Until soon, Elaine."

I blast into the reception room holding up my middle finger so blood won't drip on the floor. Ricker's next appointment, my doughy friend with a mole, flips me off behind his cupped hand as he passes into Ricker's office. I try to deny giving him the finger as he slams the door. The receptionist reaches through the glass with a bouquet of tissues, which I grab, wrapping them around my digit mummy-style. When I turn, everyone ducks their heads over magazines or pulls out their phones. In the elevator, Muzak picks at my nerves, and I realize I forgot my coat, but I cannot go back, not after that performance. I hurry out the exit, chased by the tinkle of bells someone tacked above the door. Ricker's office is in a bland building sandwiched between a Dunkin' Donuts and a musclehead gym. To get to your car you have to cross a tiny patio with a bench in front of a fountain covered by a skin of ice. I sit on the bench and pull out my marbleized notebook and flip through chunks of paper to find a clean page in the back. My butt is freezing, I am freezing, but if I start to have a daymare, a *regressive memory*, I can control it now. No big whoop.

If Ricker won't deconstruct my memories, I will.

More Things I Know About Donald Jessup:
- Had two sleeping bags
- Said I was not her
- Gave me a head start

A shadow falls across my lap. I slap my notebook shut.

"Whoa. I didn't peek, I swear." Kellan is bundled in a scarf and a hockey sweatshirt over oxford shirttails. He hooks his thumbs (always the thumbs) into his jeans pockets, kicking the air, looking out from under a fringe of ginger lashes. "Finger okay?"

"Fine. How did you know I was here?" I say. Smooth.

Kellan twists his sneaker (always the sneaker). "I may have stopped by your house."

"Did I forget something again?" I can't act flattered, because I will humiliate myself. He's made it clear that I'm just a noteworthy oddity, with my misplaced freckles, ghostly complexion, and freakishly big feet. After transferring from private St. John's Prep to public Shiverton freshman year (an easy social transition, since he knew half the boys already from regional hockey teams), he could have scored any GIRL. He scored Liv. His latest dalliance, the GIRL with the Apple Face, looks like she should be milking a cow and wearing a skirt embroidered with bric-a-brac trim. What business does he have with an un-GIRL who slips in and out of the present on a daily basis and rocks a black thing in her belly?

Yet he does keep showing up.

"You didn't forget a thing. I just thought we'd add another episode to the show of your life," Kellan says, his lip curled into a crooked smile.

"Is it going to get surreal?" I say.

"That depends. Do you consider a picnic dinner outdoors in November surreal?"

"Surreally? Where are we having it?" I ask, slipping off the bench.

"Over"—Kellan grabs my shoulders and faces me toward the gym—"there. But first you need to take this." A bustle behind me, and then darkness as he yanks his thick hockey sweatshirt over my head. I yelp, flopping the sleeves that spill over my hands, and he pulls me along by the cuff, and I laugh, letting him lead as we wend between parked cars and Dumpsters until we enter a brand-new skate park.

Stretching his arms, he affects a formal, booming voice. "This is the set."

He leads me to the center of the largest cement bowl. Someone has already defiled a wall with "Candy hearts Larry" in fresh white spray paint. He drops his backpack with a shifty thud and sits, pulling me down with him. Cold leaches through my jeans. I tug sweatshirt slack under my butt.

"An empty skate park," I say, nodding, my lips tucked. "Charmingly weird."

"I chose it because I wanted you to feel safe. Look around."

We are surrounded by cement stairs, curbs, and half-pipes; lips, bowls, and banks.

"No trees," I say softly.

"As man-made as it can get. Don't you see, Julia? I. Get. You."

Silence settles between us. For once, I have absolutely no idea what to say. But I try: "What's in the backpack?"

He unzips his backpack and removes a block of cheese, a bag of grapes, a jar of fancy shriveled pickles, and a can of beer.

"Where did you get the beer?"

"The fridge. You don't have to drink it."

"We can't sit in the middle of a public skate park and drink."

"I know. It's for celebratory effect. Oh man, I forgot the knife. You won't mind gnawing the top off that cheese, will you?"

I hold the murky jar to the sky. "I don't mean to be rude, but what are 'bitter gourdpickles'?"

"I'm not sure. I was rushed. I spent most of the morning scouting treeless locations. They call them leafy suburbs for a reason. Who knew the best one was right next door to your doc? Oh. I got you this, too." He removes a dented brown cardboard box tied with twine and sets it on the ground proudly.

I stare at it.

"Are you going to open it?" he says, crossing his arms and

patting them. "You know, not all of us have a nice thick Chief-tains hockey sweatshirt."

I untie the string and the box falls apart. Inside is a smooshed purple cupcake, the kind sold in an expensive bakery, with layers of frosting flowers now smeared on the box flaps.

"Aww, dang. It got banged up in the Jeep," he says.

I stick a finger inside and scoop some frosting. "That is so good. Do you want some?"

"It's all for you." Kellan cracks the beer and takes a sip, then tips the can to me. "You?"

"Nah."

"Do you mind if I drink?" he asks.

"There are worse things."

He grins and takes a long draft. "Steadies the nerves."

"I count stars. Statistical probabilities. Whatever's convenient in the moment."

He looks at me quizzically, then his eyes pop. "Oh hey, you're still cold! Come closer."

The soft cave under his shoulder looks like a place I'd like to spend a while. I scoot closer.

"So. You said the beer was for celebratory effect. And a cupcake is, technically, cake. What are we celebrating?" I ask.

"I hadn't thought that one through. Again, working out the treeless angle just *consumed* me." He takes another sip of beer. "When's your birthday?"

"May."

"I'm February. That doesn't work. Wait. Aren't we coming up on the anniversary of the abduction?"

"November twenty-second."

"Happy almost-abduction anniversary!" he says.

I stiffen, pretending to be furious. "That is so wrong. How dare you?"

I feel him hold his breath. Then I lose it and burst out laughing. Soon he's laughing too.

"I love that you want to celebrate the anniversary of my abduction," I say. "Sorry: 'the public's abduction' would be more accurate. And if we're getting all semantic, it's worth noting that 'happy' is relative."

"I'll rephrase: bittersweet anniversary!"

"Now that works. Bitter and sweet, like pickles and cupcakes. Because on the one hand, I got abducted. On the other hand: this."

"I like this," he murmurs.

Kellan's face is closer to mine than it's ever been. His nose might have been broken once. His ears stick out and his smile screws sideways into a dimple. Separately, his parts are oddball; together, they are devastating. Do I want to be devastated?

"But there's the question of cause and effect," I say, pulling away. "Would 'this' be happening if 'that' hadn't?"

"What are you saying?" he asks.

"I just mean, your usual . . . interests . . . diverge from . . ."

"I'm not seeing anyone, Julia."

". . . me. Like Liv. She's someone I'd expect you'd be with."

"You're still hung up on that one night with Liv? That was the littlest, nothing hook-up. I barely knew her."

His face is open and honest. Relief sweeps over me like sweet air.

I sigh and relax. "I feel like I barely know Liv lately, either."

"Because she's seeing that dirtbag Shane Cuthbert?" he asks.

"There's that."

"Dr. Phil doesn't have me on speed dial, but did you ever think maybe Liv feels guilt over what happened in the woods? I mean, you sacrificed your life to save hers."

I pull back, because his face distracts me from his words. "Say that again?"

"Maybe degrading herself by hanging around with a bottom-feeder like Cuthbert is the way Liv punishes herself for letting you take her place," he says simply, taking a long sip.

A fullness. The feeling of backsweeping, a tide rolling out to reveal gifts.

He knocks back the last of the beer and rises to his knees, his arm arched gracefully toward a trash barrel five feet away, and pitches it into the can. It clatters inside, a perfect basket. "Hey, two points!"

I reach for his waist and pull him down fast. His eyes widen. I cup his cheeks and he makes a small groan as I pull him in to kiss.

"Cold lips," he murmurs, his own lips curling to the right, aiming for that dimple.

"Suddenly I'm okay with cold. You're a really smart guy," I add.

"You're a really beautiful girl," he says.

"Lowercase letters."

"What?"

"Never mind."

"The blood in your cheeks makes you look so, I don't know. So alive," he says.

"Staying alive is kind of my thing." I rise on my knees and he rises too, and we kiss again, and instead of thinking about Liv or Shane or Apple Face, I taste the hops on his tongue, and think how I hate beer but I like this, and how good it is to taste again.

I weave my arm through his and fall against his shoulder. He strokes my hair lightly with the end of his fingertips, surreptitiously, like he thinks I don't notice.

Not only am I okay with the cold, I've become downright warm.

He sighs into my hair, and it's a vulnerable noise, and it sets me on fire. "Can I ask you one question that's been bothering me?"

I kiss him again, because none of this is real, it will shred and dissipate as soon as the black thing comes back, as soon as the memories return and the questions start.

"Just one question," I murmur.

"Who's Alice?"

SEVEN

359 Days After the Woods

Deborah's eyes flash as I stop the door with my boot.

"I need to talk with Liv. It's really important. Do you know where she is?"

"I do not. But if you hear from her, you can tell her that her electronics privileges are rescinded for a month. She never considers what her disappearances with that orphan delinquent do to me. I've been distracted for the last hour and gotten nothing done." Deborah charges back into the kitchen, shoulders scissoring as she stabs her phone, dialing. In seconds she's spelling "O-L-I-V-I-A" for some beleaguered church secretary type. As I turn to leave, she pokes her head back into the hall.

"Don't you go anywhere! I want to ask you some questions about that dope-smoking train wreck that Olivia . . ." she calls to me. "What?" she yells into the phone. "No, I'm not talking to you, I'm talking to Julia Spunk, you know who that is, I'm sure. There isn't a person in America who doesn't know Julia Spunk. Oh, now you can hear me!"

"I'll wait in Liv's room," I say, slipping through the door, past the round entrance table, and mincing up the stairs. The dimpled glass knob on Liv's door squeals, announcing me as I step inside the airless bedroom. Filthy hoodies and yoga pants lie in heaps. The only movement is swirling dust motes in sunbeams filtering through the quarter-moon window. I look for a spot on the bed to sit, but the sheets are yanked clear back and sitting feels like a violation, so I stand. The closet door swings wide. Maybe I know where Liv is after all.

I stick my head in among the clothes. "Liv? It's Julia," I whisper so harshly it burns my throat. "Are you in there?"

I tug the beaded lightbulb chain. Wool coats brush my cheeks as I feel for the panel to the secret eaves. I hold my breath and press, in and to the right. The panel slides open to darkness. I drop to my knees and crawl in, which feels safer. My fingers graze the metal Coleman camping lamp. I grope for the switch, hoping the lamp's batteries haven't leaked and corroded. The halogen tubes buzz and glow.

The eaves have always been the only place where we could go to escape Deborah's spying and listening. We'd crank the TV and slip into our soundproof hideaway, a deceptively large space inside the roof's overhang. Some days it was spy headquarters. One whole winter was spent playing squirrels. As the years passed, the eaves were where we snuck sips from a dusty bottle of Kahlua, practiced kissing the backs of our hands, and almost suffocated smoking our first butt. We'd drag in piles of Deborah's *Cosmopolitan*s and read aloud "How to Please Your Man" and sketch tattoos we'd get when we were eighteen. Absorbed by the antique Victorian, and with enough coats blocking our portal, we were invisible. Now a rough Mexican blanket and a pillow take the place of the glossy magazines. A laptop sits in the middle. The Coleman lamp, warmed now, purrs, and soft light reflects off fiberglass insulation padding the slanted walls, making the room warm and pink.

Pairs and pairs of eyes stare down at me.

Tacked to the exposed beams are a series of pictures, hand-drawn in charcoal with rips at the tops. There must be at least a dozen. I hold up the lamp: it's the same girl's face in every drawing. Her eyes are set back far, her lids are heavy. One eye is bigger than the other. The brows are mannish and unshaped. The nose is flat, the shape of the face an exaggerated heart, with a broad forehead and a weak chin. She smiles without showing her teeth.

Not a pretty face, but drawn lovingly. Instead of looking away, I'm drawn in.

In the first sketch, her hair is pulled back but for loose wisps. In a middle picture, her hair hangs around her face, drawn indecisively, as though the artist didn't have enough information. I raise the Coleman lamp slowly in front of the drawings. There is an order to things, an evolution of certainty about the subject. In the first, the girl is barely there, the eyes, nose, and mouth drawn as markers. In the second, the strokes are more confident, the lines of the jaw and the forehead more defined.

By the third, the artist has begun shading under the eyes and around the cheeks. The next four focus on the mouth, capturing her slip of a smile, closed lips forcing lines into the cheeks and lifting the chin. By the eighth, the artist tries to get the hair right, but by the ninth, he or she has given up, drawing just a few suggestive strokes. The tenth is sure, the outline firm, the shading bold. The girl looks right through me, in this tenth sketch, with her Mona Lisa smile: the smile of a girl who knows someone loves her.

I lift the lamp close to the last sketch, a busy scene set in a forest, where trees lush with fruit hold birds with feathery tails. The girl is dressed like an ancient Greek goddess, with lace-up sandals winding around muscled calves and a short toga. Her waist is encircled in a belt that ends in a snake's head. She wears a crown of leaves, and has an impossible pin-up bod. She runs, looking over her shoulder with a smile of pleasure at a warrior-type guy, an arsenal on his back. His muscled arms pull back a bow, and his thighs bulge. Animals look on from above and below, way too interested.

Why is Liv wallpapering our secret spot with soft-core porn for Dungeons and Dragons freaks?

I set the lamp down and kneel on the Mexican blanket. A pile in a spot just outside the circle of light catches my eye. I crawl closer. A stack of manila envelopes, tops torn open, the first covered in a fine dust. The envelopes are about the size of the sketches, and they are wrinkled and finger-stained in the manner of things that go through the mail. I lift one, blowing off the dust, which is thick and stubborn. The address is handwritten in careful lettering. "My Olivia," it says above a post office box number in Shiverton. There are eleven envelopes.

The ceiling presses down on me, making it hard to breathe. I set the envelopes down on top of one another and wriggle, itchy all over. The film on the envelopes is fiberglass insulation dust, maybe. Or not. A familiar chunky numbness settles behind my tongue. I feel for a beam and hang on as my eyes fill with white.

A fallen tree, like the husk of a giant dead insect. I press my body inside. Rot snags my hair and scrapes my back. I tell myself I itch not from beetles or millipedes or pill bugs or any other insect that lives in this log, and there are worse things. Hours pass as I listen for a twig snap or the suction sound of boots in the mud. Black turns to purple. It is time to run.

Deborah's sharp consonants carry up the stairs, faint, but loud enough to break the seal. I cover my face with splayed fingers.

"No," I gasp, hard, the command you give a disobedient dog. I spread my fingers and the white peels back, and I am here, back in the eaves, where I used to play.

Go. Now.

I switch off the lamp and pass through the panel door, batting coats aside for air. On the landing, I hear Deborah thank a harried school official.

"Julia?" she calls.

I thunder down the stairs, yelling, "Just tell Liv I stopped by, please!" She's screaming for me to come back as I tumble into the car, pressing the start button and miming through the window that I can't hear her, sorry, gotta run. I peel out in front of a minivan, leaving tire shred as the driver lays on her horn.

"You're home! How wonderful!" Mom yells, as though I've returned home from the war, or abroad, or college, all of which seem like better alternatives right now than dinner with the Mincae, for which it appears I am late. A dome of salmonella-white poultry sits in the lit oven. Mom looks at it with fear, then pulls herself away.

"I've been trying to reach you for hours," she play-scolds, setting out a tray of sliced cheese. "Alice and Eleanor were able to come next door for dinner on short notice. Wonderful, yes-yes?"

Alice beams at me, dumbstruck in the back doorway. Mrs. Mincus casts a sly smile, like she knows about the sketches in Liv's eaves. Like she knows I was peeping at something vaguely dirty.

"Yes. Yes!" I say. "But I have to show you something funky my car is doing. Two seconds?"

"Just two," Mom sings, following me out to the garage. The door shuts behind her, and I launch in.

"What would ever make you think it was a good idea—rephrase, appropriate idea—to invite Alice over? This is beyond weird, Mom."

"Not just Alice. Her mother, too. It's been a long time. You were best friends. I really think you could use a friend in your corner right now, someone not connected with the incident. Dr. Ricker agrees. A new addition to your circle of trust, so to speak."

"Yet another reason why I've recently ousted Dr. Ricker from my circle of trust. But apparently I don't need Ricker, because Alice is here to heal me with the balm of friend-ships past."

"Sarcasm is not useful—"

"To my healing. Right," I interrupt. "Well, you may have created this uncomfortable debacle, but we do not have to sit under your creepy microscope so you can supervise our play-date. I'm taking Alice out."

Mom's pretty eyes pop.

"Leaving. Not killing. I'm *leaving* with Alice."

Mom sighs, a ragged noise. "Fine. I'll catch up with Elea-nor. You come back in an hour." She turns to open the door to the kitchen and pauses. "Maybe more. I didn't time the chicken so well."

"Did you remove the giblets?" I ask.

She presses her knuckle to her top lip.

"Just order takeout," I say, sliding past her into the kitchen and tucking myself into my still-warm jacket. "Alice, c'mon. We're out of here."

Alice pushes back her headband and leaps up. "Where are we going?"

"Running," I say.

Mrs. Mincus buries her chin sideways into her chest, as if to say *You've got to be kidding.* I can't blame her, since running hasn't always turned out so well for me, but her expression is unflattering, and she should stop.

"Exercise. We'll run around the track." Before Mrs. Mincus can excavate her neck and object, I slip back into the garage and jam the door opener with my fist, Alice chasing after me.

"But Julia, it's dark!" Alice cries.

"It's dusk. Dusk and dark are different. Know your gradations of black." I slip into the driver's seat of my car. "Besides, the track is lit."

"We're not dressed to run."

"It's an excuse to get away from our mothers, Alice."

"Right. Of course. So we can gossip."

"Something like that."

She slides into the passenger seat and takes a deep breath through her nose. "Mmm, new car smell."

We drive across Shiverton proper in the waning late-autumn light, past mums lining walkways, past Saint Theresa's church, and past Shane's house, the neatest of them all, with mint-green vinyl siding and a Thanksgiving pumpkin on every step, his muscle car nowhere in sight. Alice blathers the whole way, excited to be in my car, my *coolest-ever* car, with its electronics that *do stuff.* And how great is it that Mom invited them over? They almost couldn't come, big goings-on at the church tonight, but Mrs. Mincus made an exception because she knew how much Alice would want to, and the boys could feed themselves.

I look over at Alice, feeling like an adult taking her kid on a Sunday drive. Alice with her Mary Jane sneakers, her Hello Kitty sweater with yarn appliqué. Alice with her headband.

"I know it's been a while since we've hung out. But I want you to know that my parents and I prayed for you every hour you were gone," Alice says.

Alice with no filter.

"I guess it worked. Thanks?" I say.

"You're welcome," she chirps, overly bright. "There's something I've been wondering. Did your mother get closer to God after last year? Considering the miracle of your return, it's hard to imagine that she's still an atheist."

"My mother isn't an atheist. She's agnostic."

She shrugs. "Six of one."

"Tomato tomahto."

"Exactly," Alice agrees, looking around. The new track is dead and dark with waves where it buckles, as though the town was in a rush and tarred it too soon. We walk for a while until Alice complains, and we plant ourselves on the bleachers, swinging our legs to keep warm. It brings back not unpleasant memories of playing outside with Alice when we were little until the streetlights came on. "I want to show you something." She shoves her coat sleeve above her elbow. The lights cast a lurid glare on her pale arm. Below the crease in purple Sharpie is scrawled *WWJD?*

"Nice tat. New boyfriend?"

"You could say that." She regards her arm for a moment. "I don't take it that far."

"Alice! JD—that's a big deal. Are you dating a lawyer?"

She kicks my shin. "It's an acronym, dummy."

"Fine, I'll bite. What does WWJD stand for?"

"It stands for *What Would Jesus Do?* Whenever I have a really big decision to make, I ask myself that question."

"So Jesus told you to wear that Hello Kitty sweater with yarn whiskers?"

"Easy for you to joke." Alice drags her sleeve down. "You don't need to be reminded of what JC would do. You do it automatically."

"I'm not following."

"When you sacrificed your own life to save Liv's."

"I see," I mutter, wary.

"In a lot of ways, you're closer to Jesus than I'll ever be."

"I had no idea. I'm . . . sorry?"

"I'm all right with it. I understand that I'm a work in progress. Most of us are. We have a lot of business to do on this earth to be our best selves. Even my mother says she isn't as close to God as some of the women she knows. Take Mrs. Lapin, for example."

"No thanks."

"My mother says she gives to her parish and her community selflessly, so she's Father Carl's favorite. She was nominated Catholic Woman of the Year by the lay board of Saint Theresa's. That's a big deal."

Alice knows she may as well be talking about Wiccan white magic when she talks to me about parishes and priests. The Spunk girls don't spend a lot of downtime in churches. Mom is a self-proclaimed skeptic, which is an agnostic on steroids. The word gets under my skin—*ag-gnaw-stick*—the way Mom overarticulates it, as if to burn it into my memory in case she's accused of witchcraft and I'm called to her defense. "Why are you telling me this?"

"No reason." She checks her arm. "Well, okay. There's a reason. Since we're coming up on the anniversary of the Shiverton Abduction, we're having a special prayer mass tonight. To thank God for bringing you home."

"Alice," I repeat, my voice tinged with warning.

"I thought you might come with me."

"Alice."

"It doesn't matter if you believe in God."

"Does it matter if I've never set foot in a church?"

"That's okay! Jesus is welcoming. And Liv will be there. She got made youth ministry leader again this year. Not that it's fair to get it two years in a row. I mean, what can she add? It's not like she'll have a fresh perspective."

"Good point."

"A sympathy vote after the Shiverton Abduction, if I might be so bold. At school, she might be queen bee to my drone. But in youth ministry, I could stage a coup at any time and be named leader. No one in youth ministry likes her. They think she's bossy. And that maybe she doesn't have the right intentions in her heart. But *never* repeat that!"

"I can guarantee I will not," I promise.

"She wouldn't have won reelection if it wasn't for the Shiverton Abduction."

"You can stop saying the Shiverton Abduction now."

"Right. Sorry. So, like I said, come. Everyone would be praying for you. It's nice. Not creepy at all."

Alice is wrong: I never thought of prayer as creepy. More like a built-in advantage religious people have, a higher probability of their wishes being granted over nonreligious people.

"I'll think about it," I say.

"Cool. Speaking of Liv, what's up with her dating Shane Cuthbert? He smells like a skunk's butt."

"That would be weed, Alice."

She giggles. "Not that I think it's so out of character. You don't play Prey without a little bit of a dark side."

"That was ages ago. And everybody plays Prey, Alice."

"I don't."

I jump up. "We should run before it gets too cold."

"I have bad shoes."

"Okay, then. Jumping jacks!" I windmill my arms and legs in place, and Alice laughs, covering her mouth. "C'mon, Minke Whale! One, two, three—" I shout.

Alice's mouth falls open.

"What?" I whirl around.

"Is that Paula Papademetriou?" she says.

Paula approaches, swathed in a cape-style coat the color of caramel, glamorous against the stark pines. She walks with a funny hitch, navigating the half-frozen earth's bumps and buckles, her heels getting caught. Still, she's polished and gorgeous.

"Who looks like that?" Alice murmurs.

Misguided pride spreads warm across the tops of my cheeks.

"I'm glad I found you," Paula says to me, and presents a sleek, gloved hand to Alice. "Hi, Julia's friend."

"This is Alice," I say. "She's my next-door neighbor." I want to pinch myself for saying that. Could I not just say *friend*?

Alice dives to shake her hand. "I'm Alice."

"Alice—right. Got it. It's nice to meet you, Alice. I live here in Shiverton too."

"I know you do, on Central Street," Alice says, being way creepy.

Paula smiles at her obliquely for a moment, then turns to me. "Julia, I am so sorry to pull you away. Is there any chance I could have a word with you privately?"

I look to Alice, whose grin drops, then lifts fast. "I need to do a lap," she says, recovering and nodding vigorously. "It's great exercise. You go, I'll be right over there."

"Two minutes," I say to Alice, but she's already gone, shuffling backward in her Mary Jane sneakers, nearly running into a randomly placed football tackle dummy.

"Can we go to my car?" Paula says, gazing at the parking lot half a mile away.

"I don't know. That feels kind of cruel. I haven't been a good friend to Alice in a long time. I probably shouldn't disappear. You know how it is with friends," I add in a leading way. Part of me hopes that Paula will talk about the best friend she mentioned at the trailhead.

"Then I'll make it quick," she says, ignoring my beggy vibe. "I got some information on deep background that has not yet been corroborated, but I thought you should know."

I look at Alice and give her a small wave. She waves back with gusto. "Oh?"

"Apparently there's a whole subset of Prey extremists who take the hunting-humans-instead-of-animals thing to a whole new level, like it's some grand, virtual payback. Sometimes not so virtual."

"I don't mean to be impolite, but if you're saying Donald Jessup was acting out Prey in the woods, the cops figured that out a year ago. Based on the fact that he was chasing me. In fatigues," I say.

"I know Donald Jessup liked to hunt. He also liked talking off the Twitter feeds. And that's something he and Ana Alvarez, a veterinary student passionate about animal rights, with a history of . . . let's call them *unusual* interests, had in common. The police hacked Donald and Ana's direct messages. Ana arranged to meet Donald in the woods to play Prey and wound up dead."

"Are you going to say all that on the news?" I ask.

"I can't tell that story, because it looks like I'm blaming the victim. Besides, I don't have independent corroboration."

Alice swings close as she completes her first lap. I lower my voice. "How will you get it?"

"We need a source in the police department. That's where you come in," she says.

Out of the corner of my eye I see Alice, trying to read our lips and stumbling. I start toward her, but she leaps into the air, hands stretched to the sky. "I'm okay!" she yells.

I turn to laugh, and am surprised to find Paula's eyes boring into me.

"You're friendly with the son of Detective MacDougall, yes?" she says, eerily focused.

"You want me to ask Kellan to ask his dad if it's true that Ana Alvarez was playing a kinky game with Donald Jessup?"

"Like I said, that isn't the story we're going to run with. I see it as background information, a piece of the puzzle. We just need to know if it's true to decide whether or not to include that piece. Detective MacDougall was on the case initially, and rumor has it he's dissatisfied with the way things are being conducted this time around, with all new players. He's a perfect source: knowledgeable, respected, and with a motive to talk. You might even consider asking him directly; I understand he's quite an admirer of yours."

I gasp. "I'm not in a position to do that!" I catch myself and lower my voice. "I can't."

"It's your call, of course. I really just wanted you to have the information anyway. Because you deserve to know." Paula turns to Alice and waves. "I'm leaving now. Nice to meet you, Alice." From an inside pocket, she pulls a glossy headshot postcard and a pen, and scribbles across the corner. When Alice runs up, she hands it to her. As Paula walks away, Alice stares at the picture. I stare at the real thing, her pale heels slipping from the backs of her shoes, a move at once sexy and kind of icky.

"This is so incredibly cool," Alice says, holding the edges of Paula's headshot as though she might smudge the image. "What did she want?"

"Just checking in. We're friends. I guess." I walk slowly, putting distance between us and Paula.

"This is about the big police exposé, isn't it? Mom says it's awkward, because they both live in this tiny little town and Detective MacDougall is *so* not having it, he might even lose his job, and, my gosh, Paula Papademetriou is a major journalist! She wins all kinds of awards, and she's gorgeous, and she's powerful, and maybe if the local police and these guys in the state government did something wrong that put Donald Jessup out on the street, they should pay."

I charge ahead, pointing my keys at the car. "The woods. Not the street. He was in the woods."

Alice runs to keep up. "Call me Pollyanna. I guess I want something good to come. Maybe that makes me naïve. Or annoying. I think the laws ought to be toughened or something, so that nothing like this ever happens again. Paula is doing what . . . oh, never mind."

I look at her over the car roof. "You think Paula is doing what Jesus would do."

"I do!"

I slip behind the wheel and close my eyes. Alice jumps in and throws her arms around me, squeezing hard.

"Oh Julia, I was so afraid to say it. But I do! I think Paula is your avenging angel," Alice declares.

I think about that as Alice hugs me in silence. I don't hug her back, but I don't resist, either.

"Julia?"

"Yeah?"

Alice drops her arms. "I overstepped a line before, when I was gossiping about Liv. What I said was totally inappropriate. And now I feel bad."

"Consider me your safe place to vent."

"Oh, I like that. Then can I ask you a question?"

"As long as you run it by Jesus first."

Alice screws her mouth to the side. "Do you think Donald killed that other girl? Ana Alvarez?"

"No," I lie, because I can't bear to put my gory suspicions inside Alice's head, alongside all those kitties and rainbows. "Okay. Now can I ask you a question?"

"You can ask me anything."

"Do you think Liv feels guilty toward me, because I saved her and got caught?"

"Hmm. A valid question, that one." She taps her lip with her finger, then stops. "Permission to speak freely?"

"Raise the floodgates."

"Well then. There was this one time about a week after the Shiv—the unfortunate event—and youth min was meeting in the church basement. It was Liv's first meeting back, in fact. I wanted to plan a candlelight ceremony thanking God that you both returned to us. I got some dirty looks. It was kind of soon,

I guess. My suggestion was viewed as 'indelicate' by some. But I promise you my intentions were pure. Anyway, Liv got teary and ran to the bathroom. The other kids didn't want me to, but I chased after her anyway. I say, do what's in your heart, right? Anyway, I think I caught Liv at a low moment, because she said the oddest thing that I'll never forget."

I pull my scarf up over my mouth to keep from interrupting.

"I tried to say the most comforting thing I could possibly think of. I said, 'God was watching over you that day when he sent Julia.' I figured she'd agree. Instead, she snapped at me. She said, '*That* day she finds her speed. *That* day, she catches up. I needed a few simple minutes alone to make things clear.' It was like she was talking to herself, as if I wasn't even in the room. I said, 'What are you talking about?' Maybe *that* was indelicate. But she wasn't making any sense."

I tug my scarf down from my mouth. "What else?" I ask.

"She looked at me, horrified, like the way your parents do when they drop the F-bomb? Well, maybe just mine. Anyway, she tried to smooth it over, got affectionate, hooked her arm through mine, and said, 'You know how it is, Alice, when you're best friends and you're together constantly? I wanted some space from Julia. To think. That's all.'"

I cringe. Now I understand why Alice remembers this so vividly. There was nothing crueler to say to the friend I dropped than what a pain it was to be my best friend.

Alice takes a deep breath and shakes out her neck. "Naturally I never said anything to anyone. I had to respect the fact that maybe she wasn't feeling like herself. You'd both been through heck. But secretly, at the time, I thought it was strange. Almost like she was angry with you for saving her. So no, *guilty* is not the word I'd use to describe the way Liv feels about you." She looks away hard, out her window and into the night.

I want to ask more questions, get more information to process Liv's weird outburst, but Alice is trying to keep it together. The urge to flee is overwhelming. I drop my phone into the cell dock ignition lock that Mom installed so that I can't drive and text. A chirp, loud and long, my tone for missed calls, makes us jump. I shut off the car and hit Play on speaker.

"Julia, it's Paula."

Alice explodes into tiny, soft claps.

"I forgot to tell you. I thought you'd like to know your friend Olivia has been admitted to Saint Rose of Lima Hospital."

EIGHT

360 Days After the Woods

Shane refuses to acknowledge my glare across the hospital waiting room,
his pale eyes fixed on the high-mounted TV. I search for guilt
in his mouth, the angle of his shoulders, the set of his cheeks
with their spray of rosacea bumps, but there is nothing. Eventually, he tosses his chin, remembering I am Julia Spunk and
he's known me since he was little, or, more likely, that I have
a murky relation to the girl he's hooking up with.

Beside me, a teenage sister and brother text nonstop while
their mother cries into a tissue. A guy with a new baby and a
toddler tries to jostle the baby while interesting the toddler
in an aquarium built into the wall. On TV, a woman with
saggy chins is told to pack her knives and leave a reality
cooking show. The baby shrieks like a cat. Over the din, I hear
Deborah's tinkly laugh, followed by her struggling to push

an empty wheelchair alongside a jacked orderly who resolves the problem by kicking up the chair's metal feet.

Deborah stops short and coos, "Why, it's Shane Cuthbert! And Julia!" oozing charm in front of the handsome orderly with the pipes. "You're a little late for a visit. Liv is about to be discharged. It was just a touch of mono." She looks pointedly at Shane. "No flowers?"

Shane, low in his seat, lolls his head to one side. "No, ma'am."

Deborah looks up at the orderly. "Everyone has been so worried about Liv. Popular girl, you can imagine. Well, this works out perfectly. You two can keep Liv busy while I sign the discharge papers. First door on the left."

Shane rises and slinks down the hall. I follow at a distance. He stands at the doorway, as if to say, *Me or you?*

"You go," I say roughly.

Hands jammed into the pockets of his shredded jeans, he sways his hips and gives me a once-over.

"What are you looking at?" I say, so sharp it slices the air.

He nods, smirking, and slides into her room. I sink to the corridor floor and wrap my hands around my knees as Liv calls out, "Shane, oh my God. Thank you for coming. I'm already discharged, believe it or not. I would have told you . . ."

The door closes partway. "You didn't answer my texts," Shane says.

I scramble to the door and place my ear flush to the crack.

"The service in here is very spotty," Liv says.

"I've been worried," he says, hangdog. "I love you, Liv."

"Oh, Shane. That's so sweet. I don't deserve you." A creak,

the sound of her shifting in her bed. "You know what I learned? The incubation period for mono is four to six weeks. You might want to get checked."

"When did you start feeling sick?" he says, suspicion threading his voice. I can hear the gears in his head turning, see the bubble over his head that says, *We starting screwing around on this date . . .* Even Shane is capable of mental math.

"Four weeks ago. I think I got worn down, spending all that time preparing for my ethics oral. Mr. Austen has been really hard on me."

Liv took ethics last year. What is she talking about?

"Austen? The guy who got caught in the sexting scandal with Gina Rubino?"

"Yes, him. Also, remember that reporter, Ryan Lombardi from WFYT? He and I have been working really hard on this story he's writing about the state's corrupt parole board."

My muscles go rigid. That's Paula's angle on the story, not Ryan's. And there's no way Liv would be working with the media; she hates the media, wants the attention to go away.

"The guy you told me you think is good-looking?" Shane's voice quavers.

Liv laughs lightly. "Did I tell you that? Sometimes I'm too honest for my own good. Anyway, I'm not sure if you heard, but the police failed me. There are so many facts you have to dig up—it's perfectly exhausting. We've been spending hours and hours together, often until very late."

"You've been with that little putz?" His words are compressed, as though his teeth are clenched.

"Ryan is a cruel taskmaster. But that's okay. You, if anyone, know I like things rough."

I spring to my feet and knock briskly on the open door. Shane whips around, close to the bed now, his ears angry pink seashells.

"Julia! I'm so glad you're here!" Liv says, flushed. "Shane was just checking in to make sure I didn't need anything. I told him I've been getting everything I need."

Shane's head snaps back to Liv. Against his thigh, his fist opens and closes.

"They're letting me out early, mainly because I gobbled up every last bit of goo they thrust upon me and washed it down with plastic cups of apple juice. Yellow custard, neon Jell-O, crystalized Italian ices. All that sugar! Deborah made puffer-cheeks at me the whole time." She says the last part to me, winking.

"I overheard you saying crazy, nonsensical things just now," I say, underscoring every word. "Because of your fever."

"Nope. Not saying crazy things, no. Shaney, could you find one of those hospital carts and steal me a tube of that hospital-grade Eucerin? It's hand cream. Everyone steals it, the orderlies, the dietary aides. I've been watching them. It's like hotel soap: you're supposed to take it."

Shane's eyes flicker between confusion and malice.

"They keep syringes in there too," Liv says.

He wipes his nose hard and stalks away in search of a cart.

"You look really well," I say, because she does.

"Yeah, well. They overfeed you here."

"I was at your house when it happened. Your mother was looking everywhere for you. They said you passed out at youth ministry?"

"Mono can cause anemia. I guess I just fainted."

"Liv," I say softly, approaching the bed, "can we talk about you and Shane?"

"I really need to go to the bathroom and get dressed before Deborah comes back. Will you stay?"

"I'm not going anywhere," I say, looking at the door. Not while Shane's here.

Liv eases from her bed, holding her johnny behind her. I hand her an orange bag with her clothes inside from the L-shaped table. A chart is clipped to a hook on her bedpost. My eyes flash over the word *ketoacidosis*. The nubs of Liv's spine snake down her neck and back, visible between loose johnny ties. As she reaches for the doorknob, her johnny parts at the back.

Across the top of her right buttock, where her back naturally curves, is a swoop of faded black marker, half a circle with half an *X* inside. It is faint, but it is there, and not only there. Half of the same is visible on the inside of her right thigh, and very lightly, nearly rubbed out, are circles with *X*s on the backs of her thin arms.

"Liv!" I gasp. "Did the doctor do that?"

She freezes, her hand high on the door.

"The marker. On your skin," I say.

She looks over her shoulder, eyes moist and bright. A housekeeper in maroon scrubs and plastic gloves bustles in and

Liv ducks into the bathroom, slamming the door shut. As the housekeeper starts to strip Liv's bed, I grab the clipboard, scanning for the word *mononucleosis*, but it's not there. There are various blood sugar counts taken over the course of the last twenty-four hours, all in the three and four hundreds, and the words *anorexia consult upon discharge* highlighted in yellow. I grab my phone from my back pocket and take a picture of the chart just as Deborah throws open the door. Shane skitters around the corner, followed by a woman in maroon housekeeping scrubs screaming in Spanish. Deborah's eyes widen, cartoon-style. Shane hands the housekeeper a tube of cream. Liv comes out in street clothes. Deborah hustles about, complaining that this whole thing has been an expensive inconvenience for her, between taking time off work and the outrageous parking fees at the hospital garage. The orderly returns and Deborah shuts up. Liv settles obediently into the chair and the orderly decides, to Deborah's disappointment, that we need nothing and disappears, along with Deborah's happy mask. Shane takes the handles of the wheelchair. Liv reaches around to cover Shane's hand with hers and we head en masse toward the elevator to the garage, one bizarre, misfit family. Deborah looks straight ahead, no doubt dying inside that her daughter holds the hand of a pale, tattooed boy with a waist smaller than hers.

I walk last. Shane leans over the chair handles, greasy hair falling forward. He whispers in Liv's ear, "I try to love you. Why do you have to make it so hard?"

Liv pats his hand.

"This isn't over, you know," he says. "I have a lot more questions."

"You're right." Liv's hands slip underneath the blanket on her lap. "I'm not nearly finished with you."

NINE

362 Days After the Woods

As if I need reminders that I am invading the personal space of Paula Papademetriou and Desh Patel and their only child.

Purple cabbages border a topiary carved into the letter *P*. Under my feet, the mat is initialed with a curly *P*. A brass knocker on the purple door is shaped like a shell engraved with another *P*. In the corner, two rockers are painted glossy white, with matching throws across the backs, one in a pastel plaid, one in darker jewel tones, embroidered *PP* and *DP*, respectively. My plan suddenly seems like a bad idea. I hold my breath and stab the doorbell. *Bong-bong-floosh!*

I ought to go.

I press the doorbell a second time: *bong-bong-floosh!*

Footsteps inside. No turning back.

The door falls open.

A boy, my age, or maybe a year younger, blinks as if the late-day sun hurts his eyes. "What?"

"Hello."

He twists his mouth to the side. "Hello."

"Is your mother home?"

"You are?"

I had planned to say I was a friend but instead I say, "She's writing a story about me."

The boy looks me up and down. "Whatever. My mother's out. It's just Dorotea."

"Hud-sohn?" a voice calls from deep in the house.

"I gotta go." He starts to shut the door.

"Dorotea?" I ask.

"The nanny. Listen, no one's supposed to come here. My mother gets stalkers weekly. You better leave."

I consider pointing out all the *P*s in just these two square feet don't suggest she's hiding her identity. Instead, I turn to walk down the porch stairs.

"Wait!" Hudson calls. "You're the chick from the woods. The one who saved her friend?"

I dig my fingernails into my palms. "That's me."

"Stay and wait. She'll be back soon."

I cross the threshold into a grand foyer. I don't have good taste. I don't think it's in my genes, though Mom's and Erik's lab-coat wardrobes make that indeterminable. But I suspect Paula's house is dripping with taste, and layers of it. The creamy damask wallpaper looks thick, the oriental rug under my feet is thick, and the polished mahogany hall table is at least ten inches thick. My reasons for being here start to feel thin. I stare at the crystal dew-drop chandelier above my head. When I look down, the dark spots in front of my eyes dissolve into a squat woman standing before me.

She faces Hudson. "You have friend?"

"Yep. This is Julie."

"Julia."

Dorotea plants her hands on her vast hips and looks at Hudson.

"She's staying," he says.

"Door stays open, your mom say!" She faces me. "You eat?"

"No, thank you," I say, but Dorothea has already vanished into the kitchen, where Judge Maria Lopez is haranguing someone on TV.

Hudson ambles away. "You must feel lucky, considering what happened to the Spanish chick."

"I guess." I follow Hudson through a dining room set with gold-rimmed china, massive leather chairs, and a crystal vase overflowing with yellow roses. "I shouldn't stay. You're having a dinner party."

"What are you talking about?"

"The table is set for a party."

"It always looks like that. Come on, you can wait in here." We enter a dark back room decorated like a pub, with a glossy wooden bar and neon signs that say things like DESH'S GUITAR LOUNGE and more *P*s etched into the glass mirror above the bar, sewn into throw pillows, and printed on cocktail napkins. Hudson collapses into a leather L-shaped chair with cup holders. It faces the widest flat-screen I've ever seen.

"Sit!" he says.

I sink into an identical chair. I could sleep in this thing, but something tells me to keep my guard up.

"This used to be the trophy room." He jerks his thumb at the empty shelf. "Now Mom keeps her awards at the office. Otherwise she'd never get to enjoy them. You want a Coke? SoBe? Dorotea!" he hollers.

"I don't need a Coke or a SoBe. I should probably go."

"It's fine. Dorotea needs stuff to do anyway. All she does is cook and clean; it's not like she's gotta change diapers or anything. She doesn't even drive. When my mother's not home she calls a car company whenever I have to go anywhere."

"So where did you say your mom was?"

"Like I said, I dunno. Dorotea!"

Dorotea appears.

"We'd like Cokes," Hudson says.

Before I can protest, Dorotea bustles behind the bar and pulls two sweaty Cokes in old-fashioned glass bottles out of the fridge. She opens them with a bottle opener and hands them to each of us. Hudson grunts. I turn to thank her, but she is gone.

Hudson slugs his Coke and wipes his mouth with his arm. "So let me guess. You think my mom is your new best friend."

"What makes you say that?"

"You show up at her house desperate. Acting like she's your crack dealer."

"Excuse me?"

"Jonesing for a little attention from Paula."

"That's rude."

"Trust me, I'm used to your type showing up on our doorstep. Paula brings her work home. Remember that baby that got kidnapped by the father and taken to Saudi Arabia? The mother spent a month crying at our kitchen counter. Total story immersion is Paula's thing."

"That's called being a professional."

"A professional enabler. Also among her skills: doing everything she can to remain—what's the word she uses? Oh yeah, *relevant*. And by that she means young."

"You're talking about your own mother."

"My own mother is the scrappiest dame you ever met. Did you know they were going to fire her when they hired that hottie she co-anchors with now? Laura Underpants."

"Underwood."

"Whatever. Paula fought hard. And dirty. There weren't three chairs at that desk, only two. In the end, they fired Harry Case—the guy with the mustache, who was never in danger of getting axed in the first place—and let Paula stay on. She had a lot to be thankful for when your story came along."

"Meaning?"

"She was tanking. To begin with, no one even watches local news anymore, and when they do, they want to see a smoker, not a forty-something has-been."

"Your mother is a Shiverton legend. People love her."

"Loved. Taking down a popular police detective and

department full of guys who moonlight as the coaches, boosters, pub and liquor store owners doesn't exactly endear you to the masses. I'm just telling you the facts." He waves a remote at the screen and it blasts Cartoon Network.

I struggle to release myself from the pod chair. "Thanks for the Coke. I'm out of here."

"So you get that she's using you, right?"

I check for Dorotea. The coast is clear. I cock my head. "Has anyone ever told you you're a little prick?"

"Am one? Yes. Have one? No. Would you like to see the evidence?" He pulls a lever and his seat flies backward, his socked feet under my nose. I make a face at the tang and back away.

"Here's the thing," he says. "If the Latina in the woods can be connected to the same perv who attacked you and your buddy, the police are screwed. The parole board chief and maybe the detective in charge of the case will get axed. Blowing open a story like that with actual consequences? That makes you valuable. Rel-e-vant. Uncannable, even. At least for a while longer."

I swipe the clicker and shut off the TV. "You are a rotten little punk."

He extracts a different remote from the crease in his seat and flicks on the TV. "Problem is, she's getting shut out. Everyone in this sleepy town is pissed at her for crucifying the good guys. That's not to say they don't feel sorry for you. And beyond Shiverton, who cares if the lazy cops go down? But this is a local story, and Paula needs her local sources. The common folk. They figure, the perv is dead. Let sleeping dogs lie. The cops know better now, so they'll be more careful about where their sickos wander. Even Tufts has a no-Paula policy, now that she's suggesting their vet student had some, shall we say, sketchy leanings."

"How do you even know all this? You're just a disrespectful, spoiled private school kid."

"You hit the nail on the head, Julie. I need to keep tabs on the money flow. Don't think I'm not fully aware that if my mother loses her job I don't get to stay at Governor's Academy. Tuition is thirty-eight thousand. That's one year at a subpar college. I say a prayer of gratitude every day that you got away from that twiddler in the woods and lived to tell about it." He straps on virtual reality headgear, goggles that look like the ones Donald Jessup wore in the woods. I recognize the opening sequence of Prey, a garden of Eden unfolding in technicolor, then the scene grows dark, the music ominous. Hudson chooses weapons for his character, a hunter in fatigues with outsized muscles and a crew cut.

I force myself to look away from the screen. "Don't think I won't tell your mother everything you said about her."

He tilts his controller and jams his thumbs into the buttons. "And who do you think she's going to believe? You might be important, but I'm all she has in this world. The only thing she and my dad share these days is an initial." His avatar gets sliced in half by a centaur bearing a samurai sword. He swears, shoving his goggles to the top of his head and fixing cold eyes on me. "Oh, and if you think I must be stupid because it's not in my interests to tell you the truth about Paula, you're wrong. It's just a hunch, but given what I know about human nature, I'm pretty sure you're more interested in revenge on those incompetent cops than in the fact that Paula might be using you."

"I don't think you're stupid. I think you're a sad, lonely kid who feels neglected by his mother and sees every person related to her career as a threat that you must take down." I storm away, stopping in the kitchen to leave my Coke on the counter and thank Dorotea, who jumps away from the TV and hides her head in the dishwasher. Niggled that my sign-off feels lame, I fly back to the media room. Hudson torques his shoulders right to left. I yank his goggles off, giving his ears a good hard tug along with them.

"Ouch!"

"Just wanted to point out that it's easier to win at Prey when you have opposable thumbs."

"Touché, be-atch!" He pulls his goggles back down and gets back in the game. "By the way, I lied. My mother's in the study, taking calls."

"You—she's been here the whole time?"

"I just wanted us to have a chance to talk. We're done now. Goodbye." He waves me away without looking.

I wander into the short hall before the dining room, wondering where the study might be in this massive house where it feels like nobody lives, despite all the initials everywhere that remind you someone does. And if I find the right door, do I knock? Or do I find Dorotea again and ask her to introduce me? Before I met Hudson, I'd been worried about the decorum of showing up at Paula's house when I couldn't even put a name to what I wanted (comfort? answers?). Then I got pissed. Now I'm back to sheer, cold anxiety, and I shake my hands to warm them. My notebook weighs unnaturally heavy in my bag—it's the only thing inside—but none of Hudson's "facts" are worth recording, little bastard. As I still myself, I hear a murmur coming from behind a door off the dining room. Paula's voice. Is she with someone? Little Bastard said she's on the phone. I will wait.

Two minutes, then five. I slump against the wall. I begin to worry that Dorotea might come through to clean, or that Hudson will emerge from the man cave and rat me out for being a stalker. Though stillness also feels like the norm in this house. Finally, the murmuring stops. I tap the door lightly.

"Come in, Dorotea!"

I ease the door open to see Paula sitting behind a mahogany desk. But I was wrong; she's still on the phone, just listening. Her eyes widen, pleased, and she waves me in with gusto, phone to ear. Everything besides the desk is white: rug, wing chairs, couch, and pillows. I fix on three framed photographs: Paula with President Obama, Paula with the governor, and Paula next to a blonde with a tepid smile. Paula catches my gaze and points, mouthing, "Elizabeth Smart." She talks into her neck. "Don't worry, even if he manages to stay on point, he still looks bad. I need the questions no later than six." Paula hangs up and stands. She's dressed for the evening news, in a sheath dress with a leather panel at the waist. "To what do I owe this visit? Sit, sit."

"I know you have to go on air soon."

"I have time for you! Make yourself comfortable," she says, waving me into a white wing chair studded with nailheads as she rises, sitting on the edge of her desk. She's wearing Ugg slippers over black hose, and she holds them up, flexing her ankles playfully. "Another one of my maxims: Never wear heels unless you absolutely have to. Can I get you anything? Sparkling water, Coke? Something warm, perhaps?"

"I'm good."

"Dorotea!"

"Please, no!" I shout. "Really. I'm all set. You're probably wondering why I'm here."

"I know it's one of two things. Either you have something you want to tell me, or you just want to spend time with a friend who understands you. Honestly, I'm hoping it's the latter." She smooths her hair back with her hands, and her face looks young and sad. "You could say I'm a little burned out on this case."

"Burned out? How come?"

"Don't worry. I haven't given up on bringing justice to your case, believe me. I'm just hitting roadblocks. Confirming Ana and Donald's relationship before my big interview with the parole board chief on Thursday."

It finally occurs to me, in flashing neon, that she thinks my reason for coming is to relay the conversation with Kellan's father that I didn't have. I scan the room, desperate for a notable item on which to comment and change the subject. "Your son was so cute!" I choke, pointing to a photo of an olive-skinned baby in a silver frame.

"Oh no. That's the Agarwal baby. Do you remember the story? He was abducted by his father in 2010. His mother gave me this as a token of gratitude." She lifts the picture to her lap. "She claims my reporting just after the abduction helped find him. Baby Sam would be living somewhere in Saudi Arabia by now, convinced his mother abandoned him."

"They must be really grateful."

Paula gazes at the picture. "My work is everything to me. If my reporting isn't making positive change in the world, I may as well not do it."

Silence settles between us. Somewhere, a TV buzzes, a drone interspersed with applause like a crashing wave.

"You said once, in the woods, that if there was anything you could do for me, you would," I say.

Paula folds her hands in her lap earnestly. "That hasn't changed."

"Something's not right with my friend Liv. The other girl . . ."

Paula stops me with a smile.

"Right. You know who Liv is. Sorry." I shift in my chair. "Liv was in the hospital for ketoacidosis, though her mother and she both lied and told everyone she had mono."

She runs a finger over her chin. "Remind me what keto-acidosis is."

"It's when your body is so starved of sugar it begins eating its own reserve of fat, causing a metabolic chemical reaction."

"I see." She grabs her phone off her desk and jabs at it. When she's done, she looks up. "And she's not diabetic?"

I shake my head.

"Okay. Is that it?" Paula asks.

My face contorts. "Not really, no."

Suddenly the details of how I found the sketches in Liv's room sound silly, and paint me as a straight-up snooper besides. And sitting there surrounded by Paula's sophisticated ether, mentioning Liv's bad-boy hook-up would make me sound like I think I'm starring in a soft-focused women's movie. What's she going to do anyway, besides tell me to call an abused women's hotline? No, best to stick with the flat-out mystery. "I mean, yes. I need you to look into what's going on with Liv. Maybe her mother, too. Inside their house."

"You think something's off?"

"Let's just say everyone wants me to be content with what they're telling me."

Paula slips off the desk and settles deep in the wing chair opposite me, pumping her shin, fleece slipper rising and falling like a metronome counting the beats until I crack. I grow conscious of new tics. The way my knee jitters. The eyelid twitch that feels visible. The compulsion to flex my own ankle every few seconds.

Finally, she breaks the spell. "We're a lot alike, you and me, aren't we?"

"We are?"

"Information is our oxygen." She rises and closes the door. "If I do this for you, can you do something for me?"

"I can't ask Kellan to ask his father about Ana Alvarez."

"Then this." She grabs an index card from her desk and scribbles a note, folding it once. "There's someone I haven't been able to get through to." She presses it into my hand. "But she might talk to you."

I squint as I unfold the paper. On it is the address of a house I know. Windows fogged with filth. Car on the lawn. An only son, sleeping under its roof no longer.

My palm falls open as if singed, and the card drops to the floor. "You want me to talk to Donald Jessup's mother?"

"I know it sounds crazy. But it might bring you closure. It's not as unusual as you might think, speaking with the relatives, especially the parents, of your perpetrator. Particularly when the perpetrator can no longer harm you."

I look at the note, white-hot on the dark paneled floor, nearly flashing. Paula sees only me. "Yvonne Jessup would never talk to me," I say.

"I'm only asking that you try. One question, and then you can hightail it out of there."

"You mean I have to go inside?"

"Yvonne Jessup is something of a shut-in. Honestly, Julia, if there was anyone else I thought she would talk to, I wouldn't ask you. She has no love for the press. Heck, she has no love for me. I simply need you to ask if she ever met or saw Donald's parole officer. I believe that the police may have created a false record of visitations," Paula says.

I envision a muddled, ancient woman dressed in fatigues in a room teeming with cats and trash. "What if she doesn't remember things exactly as they happened?"

"It's only anecdotal evidence I'm looking for. Something that will strengthen my hunch and confirm taking my investigation in that direction."

"I do this, and you'll use all of your resources to help me figure out what's going on with Liv?" I ask.

"I promise. There's another thing." Paula drags the wing chair closer to mine and sits. "I need you to let me interview you afterward. An exclusive. You speaking to the mother of your attacker is a human interest story. Every worthwhile story contains tension between victims and perpetrators. Part of my job is to frame that conflict properly. I wouldn't be doing my job as a reporter if I didn't."

I bite my lip, staring at the piece of paper.

She leans over her knees. "There's no guarantee we'd even use the interview."

"Tell me how you'll look into Liv."

"I'll start at the hospital, for one. I have sources inside. Let's see where that gets me first." She plucks the note from the floor with two fingers and holds it in the air. "Just promise me one thing: if you do speak with Yvonne Jessup, call me first and let me know. As a matter of personal safety."

"Thanks," I say, taking the folded slip of paper, "for looking out for me."

She covers my hand with hers, cool and light. "You have no idea how important you are to me."

She holds my eyes, then checks her watch and rises, changing slippers for pumps. I take that as my sign to go. Anything I say now will be awkward anyway. I leave, closing the door softly behind me, and am enveloped in darkness. It seems Dorotea has drawn the heavy striped silk drapes and turned off the glass chandelier. Somewhere, a clock ticks heavily. The rose centerpiece forms a massive shadow in the center of the table. I lean over to smell one, but it smells like just the faintest whiff of grass.

"Get with it, Julie. Roses don't smell anymore. The smell got bred out so they can be grown farther away, be bought cheaper, and last longer."

I spin around and stagger. Hudson leans against the wall near the light switch, his arms crossed.

"Jack off," I say, my voice shaky, rushing past him and making for the door.

He calls after me, "There's always a price."

TEN

363 Days After the Woods

Alice drops her sleeve, nibbling long and hard on her bottom lip. I hum the *Jeopardy!* theme music.

"Jesus would tell you to help thy friend," I say.

She shakes her head, knocking her headband over her eyes and jamming it back up miserably. "Please stop! I won't even think about going. Besides, I have to work at the rectory."

"You yourself said Father Carl lets you leave and come back all the time, no questions."

"Not to drop in on the mother of a murderer." Alice scans the emptying hall. "You're making me late for my bus."

"Paula says it's not unusual for victims to meet the parents of the person who committed a crime against them. Yvonne Jessup might not even be surprised."

"And how does Paula know it's safe? His sickness was probably inherited! Mother Jessup could be a psychopath herself!"

I can't tell Alice that, according to my research, no one knows exactly what causes someone to become a sociopath. While some contend it's due to a genetic disposition in families—i.e., if one parent has it, you're more likely to have it—others believe it's caused by an emotional detachment in early life, resulting in a disconnection with society.

On the other hand, it could be a combo deal.

"Sociopath. Donald Jessup was a sociopath. Specifically, an amoral sociopath: the kind that doesn't understand pain, and likes to torture animals, and has a vivid fantasy life where he is in control."

"I don't care if he was a sociologist! You're not getting me in that house of horrors." Alice swings her backpack over her shoulder and strides toward the lobby.

I chase her down the hall and block her way. "I need you, Alice. I can't go alone."

"You can't go, period! I'll call your mother and tell her what you're planning."

I grab her arm. "You would never do that."

She shakes her arm loose and slips her hand up her coat sleeve.

"Please, Alice. You said you prayed for me. If you care at all, help me do this. This is the last time I'm asking."

Alice blows hard through her teeth. "All right, I'll go. But you have to promise me something. We talk to her from outside. I'm not stepping foot off her porch, or front step, or yard, whatever."

I latch on to her arm and walk toward her waiting bus.

The driver yells something unintelligible. I stop a few feet before the stairs. "She probably won't even invite us in," I reassure her.

"We won't drink anything if she offers."

"We'll say we drank before we came."

"We won't eat, either," she says.

"Clearly. That scone could be a shrunken head."

"We should tell someone where we're going."

"That's already taken care of." It sure is. My call this morning alerting Paula was worth it, I tell myself. Quid pro quo. I can't expect Paula to just give without getting something in return. Asking Yvonne one tiny question about visits made by Donald's parole officer isn't a huge deal. Paula promised a quick, painless interview that she probably wouldn't use, would probably just be for her own "deep background." And did my mother consent? Of course. We're a progressive family, as you know, Paula. Concerned with justice, for all.

I won't let myself be bothered by Paula's suspicious number of *probably*s or my own blatant lies. Eyes on the prize.

"I'll tell my little brother just in case too. As a backup," Alice says.

"You will not tell your brother," I say firmly. "You will be with me, and we will be fine. I'll see you in two hours."

Alice turns and faces the bus. "It'll be hard not to say anything to anyone."

"Friends do things for each other. I'll owe you. Quid pro quo."

She dips her chin and looks deeply into my eyes. "It's not

like that. You don't owe me." She rubs my arm awkwardly. "You're my friend," she says, and skips off toward the bus without looking back.

I spend the next two hours weaving a four-part lie that will keep Mom off my trail. It involves the Y, a mall visit, a stop at the deli, and bringing Alice dinner at the rectory, the sum of which would take at least three hours. That's plenty of time for a visit—quick (as promised to Alice), and fruitful (as promised to Paula).

If Paula's word is good, my reward comes later.

Donald Jessup's house is six blocks away from Saint Theresa's, a squat brown house on busy Washington Street with two doors in the front. Lawn chairs, the kind with fabric straps that fray, dot the front yard, along with a picnic table with a frosted plastic top and thumbprint dents; a wheel-less wheelbarrow, a cracked terra-cotta pot, and a faded plastic Santa holding a lantern. There is no backyard. Instead, the house backs up to another house. Alice parks her beat-up sedan on the street and we pick our way across patches of dead crabgrass.

"All this time he was right there," Alice murmurs, fingering the zipper of her pink down coat. "Which door?"

"I'd go for that one." I point to the one next to a lift-top mailbox stuffed with yellowed mail. We climb a few steps to stand on a rotting porch in front of a molded number 277 like black metal turds. Above the knocker, a sign written in red grease pencil reads: NO SOLICITERS & NO PRESS!

"We're neither," I remind a fidgeting Alice as I ring the

doorbell. I listen, hear nothing, and ring again. We wait a minute. I pull off my glove and knock on the door.

"She'd have a car, right? Well, the driveway's empty. That means she's not home."

"Shh!"

"I'm outtie." Alice steps down from the porch as the door creaks open.

"Mrs. Jessup?" I ask.

Behind the screen stands a woman no taller than five feet. She wears an orchid-and-green calico housecoat with a yoke collar and snap front, and Keds sneakers, baby toes pushing through holes on the sides. Her pink forehead is smooth, exposed by a shock of white hair combed straight back, and her mouth is tucked and lined. Enormous glasses magnify low-set blue eyes.

"Girls, is it? I wouldn't have answered if it was boys." Her voice is crusty from underuse. "What do you want? Money for soccer? Softball? What?"

"We're not here to sell you anything. My name is Julia." I clear my throat. "Julia Spunk. I'd like to ask you a few questions."

She looks me up and down, rubbing her gums together. "Am I supposed to know you?"

My plan to tell her I knew Donald from work might not pass muster, because she seems sharp. I go with the truth.

"I'm one of the girls from the woods."

Alice catches her breath. Yvonne can't hear it, but she heard me, because her eyes grow enormous and she backs into the house.

"What do you want from me?" she cries, her hand feeling for a metal walker I didn't see before.

"Nothing!" I say in a rush. "I'm not here for anything bad. Your son . . . your son didn't hurt me. Not really."

Her head starts shaking, a loose-necked bobble, and I wonder if this is a mistake.

"I wanted to say I'm sorry for your loss," I blurt.

She sputters. "You'd be the only one who said it."

Alice touches my arm. "We should go."

"You live here alone, don't you?" I say. "I mean, since Donald passed?"

"I have a big dog and a panic button linked to 911 right in my pocket!" She pats her coat pocket. I have stumbled onto her list of things intruders say to figure out if you're home alone before they burglarize/rape/murder you. I'll chew on the irony that Yvonne Jessup should be concerned about such things another time.

She moves to slam the door.

"Wait!" I shout. "What I meant is, it must be very lonely, with just your memories. I was hoping you could share some of those memories with me. My therapist says that viewing Donald as a human being will help with my recovery. But I don't know anything about him besides what the press says. That he was a terrible monster who attacked women, and may have killed one."

Yvonne's eyes flare behind her glasses. "My Donny wasn't

capable of killing anyone. He had his demons. But he would never kill anyone. I will go to my grave saying that."

"We should leave," Alice whimpers.

"That witch Paula Papa-whatever!" Yvonne shouts. "Made him out to be a murderer when the police said he didn't kill that girl, she fell into a hole and got stuck! The evidence was right there!"

I hear a noise and turn slightly. A group of boys in striped shirts walking from the soccer field next door nudge each other and stare. I look back at Yvonne. "May we come in, Mrs. Jessup?"

"No, Julia," Alice whispers.

Yvonne crosses her short arms and rests them on her belly. "Tell me why I should let you in here?"

My belly roils, the black thing pokes. *How dare you, old woman?*

"Because it's the right thing to do," I say, looking hard at her.

She stares at us for a minute, gumming silently. Finally, she throws her walker in front of her, its feet sliding on tennis balls, and shuffles into a dark living room.

I follow while Alice stays on the porch. "Alice!"

She bends her knees inward and bounces, like she needs to pee. I grab her by the arm and drag her inside, past center stairs rigged with an electronic moving chair. We follow the *creak-drag* sound into a living room. The smell is antiseptic with an herbal, Tiger Balm tinge. The living room has heavy mauve drapes over dingy yellow sheers, and it's dark but for lamps in the corners, which Yvonne doesn't bother to turn on. At some

185

point, someone made it possible for all of Yvonne's most basic needs to be met in here, including a tiny, humming refrigerator set on the fireplace hearth, and a toilet, which Alice stands next to looking like she might die.

Yvonne heads for a blue chair, its arms rubbed silver. I choose the couch, patterned with faded bouquets that match the drapes. Alice sits as far as possible on the couch's edge looking weepy. Yvonne abandons the walker and sits with a grunt, lacing her fingers and resting them across her tire-bump of a chest. The chair and its matching ottoman are positioned across from a flat-screen TV hung on the wall behind our heads. On the fireplace mantel framed in brass are photographs of a young Donny, looking away from the camera. Thick glasses appear around the age of nine or ten. The pictures stop around age eleven.

She points above our heads with a bent finger. "Donny bought me that so I could watch my shows."

Alice makes a tiny noise. I cross my legs and pat Alice's knee, working up my most GIRLy smile. "What kind of shows do you like to watch?" I say.

"Game shows mostly. At night, I like *Raymond*. It's still on, in repeats. The *CSI* shows. The close-ups, they show up real well on this new screen."

CSI? Worries about rapists coming door-to-door? Is a hidden camera filming this as a joke? Immediately, I think of the truth in Kellan's words: it's like I'm forever being punked.

"I bet," I say.

"You said your shrink wants you to hear nice things about Donny, not what shows I like."

The thing shifts again, a quiver in my gut. The speed with which I could snap Yvonne's chicken neck isn't such a bad thing to think of, not when you're just thinking about it. It would take the police a week, maybe more, to notice anything amiss. Even the postman knows Mrs. Jessup never collects her mail, just lets it pile up in rain-soaked wads in her mailbox, and if you don't have a car, you're basically a shut-in, so nobody's out looking for you, and those Peapod bags near the front door mean food gets delivered, so she must barely leave the house, probably doesn't leave the house, there isn't even a pet, no animal to feed, at least not now that Donny's gone, hardy-har-har . . .

"He must have had hobbies." Alice breaks the silence.

My fingers tingle. I release my grip of the couch arm, letting blood flow back into my fingers. "Right. He liked gaming, isn't that true?"

"Ack, Donny and his computer!" Yvonne's eyes go someplace else for a second. "You couldn't get him away from that thing. He hardly ever left his bedroom. Kept him out of trouble, I figured."

Alice coughs. I slap her back a smidge harder than necessary.

Yvonne's head bobs. "What was I saying?"

"You were talking about Donny's hobbies," I say. "Did he have other ones, besides gaming?"

"What did you call it? Gaming? He wasn't playing games.

He was working on his computer. That was his job! They paid him big bucks to work from home. He could work in his pajamas and fuzzy slippers, he'd say. It made me feel safe to have him here all day, not going off into Boston, riding the train and getting mugged, or worse. Now every noise I hear sets me on edge, and there's been a lot of it, those good-for-nothing kids partying in the woods behind the soccer field on Saturday nights. Any one of them knows an old woman lives alone here, they could get it into their drunk minds to break in and steal my TV. You can see the screen flashing through the curtains from Washington Street at night. I told Donny that wasn't a good spot for it, it's too tempting for burglars, but Donny insisted. He was trusting."

I don't remind her that as a condition of Donny's parole he probably couldn't travel as far as Boston. Not that anyone was paying attention to the electronic breadcrumbs left by his monitoring bracelet. I also don't tell her that Donny hadn't worked a day since he left GameStop on disability for a back injury. I wonder what Yvonne lives on, cash-wise. Probably some dead husband's pension. Then I remember not to care.

"Plus his sponsor liked him to stay close," Yvonne adds.

"His sponsor?" Alice chimes in, before I can.

"Donny got into a little dope problem when he was younger. Typical teenage stuff," Yvonne says, shaking a gnarled finger at us in turn. "Now don't you go thinking he was a druggie."

"Never," I say. "You said he had a sponsor?"

"From a support group. Narcotics Anonymous. Said they met at the church. Guy would pop in and check on Donny once in a while. But he didn't need to; Donny'd been clean for years," she said.

I shift in my seat, barely able to stand it, remembering the joint between Donny's thick fingers. Alice senses my distress.

"Are you sure he didn't have to stay close to home because he wore a monitoring ankle bracelet?" Alice says sweetly.

My head snaps. *Alice*, I mouth.

"You mean the thing on his leg? That was some device his sponsor gave him so that Donny could be in touch immediately if he had the cravings. Some crazy techno-thing. Worked like my Medical Alert pendant. You know: 'I've fallen and I can't get up!'? Donny tried to explain how it worked, but I couldn't make sense of it. All I know is that he couldn't take it off. Whatever that guy said to him about drugs, it worked, because Donny was clean and sober, he was."

"His . . . sponsor . . . must have been real broken up about what happened," I say tentatively.

"Nah. Guy hadn't been around in years. Guess he knew he'd done his job right," Yvonne says.

This has to be enough information for Paula. I start to stand and make excuses to leave when Alice, who apparently believes my lie about a therapeutic mission, pipes up:

"That's impressive, that he was clean and sober. Say, did Donny like to jog? Or bike ride? Maybe go to the gym? Lift weights?" She spits out every unlikely suggestion pertaining to that fat lard until Yvonne finally interjects.

"Donny didn't waste money on a gym. He liked to hunt.

Had a real nice BB gun. Expensive. Saved for it. He liked to hunt birds, squirrels . . ."

Humans.

". . . larger prey too."

Alice drops her forehead into tented fingers. I kick her.

Yvonne shakes her finger at Alice. "I watch my *CSI* shows. I know what they say about people who hurt small animals. It wasn't like that."

"Of course not," Alice says.

"Donny had a sensitive side too." Yvonne points at me. "You should know that. He was a real good artist."

A ping of recognition. My eyes snap into focus.

"What did he like to draw?" Alice asks.

"Well, it varied. When he was little, animals, like dogs, ducks, horses. Then later, fancy ones, like dragons and unicorns and—what do they call those things? Half horse, half man? I can't think of the word. I guess those last two count as horses. He definitely liked horses."

"Did he continue to draw? As an adult?" I say.

Yvonne chuckles softly. "Oh yes, he got pretty good, let me tell you. Especially at faces. He could draw real realistic. You know that man who used to be on the PBS channel? *The Joy of Painting*, that was the show. I can't remember his name now, but he always talked about 'happy little clouds' and 'happy little trees.'"

"Bob Ross," Alice says. I stare at her. "My parents loved him. You can still watch him on YouTube."

"He'd whip those landscapes out in a few short minutes. My

husband, Don, never missed him—Bob Ross, that was it. I always said our Donny was better than him. It took Donny longer, but he could capture anyone. Particularly around the mouth." She rubs her fuzzy chin, lost for a moment.

"That's wonderful, Mrs. Jessup," I say. "That's just the kind of thing my therapist thinks I ought to know. I would love to see some of those sketches. Would that be possible?"

"Well, I suppose Donny can't mind now, God rest his soul. The whole sunroom is covered in them. Can't bear to take them down, never mind throw them away. They'll still be here long after I die, so whoever buys this house after I'm dead and buried will have to decide what to do with them. Might even make them a bit of money; he was that good." She rises with a squeal of springs and metal. "You first, I'll tell you where to go."

"I don't think that will be nec—" Alice starts.

"We'd love to." I pull Alice up by the wrist. We step past the kitchen into a sunless sunroom. The Tiger Balm gives way to something fetid. Squirrel droppings lie in small black piles in the corners of the room. Alice stretches the front of her jersey over her nose. The walls are paneled in wormy wood with holes among the knots. Spanning the south-facing wall are jalousie windows, slats of glass shut tight by rusted crank-handles. Moisture has overlaid a cataract haze. I rub my shoulders as the cold pours in through the glass.

Behind us, the walker halts. "You're not even looking at them. Behind you."

We turn slowly. Framing the door we just stepped through is sketch after sketch, dangling from pushpins tacked into the door frame, a child's drawings pinned proudly to a kindergarten corkboard. The subjects include the animals that Yvonne described, plus sexy fairies, hobbity things, and warriors, the latter with some Jessup DNA mixed in.

"Not the best spot, but that darn paneling is impossible to stick a tack through. They kept falling down. I'd come in, and they'd all be on the floor. It was like they were sad their maker was gone."

Another breeze blows through. The sketches sway on their tacks.

I feel Yvonne's warm breath on the back of my arm. "I wasn't bragging when I said he was talented, was I?"

I wrap my arms around myself and move away, fighting nausea. "So talented," I nearly choke. "Are there any other pictures? Perhaps something more recent?"

Yvonne thinks for a minute, chewing something imaginary. "Well, I suppose there's what he was working on before this mess got started," she says.

"And where is that?" I am terrified she's going to say his bedroom. Because there are limits to what Alice will do— limits to what I can do. And we are right up against them. I focus on a sketch at eye level and try to breathe. An ancient hunter holds a rabbit by its feet, its belly lax and long.

"In the dining room. Donny had a whole set-up in there. It's the only room that gets good light in the whole house, he said. Got mad at me about that, like I could control the sun. Like I'm God."

Alice laughs, a sound like dolphin chatter.

"It might bother other mothers, fussy-tidy types. But it was fine with me. It's not like we had fancy dinners or anything, it's been just us these last twelve years. He'd shut himself in there for hours, even jam rolled-up towels under the French doors. Said he needed 'ultimate quiet' so he could concentrate. By that I think he meant my TV—I like it loud, at least twenty-five on the volume."

"Can you show us?"

"The French doors back down the hall. You go on ahead."

I walk fast, Alice at my heels.

"We need to go," she whispers. "Father Carl will be back from dinner at eight."

I press on the brass door handle. Double doors squeal open to a tiny dining room wallpapered in velvet. Olive drapes still on their rods have been removed from the windows and propped vertically against the wall. Three chairs have been pulled from the table and stacked roughly; the fourth is angled like someone got up and left minutes before. A built-in cabinet with flowery china behind glass is the only piece of furniture besides a table with a sheaf of thick blank paper. To the left of the paper, charcoal sticks lay in perfect size order; to the right is a chamois cloth, a sanding block, a foam brush, a knife. The sweet smell of stale weed lingers. In the far corner is an ashtray filled with seeds and a pack of E-Z Wider rolling papers. The walker creaks up behind us.

"It's like a memorial," Alice says quietly.

In front of the chair is a half-completed sketch. A bit of charcoal sits on top of a few tendrils of hair, drawn with heavy, saturated strokes.

Yvonne creaks into the doorway. "Who is the girl in that sketch?" I murmur without turning.

"Why, that's Donny's girl," Yvonne says, out of breath. "He was in love. Said she was the best thing that ever happened to him."

I stare down at the girl from Liv's eaves. Thick-lidded eyes stare back, one bigger than the other.

"Is this the last picture Donny ever drew?" I say, facing her now.

Yvonne sniffs and pulls a wad of Kleenex from the pocket of her housecoat, lifting her eyeglasses and dabbing underneath.

"We don't mean to be insensitive," Alice says.

"No. I needed to come into this room sometime. Probably better not to do it alone," Yvonne says.

Alice makes a sympathetic noise. I gaze down, realizing I'm looking at the final version of the sketches in Liv's eaves, with all the details he had decided were right. The masculine brows and the flat plane of the nose, the shy smile above the undefined chin. This was Donald Jessup's girlfriend.

"He really was talented," Alice murmurs.

I pull my eyes away and turn to Yvonne. "Do you know how they met?"

"How they all meet these days. On the computer. Donny was a nice boy, handsome. He took care of himself, a very neat dresser. Just shy. Not great at talking one-on-one. They had a number of things in common, he said."

"Did you ever meet her?" My voice is strained.

"Naw, Donny was a big boy. He didn't need my approval. Besides, he said she was shy too."

Alice lifts her sleeve and taps her watch with one finger.

"My therapist will be real pleased that I know this about Donny. He was a gifted artist," I say. "But we've taken up an awful lot of your time, Mrs. Jessup. We ought to go."

"It's kind of you to say that. Not everyone's so kind no more." She turns and hoists her walker forward, leaning heavier than before. Her shoulders are round and small and I walk extra slowly, so as not to step on her heels. As I detour into the living room and scoop up my coat, I glance at the photos on the mantel, and find myself wondering if there really is anyone in the world who would notice if Yvonne Jessup disappeared.

As Alice and I let ourselves out, Yvonne stands to the side, looking down and away, head bobbing.

"Is there something else you want to tell us, Mrs. Jessup?" I say.

Yvonne stabs her pocket with her hand looking for another Kleenex. Alice pulls a tissue from her jacket and hands it to her. She blows her nose, a dry squeal, and stuffs the Kleenex away.

She grabs my wrist. "I'm sorry for the way he chased you. In the woods. Donny was never a bad boy. He just got his signals mixed up."

Signals? Again, the *Candid Camera* moment. I am supposed to agree with this woman, this still-grieving, delusional woman, that her Donny was confused by my begging and my cries.

"I'm sorry for your loss," I manage, wriggling from her gnarled hand.

"At least he's with our Lord," Alice says.

Yvonne looks at Alice sideways. "You know Donny killed himself, right?"

Alice's jaw falls open, then she snaps it shut. "I mean to say, it's a good thing, I don't mean it's a good thing. I mean, as far as society in general is concerned, it's a good thing . . ."

But Yvonne has stopped listening. "The truth is, I don't know what I believe anymore. Or where Donny is right now. I just know I'd rather he was upstairs."

"Of course," Alice says, nodding. "In heaven."

"I meant in his bedroom!"

I say goodbye and drag Alice down the front steps, feeling our way, because the porch lightbulb is out and the streetlights on Washington Street are dead.

"Girl! Wait," Yvonne yells, ducking inside. The door swings wide and a yellow glow pulses in her place. We trudge back up the stairs and linger unspeaking for what feels like forever. Finally, the *creak-drag* of the walker grows loud.

Yvonne hands me a piece of paper. The front of her coat dress is smudged with black charcoal. "Keep this. To remember he was human."

She slams the door and a lock scrapes on the other side. I stare at the sketch of Donny's work in progress for a moment before slipping it carefully into my bag. The opening credits of a cop show blast and a blue light glows in the front window. We turn to leave. Across the street opposite and a house down from Alice's sedan is the black SUV, lights off. A shadowy figure sits in the driver's seat, head down over the wheel, waiting to exact her agreed-upon request, my half of the bargain. The exclusive post-Mama Jessup interview-interview.

Alice stops. "Hey." She points. "Is that . . . ?"

I turn to Alice. "I need you to go home now, Alice."

"What does Paula want?"

To frame the conflict. To do her job.

"To help me."

ELEVEN

Later

The cabin of Paula's pristine SUV is hermetically sealed to highway noise.
If I start to speak, Paula gently hushes me, telling me I ought to
let my conversation with Yvonne marinate, an expression that
strikes me as vaguely gross. I sink into my seat, smelling like
Yvonne's Tiger Balm and counting exits, Donny's unfinished
sketch screaming to me from my messenger bag. I've already
decided I will not be sharing Yvonne's gift with Paula, not
before I confirm what I think I know. At the eighth exit the
WFYT News studio rises like a spaceship made of steel and
tinted glass. A parking attendant in a booth bundled against
the cold waves us in, and then we're on the move, me rushing
to keep up with Paula in her heels that click fast over the cold,
contracted pavement. In the lobby, a guard in an office walled
with grainy security monitors watches *Jeopardy!* on the flat-
screen in the waiting area. He greets "Miss Paula" with a

gold-toothed smile. While Paula asks him about his hospital-ized mother, I slip my phone from my pocket to check for texts from Alice telling me our gig is up; from Mom, checking in on me; and, in truth, from Liv. There are none.

I walk over to the elevator and jab the button.

"We're taking the stairs," Paula says, blowing past me and leaning backward against a heavy door.

"How long will it take?" I say, following her through the door.

"An hour tops," she says.

"Then the interview will be on the ten o'clock news, or the eleven?" I ask as we mount the stairs, calculating the time I have to prep Mom for the inconceivable act of allowing Paula to interview me.

She yells back, "Eight Eastern Standard!" There's some-thing peculiar about calling it Eastern Standard, but I can barely keep up, never mind ask another question. She's at-tacking the stairs now, elbows tight at her sides, up three flights, her pace unforgiving. It feels a bit like punishment for the day in the woods when I outran her. Tonight, she's in the lead. As she hits the third landing ahead of me, I call out, "Paula!"

She turns. "Yes?"

"What do you mean, Eastern Standard?" I pant.

"This isn't going to be on tonight's news, Julia. We're re-cording tonight, but it's going to be on Friday night. The eve of the anniversary."

"Naturally," I mumble, bleeding sarcasm.

She steps back down to my landing, speaking as she walks. "We all had to spin into action after you called me. But your interview fits the *Dateline* NBC format perfectly: telling true-crime stories via interviews with the people involved. New York was willing to wait to wrap production until the last possible minute."

"*Dateline?* But"—I falter—"you work for WFYT."

"I do. I'm being billed as a *Dateline* guest correspondent. Your interview is part of a larger segment on the Shiverton Abduction being produced in New York as we speak. I'm sure I mentioned it."

I grip the railing. "I'm sure you did not!" My voice echoes in the stairwell.

"The news is the news, Julia. You agreed to an interview. If I didn't mention which news show it would be aired on, I don't see how it makes a difference," Paula says.

"*Dateline* is a national show. That's shown everywhere," I say, feeling like someone stepped on my chest.

"Indeed. You seem nervous about that. If your mother truly gave consent, I don't see what the problem is," she says. "Or is that untrue?"

"Of course not," I lie.

"Not that I'm worried about lawsuits. Your name and face have been in the public domain for so long. And the police angle makes the Shiverton Abduction a matter of public concern. The whole thing's been vetted by Legal here and in New York. When I pitched this to *Dateline*, and they bit, well, this is something of a game changer as far as my career is concerned."

She studies my face. "You're getting cold feet. It's not uncommon. But consider this: How fitting is it that, on the eve of the anniversary of the abduction, the police will be revealed for their culpability in the crime? *Dateline* has gravitas, Julia."

She pauses to judge her effect. I look at the floor.

"You can set things straight," she says, an edge to her voice. "Get justice."

"You said the interview would be quick," I say, wary.

"It will be. I've been working on this story for the better part of a year. I have plenty of material, believe me. Your talk with Yvonne is frosting." She leans forward and touches my hair, softening her tone. "Let's see how it all turns out."

I turn to look over my shoulder. I could leave now, run right down those stairs and call Alice to get me. Mom would never know. No explaining my visit to Yvonne, no explaining why I agreed to an interview with Paula for national television. Suddenly an image pops into my head of Yvonne on Friday night, the blue light of the television flickering across her lined face, watching *Dateline* in her threadbare chair near the toilet. Of course they aren't worried about a lawsuit from Yvonne Jessup.

I take one step down.

Paula stiffens. "I meant to tell you," she says. "My research turned up an interesting discovery about Liv's connection to Donald Jessup."

"What kind of discovery?" I say slowly.

"We can talk about that after your interview," Paula says.

A second scenario hits me. If Paula has been researching

my story for the last year, surely she plans to include the peculiarities she's discovered—with my help—about Liv.

I blurt, "You cannot talk about Liv's problems on national TV. You cannot."

"Don't worry, Julia. My story has nothing to do with our recent discoveries about Liv. My story is about Shiverton law enforcement and the sex offender they let loose. That's the story I sold, and that's the story I'm running with."

I swallow. "You have to tell me this new thing you learned about Liv. First. Before I give you the interview."

Paula sighs, as though I'm making a big deal over nothing. "As you like. We can talk in my office. But we must be quick. They're setting up to tape us as we speak."

Paula opens a door and we step from the cinder-block stairwell into full-blown color. The third floor is a narrow hallway that stretches the perimeter of a sunken area three levels down, reached by a vertigo-inducing open iron staircase.

Paula leans in. "I suggest not looking down."

I do anyway. In one corner, a weatherwoman gestures in front of a blank green screen. Computer stations are manned by men with sweat stains and women in ponytails pierced with pencils. Red Bull cans litter desks and fill mesh buckets. A pale young woman in a pinstriped oxford stares up at me wanly as she pours a packet of Emergen-C into a glass of water. On the wall, an oversized digital clock ticks off 120 minutes and 16 seconds until airtime.

Everyone looks as abused as I feel.

Paula leads me through a frosted glass door and strides to

her desk. The office is the mirror image of her home study, in dark chocolate wood and cream accent rugs and pillows, but the furniture is less expensive-looking. She waves me toward a chair and sits behind her desk, moving a manila folder toward me. I examine the folder. Clipped to the front is one sheet of a computer printout, a long chain of code, gibberish, strings of nonsense with abrupt endings, as if the inputter kept hitting walls. On the side of the folder is a typed file tab that reads LAPIN/JESSUP/CHAT ROOM.

I clear my throat. "I didn't think chat rooms still existed."

"Neither did I. But that's not saying much."

"There are so many other ways to talk," I say.

"Not if you don't want anyone listening. Remember I told you about the deep background we had but couldn't confirm?" Paula asks.

"About Ana," I say.

"And the Prey fan forum. The police aren't the only ones capable of tapping into Donald Jessup's private conversations. I happen to have a really savvy intern. According to him, there's a fan forum for Prey gamers set up like an old-fashioned chat room. You access it through an app. Usually, the conversations drift off into IM space. Unless you happen to like reading your old conversations. In which case, you make certain changes to your settings."

"You save your conversations."

"Specifically, you check off the little boxes called 'Log IMs' and 'Log Chats.' Guess who checked off the little boxes?"

I stare at the folder, afraid.

"Not Donald. We hoped so, but no. However, he did install a third-party software program called Monitor Sniffer, which monitors, records, and captures AIM conversations on all computers in a network, exporting intercepted messages to HTML files. Once you close a chat window, Monitor Sniffer automatically logs all of your chats."

"What does this have to do with Liv?" I ask.

Someone knocks at the door, a fast rap. Paula yells to come in. A slender guy not much older than me with a Bluetooth and an electronic tablet in the crook of his arm opens the door. His eyes are dark-rimmed and match his mossy green sweater vest. When he gets closer, I realize they're tattooed with eyeliner.

He offers his hand. "I'm Josh. Production assistant–slash–intern. You're Julia Spunk. Of the Shiverton Abduction." He pumps my hand, his starched French cuff unmoving. I wonder what else he knows. "I give Paula the time."

"The time?" I say.

Josh presses his knuckles to his head. "I alert Paula to the number of minutes until we go on air. As you know, Paula's on the ten o'clock news. So: one hundred twenty minutes!"

"Josh will also help tape our interview downstairs. I'm just prepping Julia; we'll be downstairs in five minutes, Josh."

Josh rocks on man-heels and hugs his tablet to his chest.

"That's all, Josh," she says.

He grins. "Of course. Can I get you anything before I go? Tea? Red Bull? Matcha for you, Paula?"

"No, thank you. You can go now."

He backs out of the room and leaves the door open a crack.

"Josh is eager to please. And maybe a little starstruck by you," Paula says.

"Starstruck?"

"We've all spent a lot of time thinking about you over the last year. Your story didn't end for us after the woods. Actually, that was when it started," Paula says, then flutters her hand at me. "Now open the file."

The folder contains one sheet of paper. Above a string of code that looks like an IP address is one line of text:

"Shy SWF looking to meet Preymate for chat, play, more. E-mail direct rabbit15@rabbit15.me"

Paula stares, pupils big, waiting for me to say something. But I don't trust my voice.

"Do you want to know who that IP address belongs to?" she asks.

I nod.

"It's registered to the Lapin household," she says gravely.

I reread it, and am quiet for a moment. Then I sputter, "Liv's toying, killing time. She probably sent it during school."

Paula points at the time stamp: July 12, 2013, 8:30 p.m.

"That doesn't mean anything. Liv gets bored and does dumb things constantly to piss off Deborah. Like seeing this loser guy named Shane. In fact, maybe that's how she and Shane hooked up. He answers the message, and they realize they're a match made in heaven. See, that makes a lot of sense." Even as I say it, I know how lame it sounds. There are a lot more direct ways to hook a bottom-feeder like Shane than playing a misogynistic video game.

"Julia, think," Paula says. "My intern found this message in Donald Jessup's saved cache of private forum messages. We can't crack his e-mail, but I think the import is clear: that message is like an invitation for any creep to come find you."

The silence fills with computer clacks and shouts wafting up from floors below. Paula is crouched in front of me, moving a hunk of hair from my face. Suddenly everything is blurry; I'm tearing up. Because I know ancient chat-room messages aren't the only connection between Liv and Donald Jessup.

"It's just esoteric code in the electronic ether, even if it is caught on a printout." My voice cracks and falters. Maybe, but charcoal and paper sent through the old-fashioned postal service is real.

"Julia?" Paula says. "We can make this right. Even if Liv somehow invited Donald Jessup into your world, you can make sure it never happens to another girl. Because the fact remains that he did not belong on the streets." Paula grabs my shoulders and gives me a firm shake. "He did not belong in the woods."

Get yourself together, Julia.

The black in my belly slithers, spreads, takes up space. It rises, but not for Paula.

Josh raps at the door, and calls, "Ready for taping."

Paula slaps her knees and stands. "Let's do this."

I don't feel myself leave her office, but I must, because suddenly I am banging down the fire-escape stairs, past Josh, who presses his whole self against the landing rail with a thin smile, past the editor buns and sweat stains, past the weather GIRL who is on camera right now but loses concentration as I blaze by. I am in a daze as they sit me in a chair, strip off my jacket and scarf, brush my hair away from my face, and sweep a puff over my nose and forehead. Someone clips a microphone to the V-neck of my sweater and tucks the attached battery pack under my leg. When I look at the camera I see Josh, who makes a small wave, and a video screen in front of the camera lens mirroring me in my chair.

"Don't look at the camera. Look at me," Paula instructs.

Her questions are simple and straightforward. There are ten or maybe fifteen; I lose count. Every so often we stop taping because I slip down in my seat, out of the camera's frame, and they remind me to sit up. There's no way Mom would allow this, yet it's not altogether bad. It's nice to download my weird evening with Yvonne, minus my revelation regarding the sketches. I don't mention Alice, either, because it feels wrong to drag her into it. Once I start talking about Yvonne, I find myself warming to her. It seems like people should get to know her. I don't know why things turn in that direction, but once I start, I can't stop. Paula doesn't say much herself. In the interest of getting me home quickly, she will edit in her responses later, she says. They often do it that way.

At the end, I feel cleansed. When the man behind the camera says "And. We're. Out," Paula leans forward to push hair from my face.

"You did good," she says, closing a manila envelope of questions that I hadn't noticed until now. I remember the real reason I am here.

And I scramble from my seat. And now I'm running from the studio, the battery pack dragging then falling on the ground, past the man with the gold tooth, and I don't know Paula's chasing me until I am standing in the parking lot and I realize I have no car.

"Let me call a car for you," Paula says, brushing hair from her temples. "If you need help talking to your mother about this, our legal department is always on call."

I shake my head violently. "No! It has to be me."

"Listen, whatever you wish. But there is one more thing." She shoves an envelope into my hand.

I open it slowly, as though the paper is coated with ricin. In my hands are receipts for four tickets, two for a flight departing from Logan Airport in Boston arriving at Viru Viru International Airport in Santa Cruz, Bolivia, dated November 28, 2014, and two from Viru Viru back to Logan, dated December 28, 2014, in the names of Deborah Lapin and Olivia Lapin.

Liv neglected to mention she was traveling to South America, never mind missing school for a whole month.

"How did you get this?" I ask.

"That same whip-smart intern noticed that Deborah Lapin doesn't clear her browser history. Ever," Paula says.

"What does it mean?" I whisper.

Paula shrugs. "It means they're leaving."

It dawns on me that she no longer cares, because Liv and Deborah are not her story. I am, and I have proven more than enough. Paula turns on her snakeskin shoe and marches across the lobby.

I stare at the hacked ticket receipts incredulously as she turns and calls without looking back, "You did the right thing, Julia."

Doing the right thing was unavoidable, since I pulled up to my front door in a town car.

I came clean immediately. Mom shook her finger, wordless, and then disappeared upstairs, speed-dialing Ricker. I trudged upstairs and collapsed on my bed with my coat and shoes still on. A bedroom away, I stared at the ceiling, counting the seconds until Mom came crashing through my wall like the Kool-Aid Guy, but angry.

She chose the door.

"What did Ricker suggest?" I said. "Am I past the point of being fixed by her traditional cognitive behavioral therapies? Are we moving toward electroshock therapy and a lobotomy?"

Mom's phone was still clamped in her fist. "Honestly, Julia! What were you thinking? Going to that house was so unsafe! There are ways to find closure besides talking to the mother of the man who—"

"The man I got away from. I was never in any danger from Mrs. Jessup. I even learned some things." I patted the edge of my bed.

She sat, rigidly, clutching the phone as if it was a lifeline to Ricker. I saw everything on her face. Not just her worry about me that night, or over the last year, or when I was in the woods. Her worry for my whole future, all in the furrow of her brow and the downturn of her nose, and her sad, pretty mouth ridged like a clamshell on top. The black inside me uncoiled, and I remembered this was my mom, and she was warm, and she was that only thing I wanted when I was in the woods counting stars. I told myself it would help her to see that this interview wasn't about me at all, but about setting a system right. I was incidental, and incidental is safe.

I scooted over in my bed, and she slipped in beside me.

"If that Pantano guy had just done his job, none of this would have happened," I said. "You can be mad at me. But aren't you mad at the cops, too? Even a little?"

She stared at the point where the ceiling met the wall. "I spend my time focusing on things we can control. Like press access to you." She rolled over and propped up on her elbow. "Tomorrow, Dr. Ricker will come over, and we will sit around the kitchen table and you will explain to us, in detail, what you said to Paula Papademetriou, and more importantly, why." Her eyes went clinical then, all reserve and scary control. No "Oh yeah!" Kool-Aid Guy; this was Mom as badass, a combination of Morgan le Fay and Gwen Stacy, her special brand of cool cerebral coping. "Then Dr. Ricker will suggest next actions. Those may include complaints against the reporter and the TV station; they will most certainly include some kind of consequences for you."

"You're saying I'm grounded," I said, pulling the comforter over my head.

It would be good, I thought, to stay in bed like that. Just a day or two to let the smoke clear, let Liv be confused, Kellan be incensed, Ricker be elegantly outraged at my disobedience. The only necessary ally is the person who gives me information, and that is Paula.

Still, the interview hadn't yet aired. In other words, the shit hadn't hit the fan.

But Mom wasn't through. "You still have not given me one logical reason for why you went to see Yvonne Jessup, and why you agreed to be interviewed by Paula Papademetriou," she said.

I pulled the comforter down and folded my hands elaborately, buying time to think. I made steeples with my fingers and focused on the pink shadows inside. "I went to see Yvonne Jessup out of curiosity. For closure. Paula Papademetriou must have been driving by, or got some tip. She ambushed me. I gave her short answers; nothing I haven't said before. You would have been proud, actually."

"You will lie low this weekend. I've invited Erik to come tomorrow and stay for a while." Then she snuggled up against me, which was nice. "We could use the time together."

I focused on my fingers. Normally I'd be wondering if "we" meant "three," as in Mom, Erik, and me. But I wasn't. I was thinking about forgivenesses to be begged. Explanations to be made.

Revenge to be sought.

TWELVE

365 Days After the Woods

I haven't left my bed since.

It's been less than twenty-four hours since the Shiverton Abduction episode aired, and already Ricker has made complaints to the Federal Communications Commission and the Society of Professional Journalists and the White House (though it's fully believable, I made the last one up). Erik's friend's legal opinion is that we can't sue, because Paula was under the reasonable impression that my mother had consented, and besides, the interview would likely be considered in the public interest, since it was about police misconduct. Liv was easily airbrushed out of the story, which is the advantage of running away from the scene of a crime. Paula kept her promise not to reveal the facts she's turned up about Liv.

That was the only promise she kept.

The interview was a human interest story to the extent that

Paula is a human and she was interested in creatively editing and contextualizing everything I said. Every worthwhile story contains tension between victims and perpetrators: I was the victim, and the parole board and the Shiverton Police Department were the perpetrators. Donald was mainly an off-the-hook closet deviant running around foaming at the mouth. Paula's job was to frame the conflict properly, and she selected the frame.

The finished piece included these highlights. I break them down into three categories: *What I Actually Said*, *What You Heard Me Say on TV*, and *What Paula Said on TV*.

What I Actually Said: Mrs. Jessup said Donny had his demons, but he wasn't capable of killing someone. She said she would go to her grave saying that.

What You Heard Me Say on TV: Mrs. Jessup said Donny had his demons. She said she would go to her grave saying that.

What Paula Said on TV: So Yvonne Jessup knew that her son was a clear danger to society.

What I Actually Said: His mother said he didn't waste money on things like a gym membership. His main hobby was hunting birds and squirrels, and other animals with his BB gun.

What You Heard Me Say on TV: His mother said his main hobby was hunting animals with his BB gun.

What Paula Said on TV: In other words, he took pleasure in maiming and killing small, defenseless prey animals.

What I Actually Said: There were lots of framed photos on the mantel of him, only up through about age eleven. He looked like a happy little kid.

What You Heard Me Say on TV: There were framed photos on the mantel of him only up through age eleven.

What Paula Said on TV: So the photos vanished after age eleven, the last age at which Yvonne wished to remember him, before he receded into the dark recesses of his mind.

What I Actually Said: She said he liked to work in the dining room because it had the best light. Mrs. Jessup joked that he thought she could control the sun, like God.

What You Heard Me Say on TV: She said he thought she could control the sun, like God.

What Paula Said on TV: In other words, he suffered from the delusion that his mother was God.

What I Actually Said: She claimed she had a panic button and a guard dog. She was paranoid about her TV getting stolen by kids who partied behind her house. To tell you the truth, I think she watched one too many *CSI* shows.

What You Heard Me Say on TV: She had a panic button and a guard dog. She was paranoid.

What Paula Said on TV: It sounds as though Yvonne Jessup lived in fear of being raped and murdered by her own son.

What I Actually Said: I don't think she understood her son was troubled. She definitely knew nothing about him having a parole officer. I think she was in the dark about his past crimes. And she apologized for what he did to me. That was big for me to hear. I'm still thinking about it.

What You Heard Me Say on TV: She definitely knew nothing about him having a parole officer. That was big for me to hear. I'm still thinking about it.

What Paula Said on TV: Nothing. She winced a millimeter and shook her head almost imperceptibly. It was an expression of disbelief, sympathy, and outrage deserving of an Oscar, all without a sound.

For the record (and I'm guessing there is no longer one beyond my notebook, which is where I wrote this), here are the

Things I Know About Yvonne Jessup:
- *Didn't want to let me in, but I told her it was the right thing to do*
- *Likes Bob Ross*
- *Was sorry for the way her son chased me*
- *Was afraid of a lot of things, but not Donny*
- *Wishes he was back upstairs*
- *Doesn't know if she believes in a God anymore*
- *Wanted me to remember he was human*

On the next page, which happens to be the last page of my notebook, I've written:

Things I Know About Donald Jessup:
- *Bought his mother a TV*

- Was trusting
- Needed quiet so he could concentrate
- Was good at drawing faces
- Drew pictures of his girlfriend
- Liked the same things as his girlfriend
- Was in love

Even if I'm the only one who will ever see it, there is now a record of the truth.

In the woods, I tried to count the stars, and when I couldn't make them out, I divided numbers in my head to keep from screaming. My research is done. I have no more things to count. So I can no longer keep from screaming.

The first time the scream came, I was riding home in the town car from WFYT, and the words came to me, Liv's voice, lilting in my right ear.

chat, play, more

And all the uncertain things became certain. I threw back my head, bared my throat, and wailed. The driver almost crashed. Dr. Ricker calls them primal screams, says they're a form of letting off steam and will bring catharsis. They seem to be having the opposite effect. Every time I scream, I get angrier, a wave crashing onto shore followed by another, bigger wave.

chat, play, more

And now I'm angry enough to torch a prom with my mind. Boil a bunny. Bark like a dog. I am all three Furies, breath burning and eyes dripping with blood, waiting at the mouth of Hell to wreak vengeance. Prayer and tears won't move me.

There is an upside. Erik has moved into our guest room, ostensibly to help Mom deal with my madness. I hadn't seen him since that night Kellan showed up at my house: the music, the laughter, Mom's sloppy gestures. I assume some line got crossed while Kellan and I weren't paying attention, and awkwardness ensued. But any awkwardness has been forgotten, now that I've had what I heard Mom tell Erik was a "psychological break."

As if I'd be this upset over a stupid interview that I agreed to from the beginning. I like to think it takes a little more than being violated by Paula Papademetriou to send me stomping around the house, pulling out my hair, and yelling into pillows.

Being violated by my best friend: that's different.

I've taken to locking myself in my car in the garage, or slipping into the thatch of trees behind our house, just to save Mom and Erik from witnessing the ugly. Especially Mom. Among my other new habits: slipping the Klonopin Ricker gave me between my teeth and burying it in my spider plant. Which is looking very relaxed. I had to keep my wits sharp, to finish my research.

I've been studying the sketch Yvonne gave me. I scanned it into Roboteye, a reverse-image search engine that lets you find out where an image came from, how it's being used, and if modified versions exist. The way it works is surreal. Facial recognition algorithms identify features by extracting landmarks from an image of the subject's face. For example, an algorithm may analyze the relative position, size, and the shape of the eyes, nose, cheekbones, and jaw. Those landmarks are used to search for other images with ones that match. It's freaking brilliant. And it's free. But the subject of Donny's sketches never made her way to the Internet, not even as a driver's license photo.

This was just me proving my hypothesis. Now that my research is complete, I know the girl in the sketch never existed.

Though Donny's girlfriend did.

It's this funny inverse of a cliché. Usually when a person lies online about their appearance, they pretend to look better than they do in real life. Like the guy who posts pictures of himself on Match.com from twenty years and twenty pounds ago. But when someone you love—say, your own mother—insists other people will only love you if you're that someone's version of perfect, then you experiment a little. Prove them wrong. So when you describe yourself to a Donald Jessup / Lonely Hearts Club type, for example, you pick all the things you think would make you ugly. But he loves you anyway. Immortalizes the you he thinks you are in his sketches. Mails them to you, and you hang them in your own personal, fiberglass-insulated trophy room. *Winning!* you think. *Eff you, Mother.* He drives all around town trying to see you in person, but you provide exactly enough wrong clues that he always just misses you. The whole experiment works, until one day, simply flirting with danger isn't enough. You decide it would be fun to let him see what you really look like; let him in on the experiment. Unfortunately, the subject you picked for your experiment turns out to be a murderous psychopath.

Whoops.

I've had lots of time to think of next steps. In fact, I titled this chapter "Next Steps" in my notebook, where I've had to start over from the beginning, along the margins. On the early pages, my handwriting is vigilant and tense. Now it flows. On the very first page, the page with the bisected cat's eye, I wrote along the side "Keep your friends close and your enemies closer" as a personal reminder of my new MO. (Everyone attributes that to the Chinese general Sun Tzu in *The Art of War*. But what he was really saying was, Know your enemy and know yourself and you will always be victorious. The original quote is actually from Machiavelli's *The Prince*, the ultimate primer on how to be a sneaky liar. You use the word *Machiavellian* to describe someone who manipulates others in an opportunistic and deceptive way to get what they want.)

I will confront Liv for throwing me into the path of a psychopath for a sick thrill, for her own proof to herself that, contrary to Mommy's lies, she could be loved no matter how she looked. Only I have to figure out how, and I don't have much time. But I can't think on that now, because Erik is here, and I have to make him not worry quite so much.

We sit in Adirondack chairs on my back deck, bundled in blankets. I insist on being outside these days, and Mom seems to like the idea. Which is totally in character, since fresh air was once a cure for female hysteria along with bloodletting, cold douches over the head, and lobotomies. For the nth time, I re-count the trees that line the end of our property, my mouth moving silently until Erik interrupts.

"Your mom says you're planning to go to the Lapins' house for a Monday-night holiday party. Think you're ready for that?"

"Can we talk about something else?" I ask, picking at invisible lint on my blanket.

"Absolutely. How about this: Why would you ever go see the mother of Donald Jessup?"

"Dr. Ricker told Mom the impulse to reach out to the relative of my perpetrator was natural. I quote: 'The urge to connect Donald Jessup with some evidence of his own humanity is a sign of healing.'"

"It was completely reckless," he says.

I turn in my chair. "Seriously? You were the one supporting my 'need for information' before. Maybe my need for information is okay to a certain extent, but when it gets a little freaky—"

"A dumb, dangerous move. Period," he says in a definitive way I sort of admire.

"Yvonne Jessup can barely see past her glasses and gets around on a walker on tennis balls. The only thing that could have hurt me in that house was an allergy attack from all the squirrel droppings."

"You were exploited, Julia. On national news. Yvonne Jessup could have sued you for harassment. She still might sue—who knows? More importantly, we can't predict the psychological effects of meeting with that woman alone." He leans in and says in an undertone, "I would have gone with you. If you really wanted to talk to Yvonne Jessup, I would have considered going with you."

I soften. "You would have?"

"Yes. Probably. I also could have saved you from what happened afterward. At the very least, being ambushed and coerced into Paula's car should have been horrible enough to change your perspective on the reporters covering your story," Erik says.

"If by 'changed perspective' you mean 'distrust,' sure," I say.

"That's huge. It lets you move on."

"Where am I going?" I ask.

He shakes his head at my brand of throwaway sarcasm. It stings, and I regret it immediately, because I'm starting to feel very alone in this world, and I need Erik to stay close. My allies are dropping like flies: in great, skeevy numbers. There's Paula, who blatantly used me. Liv has not been my true friend in a year, likely more. My nationally televised, police-damning interview ensures Kellan won't be coming around anytime soon. Even Alice has been afraid to knock on the door, probably having overheard my primal screams in the backyard.

"I've found that when life-changing events happen, it becomes time to shed your skin. Like a snake—" Erik says.

A snake? Really? I search the woods for the cameras. My chest pangs for Kellan; I so want to tell him this. But then I'd also have to explain the black in my belly . . . never mind.

"—you let go of the old people around you who don't make your life better. Maybe it's time to make some new friends? Start fresh?" he finishes.

Word-for-word Mom, without a doubt. "I disagree one hundred percent. I think this is the perfect time to keep your friends close. Besides, Liv needs me now more than ever," I tell Erik.

"Because of the *Dateline* interview?" he says logically.

But nothing Liv-and-me is logical. Why not be open with Erik? He dropped everything, sped to Shiverton after Mom's panicked call, and now he's stuck playing nursemaid to my crazy. Over the last seventeen or so years, he's never complained about Mom's wacky arrangement with me, or her romantic push and pull with him, besides. Suddenly I feel bad for him. Or maybe I feel bad for all guys who get used by women.

I ought to open up a little.

I sigh deeply. "Liv's problems go back a lot further than that," I say. "Like birth."

"You mean Deborah Lapin? Gwen has told me . . . things," Erik says carefully.

"It's just the two of them, but not in a good way. I have to think if there was one more person in that household, a buffer, things would be easier for Liv." My eyes flit to Erik, wondering if he thinks I'm talking about Mom, him, and me in code.

"We can't begin to try to understand other peoples' arrangements," Erik says gravely.

Ouch.

"Though her dad is coming," I say brightly, taking a different track. "For February vacation. There's that."

Erik unwinds his long legs. Like me, he likes a little legroom. "Where does he live now?"

"He and his family used to live in the Cayman Islands. Now

they live in Provence, where all the lavender comes from, in France. He's a—what's the word?—ex-pat?"

"An expatriate. He works outside of the United States but was born here. You said, his family?"

"He has another whole separate family with little kids, two of them. They were all in *Vogue* last year. You couldn't see the kids' faces, just these black-and-white shots of their tiny toes and the backs of their heads. His wife is a lot younger than Deborah and has her own line of smelly luxury candles that her dad sends Liv once a year, along with other useless gifts that no kid wants, like Mont Blanc pens and personalized stationery. Deborah makes Liv display the candles. It's like Deborah wants so much to be associated with the other Lapins, when you'd think she'd hate them."

"Display the candles for when he visits, you mean?"

"Yeah, during February vacation, for one day total, while he's in Boston doing business. Deborah is excited about it. Liv says it's tragic, since he doesn't even plan on seeing Deborah, only Liv."

Erik frowns. "How long were they married?"

"He—his name is Leland, Liv actually *calls* him Leland— and Deborah were married for almost four years total. Liv barely knows him. But that doesn't mean she doesn't hate him."

"Do you know why she hates him?" he asks.

"Um, yeah! For one, Deborah said her father left because Liv was unlovable. That she drove him away."

"Liv told you this?"

"I've heard Deborah say it to her. Plenty of times."

"That's a strange thing for a mother to say to a kid. Do you believe it's true?"

"It's a rotten thing for a mother to say to a kid. I mean, Liv was two and a half when he left! It's not true, right? Couples don't split because a kid is awful."

Erik turns to face me. For a second, my heart stops, because I have no idea what he's going to say. *Please, God, if there is a God, please don't pair the worst time in my life with what should be the greatest time in my life. Don't mix up all the hate I'm feeling for Liv with love for Erik. No daddy confessions today.*

"You know I've never married, so I don't have a lot of experience along these lines. I can tell you that couples don't fail because of some perceived personality flaw of the kid."

I exhale a raspberry. Erik gives me an odd look, settling back in his chair.

"You know I tend to go where I'm not supposed to. Your mom will tell you that," he says. "But tell me something. What kind of person is Mrs. Lapin?"

"For one, she creates these great big fictions about herself. Like she claims she was a catwalk model in her teens and twenties. Except it's a total lie. She was in department store ads and local pageants. Liv outed her once to me, when we were nosing around her room, looking at all her creepy dried flowers and sashes. This was back when Liv could laugh about her mother. It's different now," I say.

Erik nods. "I think I get the picture. I need to ask you a question. Has Liv ever complained about her mother abusing her?"

"As in hitting?"

"There are other forms."

"If Liv was being abused, why wouldn't she talk to me about it?" I ask.

"I have no experience in psychology beyond college intro courses. But from what I remember, Liv's mother's abusiveness may be part of a lifelong campaign of control. And because people with narcissistic personality disorders are careful to rationalize their abuse, it's tough to explain to other people what's so bad about them." He rushes to add, "That is not to say I'm diagnosing a woman I've never met."

I smile. "I like when you 'go there,' Erik. You should go there more often."

The slider behind us grates open and Mom pops her head out. "Something warm to drink?" Erik checks his technical-looking watch and says he's due to call the lab.

I crank my head around to watch him angle through the door. "So it's never really about the kid? When couples don't make it, I mean?" I call to him.

He freezes in place and looks at my mother, then me. "No. It's always about the parents. And anyone who says otherwise is not telling the truth."

Erik disappears upstairs and Mom steps onto the deck holding out a steaming mug of ginseng tea. I cradle it in my hands, and she slips into Erik's chair with a mug for herself.

"People are forever offering me something warm to drink. Why is that?" I ask.

"I don't know." She presses her own mug to her nose. "Maybe because you always used to seem cold."

A breeze rustles the tree line and dips low, swirling the crisp leaves at our feet. I pull the blanket up from my legs and stand, wrapping it around my shoulders. "Thanks for the tea. It was nice of you. But I'm taking a walk."

She puts her mug down fast on the deck plank and stiffens, probably preparing to tent-hug, inject me with a sedative, or both. Then I realize: she's upset. I just talked to Erik three times as much as I've spoken with her in the past week.

"It's not you," I say softly. "I just want to be alone."

Her shoulders relax and she sinks back into her chair. "For the best, probably. There are things I should be better about doing, now that we have a guest." She lifts her mug and draws it close to her chest. "Dinner, and such."

I descend the deck stairs and cross the lawn, taking long, glidy steps. I must look dramatic to Mom from behind, I think, my hair blowing straight back like a cape at my shoulders, a heroine crossing the dark moor. At the edge of the tree line, I inhale deeply. Though Mom is still a pindot on the deck, it feels good to be mostly alone. It even feels good to be outside. I wonder about the serpent in my belly, if it went away, slipped out of me when it was no longer needed. Or did it keep rising after I left WFYT, to enervate my whole being? That feels more likely.

chat, play, more

I step more deeply into the swath of wooded land that abuts our yard. I like to be alone with my screams. Branches scatter the ground, snapped off by the heavy rain. I pick one up and walk in deeper. Another, then another, gathering twigs as I go. I don't know why. The sky is the color of eggplant, and the November air smells of early snow. I come upon a patch of ice needles pushing through the soil in a half horseshoe, short, beautiful shards. Deeper still, on a log, a frost flower blooms, long petals of ice extruding from some plant. Frost flowers are rarely seen; I know this from freshman geology. Am I really seeing these things at all?

chat, play, more

I grip my belly and scream then, leaning back and shaking my head, a howl that could bring police sirens. It still might, given Mom is on the deck, and the Mincuses' backyard is twenty feet away. When I scream, I imagine a black lava flowing from my mouth, every kind of deadly animal riding inside: lions, tigers, sharks, cobras. When I'm done, a cold sweat runs down my shirt, and my back heaves, hands on thighs. The exhaustion that follows brings peace. Sticks lie scattered at my feet like bones, but for two bunches in my hands. I am Shakespeare's Lavinia in *Titus Andronicus*, trimmed and given bundled branches for hands, her tongue cut out, all so she couldn't bring justice to her violators. But she found a way. She took a stick in her mouth and scribbled their names in the sand. She had her revenge.

Like Lavinia, I will figure out a way to make my greatest offender known. It won't be public, but it will count. I will create my own kind of justice.

THIRTEEN

366 Days After the Woods

The skate park should be the perfect place to perform an extreme stunt. Where else to explain my seeming alliance with the person bent on taking down the Shiverton police department? To make amends for being Paula's instrument? To stoke my courage, I catch snowflakes on my tongue. In the half hour that I've been waiting for Kellan, I've tested my resolve by exposing different parts of my body to the cold. Ankles, wrists, earlobes, lower back, tongue.

I let the snow dissolve. Granular, tolerable, gone. In the distance, steps approach, boots crunching in the cold dust.

"You came," I say.

"I came." Kellan shambles to me, shoulders hiked to his ears. The light poles cast a pewter glare. His eyes are coated with mistrust. Am I too late? Has disappointment calcified into hate?

"I suppose you think I'm a traitor," I say.

He cocks his chin and stares at the sky, which is worse than an answer. This is the opposite of the skate park where we celebrated before, dark and upside-down. I clear my throat, starting over. "I asked you here so I could explain why I agreed to an interview with Paula Papademetriou."

He jams his hands into his pockets. "Don't think you can."

I wasn't expecting such an absolute shutdown. Flummoxed, I stall. "How did you get out so late?"

"Snuck."

"Me? I used the front door. I'd planned something more dramatic, but it turned out to be overkill." I wait for a smile, but his mouth is set. Around us, the first snowflakes of the year fall sparsely. Everything is blurring, the seasons overlapping. It's a wavy-mirror world that suits things perfectly. "Please sit with me."

"No thanks." He says it with an edge, breath swirling from the side of his mouth. "So you said yes when Paula asked to interview you?"

"I had no choice," I reply.

He winces at the sky. "Did she hold you hostage?"

It would be easy to give him the story I gave Mom, to lie, say I was ambushed. But I have to make him understand that Paula is my last resort. "We're working together. Paula's helping to make things right."

His eyes flare with disbelief, which is awful, but better than the dull veil of before. "How can screwing the police department be right? Don't you get it? If my father loses his job, it's bad, for him and for my family. Why do you think I left St. John's? Things are tight. If you haven't noticed, we don't live on your side of Shiverton."

"Paula is trying to change a broken system," I say.

"That broken system saved you," he says.

"A guy riding his bicycle by the watchtower saved me. That broken system got me abducted. Donald Jessup's ankle bracelet told the police he was lurking around the high school, the track, and Liv's house, and still he slipped through the cracks." I say it steadily, without emotion or inflection. Just the facts.

"My father didn't create the system. He's a good guy. He cared about your case, not only for the two days they were searching for you and Jessup—and he was out there, on the ground, in the woods—I'm talking months and months after. Your case might have been officially closed, but my father always believed there was more to it."

"Your father isn't the one who looks bad. Chief Pantano is taking the fall," I point out.

"Is that what Paula says? Your new BFF?" he spits.

"Paula is the only one who can help me. There's a lot you don't understand. Ever since the woods, something's not right with Liv."

"Somehow the fact that this is about Liv Lapin makes it so much worse."

Kellan angles his body away from me. Beyond us, traffic thrums and beeps, and the cheesy gym next door leaks riffs of music. But inside the cement bowl it's just us and the patter of snow. The air smells metallic, lustrous and charged. I wonder how I can do this, remain seated and totally still, while Kellan twists and turns to stay warm, beating at his sides and shifting from foot to foot.

I stick out my tongue to test a snowflake again.

He squats, forearms resting on his thighs, and for the first time looks me full in the face. "You once said what happened in the woods made you morbidly fascinating, a freak-show oddity. But you don't get it. I never looked at you *until* the woods."

If the woods could create a snake in my belly, why couldn't it make me irresistible to Kellan? Maybe the cold forced my body to burn fat, turning me into a lean, hard fighter. Perhaps learning to hide my footfalls in the crunch of telltale leaves gave me agility and grace. Seeing through rain sharpened my vision, let me see people for who they are.

I scramble onto my knees. "Make me get it."

"When the abduction happened, I knew it was a terrible story in a vague way, because you and Liv went to Shiverton, and we were in the same grade, and the dude was from Shiverton, which was scary. It kept my father from coming home at night, and that sucked, but it wasn't the first case that's consumed him. Still, I didn't get what the big deal was until my father explained to me that you weren't an ordinary girl. You threw yourself in front of danger to save your friend's life. Then you outwitted the guy, came back, and got him arrested. Dad called you the bravest human being he'd ever met."

I hold my hand on my belly, like there's something there I need to protect, something the woods created that I don't want to let go. Not yet.

"I fell for you without knowing you. And then, when I finally talked to you, I found out you were sarcastic and funny, and dark and dry. Tough. Not just physically, but your mind, too. It's like this terrifying, shiny thing that can take anyone down. I told my father Donald Jessup never stood a chance."

I start to smile, but the sadness in his eyes makes me stop.

"And now, it's like you're an instrument of the enemy. I have to ask myself: Were you playing me?" he says.

My stomach drops. "I wasn't playing you. Not ever."

"Five minutes ago, you said the police let Donald Jessup slip through the cracks. That sounds vengeful to me."

"The reason I'm working with Paula has nothing to do with vengeance." I hold my head in my hands. "Donald Jessup and Liv are connected, but I can't prove how. Is that enough to make you understand?"

"So this is all about Liv."

"Actually, yes."

He takes my chin in his hand. "I can't share your heart with Liv. Half of Julia isn't enough for me." He rises, throwing out his hands, and paces. "I haven't stopped thinking about you since that day I grabbed your waist and threw you in my car. I'm insane about you. The crap you say. The way you look at the world. The fact that you're utterly unafraid of anything. Being with you is like injecting this rush that makes me feel alive. When I'm not with you, you're all I want. I can barely breathe."

I want to take his jaw in my hand and drag his mouth to mine, consume him whole, I ache for his mouth on mine so much, and what the heck, what difference does it make? I don't care if he throws me off of him, tells me to go to hell, that I'm a father-wrecking, home-wrecking career-wrecker. I've had worse.

He is far away now, far enough away that he might leave. He calls to me.

"In the woods, when you said 'come with me'? You meant to the place where Ana Alvarez died, but in my mind, you were asking me to fall for you. And it was already too late. I was all in." He turns and walks toward the alley.

I leap up and run toward him. He spins around just before I tackle him, wrapping my arms around his neck and pulling him toward me. His lips are cool and the tops of his cheeks feel wet, and he holds back at first, the muscles in his chest and shoulders unyielding, and I let go a little, but then he comes in fast, and I fall to my knees and then the ground, and he crawls on top of me.

"In case you were wondering, this is not one of those sur-real moments," Kellan says.

"So no audience?" I say, breathless.

"No audience. But we can pretend, if you're into that." He nuzzles my neck, and the vibration is delicious.

Long, scraping noises. A bright beam swoops and bobbles

over us like a spastic searchlight. Kellan follows my stare toward the source, a half-pipe over the ridge of the bowl.

"Kids on skateboards wearing headlamps," Kellan says.

"So we *are* being punked," I say. "This is probably not the best idea."

"The idea is excellent. It's the execution," he says. "Next time, indoors."

I laugh. He rolls to his side, and the loss of his warmth and weight feels like it might kill me. I peel myself from the ground and brush off, every inch of my body screaming, the air around us throbbing with frustration. He pulls me to his chest and holds me there for a second, the two of us standing in the middle of a big empty cement bowl against a psychedelic backdrop of light beams swooping and dancing as if to music.

He tips my chin to see him, a trick appealing to us tall girls, I expect. His eyes are soft and sad. "Seeing Yvonne Jessup wasn't safe. She could have been as sick as her monster son. She could've hurt you."

"I brought Alice."

"Of course. The famous Alice. I'm starting to think Alice is your imaginary friend."

I pretend to sucker punch him and in the process kick over my messenger bag. The junk inside spills on the asphalt, along with my notebook and the gifted sketch. He deserves to understand. I kneel down and lift the sketch. The girl's strange broad forehead catches the light, and Kellan's eye.

I hand it to him, and he tilts it, trying to see, head cocked. I expect him to make a guy face, a pure, unfiltered reaction to a picture of a girl who isn't the prettiest. But his eyes flutter all over it. Deep in my chest something plinks—jealousy?

"Cool," he says, crouching next to me and handing it back. "Who's the artist?"

"Donald Jessup."

His head jerks back, like I've slapped him. "How—"

"Yvonne Jessup. She gave it to me," I say. "Aren't you going to ask who the girl is?" Because that's the important part.

"Who's the girl?" he says slowly.

"You know her," I say. A dusting of snow smudges the charcoal. I blow the sketch with a soft puff, adding, "Just not as well as I do."

FOURTEEN

367 Days After the Woods

"Mother prefers the green foil paper with the Spirograph snowflakes."

Liv only calls Deborah "Mother" around Deborah. We are wrapping gifts under Deborah's surveillance, gifts for Leland's family, which will be mailed well ahead of Christmas to France; a gift for Father Carl, who is expected any minute; and Liv's gift for Shane, which she is in charge of because it's heavy and the corners may tear. Tonight has been declared Early Christmas by Deborah, who has the power to schedule holidays prematurely in her own house, since the Lapin girls will be in Bolivia for actual Christmas. Besides the calendar-warping, the evening is made weirder by the fact that I have been dropped into a scene straight out of *Barbie and Skipper's Holiday*, with Deborah in full makeup and a red rabbit-collared suit, and Liv in a matching red dress. I am apparently styled after little green plastic army men, in jeans, a camo Henley, a puffy vest, and the black military boots I've taken to wearing every day.

Deborah's surveillance extends to our conversation, so I cannot ask Liv about the charcoal sketches, or how she feels about my publicly outed visit with Yvonne Jessup, or how she will manage missing a month of school. We speak nothing of my interview on *Dateline*; I can only assume that its national nature has piqued Deborah's annoyance. As much as she supposedly hates the media attention, she hates me getting media attention even more. So the subject is closed, which suits me fine.

Even my pointed looks at Deborah's outfit get censored. "Pretty makes her happy, and her happy makes everything easier," Liv explains quietly.

Christmas music sung by an aging pop star screeches out of the Bose radio. Rolls of paper are spread across the dining room table—too many, since the gift count is low. I finish wrapping Father Carl's gift and set it aside. Father Carl is coming to talk to Liv and me, a "check-in" following our recent exploitation by the media. But giving him a present deflects the attention back to Deborah, and he deserves a present, she insists. What you buy a priest I cannot imagine, and I don't ask what's in the generic box, although she wants me to.

Deborah scrapes the length of a red ribbon with the edge of her scissors until it snaps into a tight curl. She steals a look at Shane's gift box in Liv's hands. "Should I guess what you've got in that box?"

"Oh, I don't think you can guess," Liv says, folding the corners into careful triangles. "It's a toughie."

"There's nothing you can give me that would equal the love and care I give you," Deborah says, arranging a pile of curlicue ribbons on top of her wrapped box for one of Leland's other children. "Besides, what can you afford?"

"It's not for you, Mother. It's for Shane." She tapes an oversized gold bow to the middle of the tie box, a tie being an excellent guess if it was for anyone but Shane Cuthbert. "What did you get Father Carl? I thought priests weren't supposed to want anything."

"This isn't for Father Carl, it's for Crystal," she says.

"Who's Crystal?" I say, stupidly. The only place I ever sound stupid is in this house, mainly because I have such a hard time following their insides and references. Though Liv is forever in opposition to Deborah, they are always on the same plane, like two comets racing to earth on the same path, scorching each other on the way down. I'm so caught up in this image that I don't realize they are both laughing at me.

"Crystal is my new little sister," Liv says with a wicked smile.

I nearly choke. "One of Leland's children?" I look at Deborah in horror. *Or is she pregnant?*

"Little sister, like Big Brothers Big Sisters. My community service hours for confirmation. She's darling," Liv says.

"We got a good one. She's a stunning girl," Deborah says.

"Crystal is eleven. Eleven is cute, not 'stunning.'" Liv bites off the word.

"I had to get her something. It's a lava lamp. Silver and purple, with glitter inside. She'll love it. It's the gaudiest thing, but she loves anything sparkly, little magpie that she is. I ought to make an inventory of my jewelry drawer at some point," Deborah says.

"So what did you get Carl?" Liv asks sharply.

Deborah looks at Liv with an icy glare, hands holding ribbon above the gift. "I believe you meant to say Father Carl. I got him a Lenox figurine of two hands joined in prayer. It's lovely; someone was selling it at a steep discount on eBay. That's why it's not in its original packaging," she says to me, as though I was wondering. "White bisque porcelain. I just think a little luxury in his life can't be a sin, not if the gift goes beyond the recipient. He can place it on his mantle in the rectory lobby, where everyone can enjoy it."

"That sounds nice," I say.

Liv grunts softly.

"I might as well reveal what I got you, Olivia. You're not a little girl who needs surprises. It's an SPF long-sleeve shirt and pants. It will help protect your skin from the sun on our vacation," Deborah says.

I force myself to listen.

"Once the sun damages your derma, there's no turning back. More than one esthetician has told me that my skin is in such great shape because I wore foundation for so many years and it shielded my skin from the sun. You know, most girls would start acting excited right about now if their mother was whisking them away from miserable, gray New England,"

Deborah says, adding as an afterthought: "Oh, and I got you those colored pencils. The Swiss ones from the Dick Blick art store."

Liv's hands freeze, a curlicue of tape dangling off one finger. "The Caran D'Ache Supracolor Soft Aquarelle Pencils? In the hinge-lid wooden box?"

"I asked the guy. I suppose so." Deborah sniffs. "This place smells like a hospital. The cleaners must have used their own supplies. Cheap and harsh." She bustles away in search of one of Leland's candles.

"So tell me about your vacation." I try hard to say it casually, but it comes out sounding pointed.

The childlike smile that formed when Deborah mentioned the pencils fades. "It's what Deborah wants," Liv says.

It sounds simple. A simple vacation to someplace warm, for a month. What's the big deal? I smile, too. "So what did you get Shane?"

"A new knife."

I drop Father's Carl's present on the table. It lands hard and rattles, like those two hands might no longer be joined. Liv carries Shane's gift—Shane's knife—with its incongruous, gorgeous fat bow into the dark parlor, setting it under the lopped-off top quarter of a skinny Christmas tree. I set the broken gift aside and follow.

The tree takes up too much room in a space already jammed with three chairs and a coffee table, on which sits a crèche stuffed with straw and porcelain figurines. I can't imagine where Deborah and Liv will sit on Christmas morning to open presents without their knees bonking. Then I remember: they won't be in this country. Two very old stockings are hung from weighted pewter angels that could be weapons in your standard murder mystery. The stockings are unnamed, which makes sense if there are only two people in the house, but makes my job harder if I'm going to give Liv the present I plan to surprise her with. Yvonne's sketch is rolled and tied with ribbon in the inside pocket of the puffy vest I will not take off, and my note, telling Liv everything I know—

You used him.
You used me.
You sacrificed me.
Merry Early Christmas.

—is under the ribbon too. But I need to make sure it lands in the right stocking.

The doorbell rings.

Liv kneels in front of the crèche and lifts ceramic Baby Jesus from his cradle. Winking Christmas tree bulbs cast her in a wash of light, then shadow.

"Do you think it was a good idea to get Shane a knife?" I ask, one eye on the hall. Deborah throws open the door and steps back to let Father Carl enter. He hands Deborah the door handle.

"You heard Deborah's theory on presents. It was an excellent idea to give Shane a knife."

"How is a knife enjoyed by all? Liv, he's not"—how do I

say this without admitting I've overheard things?—"the most stable person. You used to know this."

"Are we going to discuss questions of judgment? Good then." She turns Baby Jesus over in her hand. "Then let's start with sitting down for an interview with Paula Papademetriou."

I drop my head.

"I didn't think so," Liv says, setting Baby Jesus down with a ceramic tick. "I can't believe she got me those colored pencils. They're perfectly hexagonal. Presharpened. Most unbelievably, I actually wanted them."

Deborah takes the handle from Father Carl without looking at it, as if it's the most natural thing in the world. As Deborah climbs the stairs with his coat, Father Carl's eyes go to the cords dangling from the spot overhead where there was once a light fixture.

"I saw circles and Xs on your body. Drawn with a marker. Why did you draw circles and Xs on your skin?" I ask heatedly.

"You've got a renovation going on, I see," Father Carl booms.

"Oh, that's been on hold for a while!" Deborah yells down. "This house is a bear. Too many diversions lately!"

Liv's shoulders raise and her spine grows taut, like someone has lifted slack strings above her head. "Deborah says stick-style Victorians were high-concept houses. You can read the outside from the inside: eaves and trusses on the inside make shadows and voids on the outside. The sticks are decoration, meant to symbolize where the joints and posts are," she says.

"We're talking about you, not high-concept houses," I hiss.

"The builders capitalized on the best resources of the era. If you live in a day and age when modern tools can make something more beautiful, it's a sin not to use them," Liv says.

The room is so cold, I think I see my breath.

"And she won't spare any expense." Liv turns and waves to Father Carl. "Father Carl! Come see. What should we do about Baby Jesus? He's not supposed to make an appearance until Christmas Day."

"Well, look there." Father Carl comes in, squatting in front of the manger. "Very pretty. And God won't hold it against you, Olivia, if Baby Jesus makes a premature arrival. Though I know some people like to keep him hidden until the day he was born."

"I think that's an excellent tradition," she says.

Father Carl turns to me. "You're Julia. It's very nice to meet you, Julia."

I give him a stiff, upright wrist wave, close to the belly. "Hi."

"Olivia has told me so much about you," he says.

Liv stays kneeling, staring into the manger, and says, "An excellent tradition, keeping him hidden. Because no one ever talks about the heartache that he caused. All those other babies who died on his behalf."

Father Carl's eyebrows rise into triangle tips. "Other babies?"

"Julia doesn't know what we're talking about," Liv says. "Her mother is an atheist."

I start to correct her, then stop.

"King Herod learned he'd been outwitted by the three wise men and ordered all boys in Bethlehem under the age of two to be slaughtered," she continues.

"Be right down, Father!" Deborah calls from far away.

Father Carl pats his belly. "Well, that's the biblical story, yes. I believe modern historians put the number at about twelve." He spins on his heels to me. "Bethlehem was a very small town, you see."

"King Herod was obsessed with his legacy. He built a lot of things, like fortresses, aqueducts, and theaters. Splashy, visible projects. Like the Temple of Jerusalem," Liv says.

"You've certainly been keeping up with your Bible studies, Olivia." He glances back to the center stairwell where Deborah disappeared.

"But he was also paranoid and bloodthirsty. Especially toward the end of his reign, as he was getting older. He even thought the plots against him were hatched by his own family. He killed one of his wives, Mariamne, and three of his sons: Alexander, Aristobulus, and Antipater. What kind of monster does that to his own family members?"

"Maybe we should eat," I say.

"The thing is, no one would be sad when he died, and he knew that. That's why as he was dying, he rounded up the leading men of Israel and threw them in the Hippodrome, ordering they be killed when he died so more people would mourn. A totally immoral monster, wouldn't you say?"

Deborah rushes down the stairs with something in her arms.

"It's no surprise that Caesar Augustus said, 'It is better to be Herod's pig than his son,'" Liv says.

Father Carl forces a laugh.

Liv forces a laugh back. "Funny, right? The joke, of course, is that since Herod was a Jew, he wouldn't eat pork, so the pig would be safe."

Deborah bustles toward Father Carl with a square box wrapped haphazardly in tissue with a pink grosgrain ribbon I recognize from a pillow on her bed. She gives me a sharp look that tells me she heard the sound of broken parts inside Father Carl's gift, and if she didn't have to be on her best behavior, I'd be toast. "And you're all in the parlor. Perfect! And you've already been talking to the girls, so your counseling is done. Are you hungry, Carl? Because if you can wait, I'd love for you to open a small gift I got you."

Father Carl gushes, noting he didn't bring anything, doesn't need anything, for he has all he needs in God's love, but she insists, and does he like art supplies? Everyone likes a nice set of watercolor pencils, especially ones from Switzerland, the brand is well respected if you're into that sort of thing.

Father Carl collapses into one chair, and Deborah sits stiffly in the one opposite. I sit in the third, and no one seems to notice that Liv hasn't moved from the floor, staring at the stupid manger scene that isn't really pretty but is actually kind of shabby. The smell of Leland's candles is overpowering, a mix

245

of candy apple and wintergreen that hurts my teeth. The Christmas tree winks on and off in a sickening strobe effect. I can't understand why Liv doesn't move, doesn't blink, doesn't even give Deborah a dirty look for giving her present away, so I give Deborah my dirtiest look for her. Can't anyone see Liv's eyes are filled with tears? But since I'm the one who broke Father Carl's praying hands, maybe it's my fault.

Father Carl rips at the soft tissue paper. "These pencils are lovely! I guess I'll have to take up drawing."

"I need to call Shane," Liv says softly.

"What's so important that you have to call Shane right now?" I say, wishing she'd stay, because the minute she leaves, I will slip her gift in her stocking, and she will know, and nothing will ever be the same. Right in this moment, we are in a snow globe that's about to shatter, a moment in time that we can never go back to.

"I need to arrange when to give him his gift." She trips lightly up the stairs.

Deborah throws up her hands. "Dinner's nearly done. Come, everyone! I've even made figgy pudding."

I am left alone with the flashing tree. The lights have halos. I'm looking through tears, I realize, blinking them back. There isn't much time. I stand and walk over to the ornamental fireplace, patting my vest. Liv needs to know I know what she did. I risked my life to save her. And she risked my life to . . . what?

Which stocking? *Eeenie-meanie-miney-mo.* The one I land on feels wrong. I try again.

Not because you're dirty.
Not because you're clean.
Just because you kissed a boy behind a magazine.
Out goes Y-O-U.

I slip the stocking off the angel's trumpet hook. It's heavy. Inside is a box of Crest whitening strips, a cold eye pack, oil-control blotting papers, and a large jar of vitamins called Time Machine with "age-defying, plant-based properties that support cell health." All stuff I've seen among Deborah's things she uses and owns, just more of it. I stuff the items back in the same order and slip it back on the hook.

Stocking Two is as empty as the other is full, but for a long envelope. Please make this be a really good gift certificate, I think. Clothes or the Apple store or anything, really. Liv may be immoral, but she's a kid whose fake-Christmas present just got given away, and she deserves something.

Laughter from the other room. I slip the envelope from the stocking and face the wall. Peeking may be a violation of Liv's privacy, but she violated us.

The gift certificate is not a gift certificate but a tricolor brochure for something called Makeover Travel. It's written in stilted English, with porny photos of boobs and butts and perfectly caved stomachs and straight noses. It explains that "surgery holidays" in Bolivia are less expensive because there are no taxes and the exchange rate is favorable, where something called the "Latin Touch" means you get to recover in a "post-operative paradise" for as many weeks as you like. It talks about combining various plastic surgeries at once—a cost-effective alternative! Where else can you "go on holiday and you become the souvenir"? I feel nauseated as I tick down the menu of implants (chin, cheek, butt), lifts (face, breast, thigh, butt), reductions (chin, female breast, male breast), and ominous-sounding plasties (blepharoplasty, rhinoplasty, labiaplasty).

Plastic surgery in Bolivia?

From the dining room comes the clinking of forks and the slosh of poured wine. Another doorbell, and Liv's fast steps on the stairs. I tuck my present for Liv back into my vest pocket, and meet her as she swings around the newel-post, lighter, her mood shifted to suit our new visitor, Crystal, who has arrived in a cab that Liv runs out to pay. Deborah doesn't move from Father Carl, which leaves me as host and greeter until Liv returns.

I walk over to Crystal. "Hi. I'm Julia."

Crystal is a gorgeous child: perfect skin, bright black eyes, cheekbones to die for. Tall and limber already, her figure is filling out in ways that peg her a stone-cold fox in a year's time. Dread blooms inside my chest.

"Hi," Crystal says, shy. Afraid of me.

Deborah yells from the dining room, and Crystal runs toward her voice. Liv comes behind me.

"Crystal's mom sends her in a cab?" I say.

"Crystal's mom is a meth addict. She and her two little brothers live with her grandmother, who's on dialysis. *We* send her in a cab."

"She's afraid of me, but she likes Deborah," I say.

Liv snorts. "She thinks my mother is a benevolent goddess. And that we live in a yellow-pink-and-green palace."

"Really?" I say, though I'm not surprised. Deborah has that effect on people who don't know her well, that lethal combo of faded looks and faux-folksy warmth she projects on newbies. Crystal will learn soon enough.

"And it's mutual. Deborah dotes on her. Sometimes I don't know if she got her for me or for her," Liv says airily.

"I think it's cool that you're doing this," I say.

"It wasn't my idea. Deborah tweaked and polished my application so hard she could see her reflection in it," she says, hooking her elbow through mine, and we walk into the dining room. Steps away, she stops. Crystal is seated at Deborah's right, looking awkward and stiff, like she's supposed to be having fun but isn't. When she sees Liv, her face relaxes and she lights up. Liv turns fast and drags me close. "Listen, if something ever happened, if, say, I had to leave for a while, just to clear my head, would you do something for me?"

"Where are you planning on going?" I say, startled.

"It's an important question. Would you take care of Crystal?"

"I can't be her Big Sister. Isn't there a whole vetting process? I see a therapist regularly, I probably wouldn't pass muster."

"I don't mean be her Big Sister. I mean make sure the arrangement ends. She shouldn't start spending time with my mother."

"It's Big Sister, not Big Mother," I say. "That's not how it works."

"It's looser than you think. Just promise me," Liv says.

She drops my wrist. Crystal gives a tiny wave. Father Carl tries mightily to engage Crystal, but she only has eyes for Livvy, as she calls her.

"Just promise me," Liv demands.

"I promise. God!" I rub my wrist.

When she faces me, her eyes are wet. "Thank you."

It is the only time she's ever said it.

Liv sits on Crystal's other side and transforms back into a teenager, a cool teenager Crystal adores already. Liv and Crystal have each other; Father Carl and Deborah have each other. I am alone but for my knowledge, which I wear like a hair shirt. I sit across from the clove-spiked ham, silent. It's as though I'm not there at all. There are two tall windows in the dining room, and I find myself gazing out of them throughout the night, drinking in the velvet darkness like sanity. With each sip of wine and forkful of ham, Deborah grows softer and Father Carl grows more moist and red. She flirts with and cajoles Father Carl, skilled at using her womanliness. Liv pushes salad around her plate and makes jokes at the expense of Paula Papademetriou, whom Deborah predicts won't be showing her face around the Shiverton Chamber of Commerce luncheons or the charity circuit or the athletic fields or the country club for that matter for a good long while, given the Pantanos' long reach in this town, never mind the MacDougalls, who are darn near salt-of-the-earth-style royalty. Crystal laughs at things she doesn't understand.

Deborah expounds on all that she will do as Catholic Woman of the Year, plans for readings at the senior center, clothing drives, spiritual retreats.

"You always have to have a project," Father Carl says approvingly, between bites.

Deborah serves Crystal more ham, never taking her eyes off Father Carl, who hasn't yet offered comfort or wisdom during our post-ordeal year, maybe because Crystal is here and she is an innocent, or maybe because he has forgotten.

My breath is visible. I didn't notice it at first, and no one else seems to either, since the adults are flushed with wine, and from what Liv says Crystal is probably used to the cold, and Liv's skin always looks like poultry these days, and truth be told, the cold does not bother me anymore. When the conversation pauses, I hear metal furnace ducts whistling, hot air rushing within, but the heat pours straight through the old, wooden-sash windows. It's not just the heat that is failing. Circular brown stains on the ceilings show the heavy rains. The hardwood floor shines pale in spots, and cracked seals let moisture cloud the windows. Outside, yellow paint peels like molting skin. The house seeps and sheds with neglect.

Deborah always has to have a project.

In my lap, my hands hold a nonexistent pen above a nonexistent notebook. I mime scribbling, trying to trace the logic.

Liv's purpose for Donald was to foil Deborah. What is the purpose of Shane?

Old truths wash away like a splinter of glass from my eye.

My stomach is finally quiet. Snakes wait in weeds and holes in the ground, not in girls' bellies. They defy decapitation and are immune to their own venom. Sometimes, they have daughters.

FIFTEEN

368 Days After the Woods

I'm sure of it now. My senses are sharper than before the woods, tuned more finely. I have evolved into something that survives.

I've listened to Paula approach for a quarter of a mile, her footfalls crunching the frost. Wind whips the flag above the watchtower. As she enters the Sheepfold, grackles hidden in the tops of pines take off in a whorl. I sit on a flat stone to the side of the tower entrance, the one I palmed before hiding inside, because it was smooth and seemed like it might be the last pleasing thing I would touch before dying.

"Thanks for meeting me here," I say.

"I hadn't heard from you in a while. I wasn't sure how you felt about me." Paula wrestles her heavy hair into a ponytail. "I'm not popular around Shiverton these days."

"How Shivertonians feel about you is irrelevant. How I feel

about you is irrelevant. What is relevant is that I still need you," I say.

Solve it, or leave it.

I nod toward the crime scene. "He collapsed the pit, but the police dug it up again."

"I know. I saw it before," she says, her voice brittle. "The day we met, remember?"

The pit looks nothing like it did the last time I saw it, and the things inside. Ubiquitous yellow crime tape is staked in a rough octagon wide of the pit's original perimeter. It flaps in the breeze like sad party streamers. A perfectly excised rectangle of earth has been removed along with Ana. If Jessup closed over the pit after I escaped and before he was arrested, that means he came and saw her one last time. He wasn't experienced enough to know he should have taken her out, that you can't just leave a body in the elements. Ana's soul might have flown off long before I saw her, but her body would stay and make itself known.

The pit is too changed. It doesn't suit my purpose.

"Why did you ask me here, Julia?" Paula says, impatient.

I reach into my bag and hand her the pamphlet. "I think Liv and her mother are going to Bolivia for something called Makeover Travel."

Paula skims the text and lewd photos. "Where did you get this?"

"It was in Liv's Christmas stocking," I say, twisting my mouth grimly. "I think it's a present."

I once asked Liv what she wanted for Christmas. She scoffed, reminding me that she stopped making lists when she was six, because didn't I know that Deborah always decided what she needed?

"You like to do research," Paula says, a new edge to her voice. "What do you know about medical tourism?"

"Only that something like half a million Americans go abroad for procedures every year, and the majority of those procedures are elective cosmetic surgery," I say.

Paula hands me back the pamphlet. "So what do you need me for?"

"Confirm what Deborah's up to for me."

"What Deborah's up to? You'll have to be more specific than that."

"Confirm whom the surgery is scheduled for," I say slowly.

"Did you know I ended up with ethics infractions from complaints made by your mother and your therapist? *Dateline* didn't care, but the station took the charges more seriously than they had to, because it made them look good," Paula says.

"I'll give you something," I say. "The story of my escape. And how I found Ana Alvarez before everyone else did."

Paula stares at me for a full minute, eyes blazing. Then she digs for her phone and paces away, speaking into a cloud of breath. When she returns, the edge in her voice is replaced by exhilaration.

"I confirmed that the Lapins' travel plans were made through an intermediary, something called Swan Tours, a company that sends Americans to Bolivia specifically for the purpose of getting plastic surgery."

"Why go all the way to South America to get a nose job?" I ask.

"The cost is lower than in America. Bolivia in particular is becoming a hub for this kind of thing. It's a third of the price in some cases."

"Deborah doesn't hurt for money. She gets anything she asks for from Leland. It's always been that way."

"Perhaps her ex-husband wouldn't pay for elective plastic surgery."

"Maybe."

"There's something else. Liv is sixteen?"

"We're both sixteen."

"Plastic surgery is viewed differently in South American culture. It's practically a birthright. If you have the money, and you don't like it, you get it fixed." Paula comes closer, that old look in her eye, hot and bothered, wanting something from me. "Is there a part of Liv's body that she's unhappy with?"

I see them, in front of my eyes. Faded marks, encircled *X*s, on her bottom, legs, arms.

I shake my head.

"Well. Either way, there are reasons to be concerned. The standard for medical training isn't the same in other countries as it is in America. And there's no one on this half of the equator policing it. There are countless horror stories, deaths under anesthesia, inadequate follow-up." Her eyes glitter. I've given Paula her next story: mothers who schedule unnecessary plastic surgery for their sixteen-year-old daughters in foreign countries.

I've made my promise, my bargain. Now she gets two stories for the price of one.

The flag at the top of the tower waves to me. I step inside, met by the rank smell of piss, and climb. I hit the second landing before Paula's weight on the stairs joins mine. When I reach the top, I press my back against the wall and slip down to the floor. Paula's face appears, but it doesn't awaken me. Too late, I'm already gone. My ears seal over.

The watchtower is a green-gray cylinder framed in morning light. Patches of moss climb its sides. A wrought-iron staircase spirals upward, visible through long windows. On a pole at the top is a weather-beaten American flag, its tatters undulating in the wind. The tower means I am heading in the direction of the parking lot, where kids used to leave their cars and hike up to the tower to drink and get laid before it became too overgrown to pass. It's twenty feet away. I can do this. I hobble toward it, dragging my leg behind, using my knuckles to propel me like an ape. Cranking my neck, I fix my eyes on my goal. I think of a famous painting I once saw in New York of a crippled woman dragging her body toward a farmhouse. Christina. I fall to my hip like Christina, dragging myself with my arms, which aren't yet ruined. This is somehow faster. I am moving now, really moving, dragging my body across roots and rocks, falling and rising up again, digging in with my elbows, scuttling across the ground like a crab. The tower is closer, twelve more feet to go.

My hand falls through the earth. I freeze.

Pebbles spray from under my hand and are swallowed by darkness. I kneel at the edge of a hand-dug hole in the ground. An inch more, a shift

*forward of my weight, and I would have thrown myself into the hole be-
hind the pebbles. It is six feet across. The smell of overturned earth lingers, and it terrifies me. I scurry backward, folding my ankle back
underneath myself. Pain lances through swollen tissue. I can't go much
farther on this thing, not firmly attached.*

I turn to the side and vomit.

*Time passes. Behind me, the sun rises. My bile sparkles like diamonds
on briar leaves. A vine grows over the pit's edge and inside. I swipe my
sleeve across my mouth and follow the vine, crawling back to the lip and
peering over. Rocks poke from the sides like blisters in a throat, and there
are holes where rocks might have been but are missing, as though they
were knocked out by someone trying to gain a foothold. I shift to let sunlight past me into the hole. From top to bottom, it's the height of two men,
maybe less. Wedges of pale green and orange—cantaloupe rinds?—cut
into quarters by a human hand. Silver wrappers. Plastic water bottles.
Something was fed and watered down there. The electric buzzing of flies.
I lean closer. Two mud-covered hot-pink sneakers splayed at a terrible
angle. And something else, covered in black leaves. A dark lump curled
in the shape of a shrimp.*

*A twig snaps. I hunch my back and peer over my shoulder, feral
and alert.*

RUN.

*I clamber up and rise, but my ankle caves instantly, soft white static
filling my eyes. I drop back to my shredded knees and crawl, around the
hole, over rocks and brush, bleeding from so many places. The tower is
farther than it looks. I scuttle on, leaving a trail of blood. When I reach
the base of the tower I pray the door is unlocked, rising and swaying on
my knees like a prairie dog. I throw my weight against the door and fall*

in on my hands. *The smell of ancient piss rises beneath me, but I am past things like hygiene and disgust. Beer cans litter the floor. I look over my shoulder at the vegetation I've beaten down with my hands and knees. My blood trail will lead him to me, and I will be trapped. I know what I must do. The railing, a skeletal helix, rises from the floor. I use it to pull myself up, and it squeals under my weight. I hop to the first step on my good foot, then two, then ten. I take breaks every three steps. At eighteen I stop counting. At thirty-two, I reach the top. Someone spray-painted PURGATORY on the wall in front of me. I laugh, but the laugh loses to my breath that explodes like firecrackers in the trapped tower air. I swallow my noise, because it interferes with my hearing, and hearing is what's kept me alive in the woods until now. The first day, I listened to the man's tone, to see if he would grow affectionate toward me the longer we were together. Later, I listened as his random mutterings become more distant, as he began to regard me as less than human: something he caught, but did not want. That first night, I listened for the man's heavy footfalls in the mud, as he searched for his escapee, in the dark and through the rain. On this day, I listen for the swish and switch of a hunter cutting through brush that stands between him and his prey.*

He will come soon.

I move to the window, palming the wall. When he comes, I will listen as he pushes through the door. I will listen as his feet touch the first landing. When he gets to the third landing, I will jump, headfirst, which will snap my neck. And then he cannot keep me. Because I will be free.

I watch.

The sun travels across the sky. My eyes dull. I give the window my back and sink to the floor. On the walls are shadows, a sinister lace of leaves and branches. The patterns shift and change. I rest my head on my knees and doze. When I wake, light fills my eyes from the back window. The sun climbed over the tower while I slept. I push myself up with my hands. My ankle is twice the size of the other, heavy with blood. The calf looks fat too. I use my hands to stand. My ears ring, a tinny hum. Surfacing too fast, getting the bends. The tower walls tilt, and the spray-painted letters lengthen.

The window. I hop hard through the wooze, four hops to get me across the room. If he comes, there's no rule that says I can't jump to my death from this window instead of that window. I laugh, weaker even than before, an anemic hysteria that fades to husky sighs. A faint whoosh! from below. Different from the wind in the trees, different from the owl swooping to the ground to snatch a vole in the night. A deliberate, man-made noise: rubber tires skimming through leaves.

I throw my waist against the windowsill and flail my arms.

"STOP!"

A biker flies past. I thrust my torso out of the window and scream as loud as I can:

"HELP ME!"

The terrible scraping noise goes on forever. He braked too fast, got thrown from his bike. My heart sinks. I have killed him. Then slow, staggering footsteps. The biker in the tight turquoise shirt printed with Italian logos staggers underneath my window. His helmet sits crooked on his head, leaves are caught in the hairs on his shins, and his elbows are clotted with dirt. He leans forward, his back heaving. When he looks up, his eyes are slices, his mouth is ugly with pain.

"Are you the missing girl?" he gasps.

"Yes," I whisper.

* * *

Paula kneels on the ground holding my hand. I didn't feel her take it.

"Julia?" she says, tentative.

My head rises. "You'll use your contacts. Speak Spanish. Confirm which one of them is scheduled for surgery?" I say.

"I'll do my best," Paula promises.

"Then I'll tell you what happened to Ana," I say. "Papademetriou is Greek, right? You've heard of the Ionians? They were an ancient Greek tribe."

"I suppose. Though I don't see the significance."

I rest the back of my head against cold stone. "Have you ever heard of the Ionian word *zagre?*"

SIXTEEN

369 Days After the Woods

Each hour, the rain fell harder. I know because I stayed awake listening.

It stopped as the sun rose. By then the damage was done. The Aberjona River had overflowed. Sewage leached into backyards and playing fields. Water pushed through the foundation of a house on Lake Street and exploded its basement. The new track is permanently damaged, some say. There is talk of a FEMA intervention.

Liv's front yard is pocked in spots where the ground gives way.

"This isn't fun anymore. We should go," Alice says. After a morning spent surveilling Liv's house, Alice wants to do something more fun on our day off before the holiday.

"There." I lean wildly around Alice. "Did you see the parlor curtain move?"

"You asked me that before. The house is empty," Alice says.

"Isn't it possible Liv's car is in the driveway because they're out shopping in Mrs. Lapin's car for their trip?"

The curtains are drawn, and the lights are out, and Liv hasn't answered my calls, which means we haven't spoken since Early Christmas. It's impossible to explain to Alice, but I swear Liv is hiding from me inside.

"Liv is home. Don't ask me how I know. I just know."

"She's not. Look, I'll prove it to you." Alice swings open the car door and leaps out, shrugging her coat around her ears.

"Alice!" I hiss. "Come back!"

Alice bops up the walk and straight up the porch stairs, cupping her hands against the stained glass flanking the front door. The threshold falls away creating a gap, and underneath I see a thin line of light.

Alice gives me a thumbs-down.

I roll down the window and call in a whisper that hurts my throat. "Get back here!"

Alice mimes "I can't hear you!" and hops off the porch, navigating depressions in the lawn and disappearing into Liv's narrow side yard.

I grumble, unbuckling my seat belt and sliding out of the car. I follow her path between the holes. She stares down at the foundation, where fat paint flakes like butter shavings litter the lawn.

"See?" Alice points through the dining room window, which provides a direct sight line into the kitchen. "It's almost noon. There's no way her mom wouldn't be in there making lunch for the two of them."

"This is not a household where lunch is eaten together or served on time," I say, quietly deadpan.

"I haven't been inside Liv's house since her ninth birthday party," Alice says, too loudly, peering in.

"I remember that birthday," I admit.

"I was dying to see the inside of the Gingerbread House," Alice recalls.

I'd forgotten they called Liv's house the Gingerbread House, and the glamour that went along with it. With its salmon-colored boards that divided the house into bright yellow puzzle-pieces with dark green trim, it was conspicuously cheerful.

"I totally forgot people called it that," I say.

"My mother didn't. She called it the Painted Lady. Said it was garish," she says.

"It's actually a stick-style Victorian."

"Sticks because of the boards?"

"Yeah." I rise on my toes to see plates in the sink and the coffeepot on its burner, half full. "You can read the inside from the outside. The boards are just decoration to symbolize where the supports are."

"You know a lot about architecture." Alice looks at me, with her lack of filter, and that absolute sincerity that is somehow endearing. "You know a lot about everything. I kind of forgot that about you."

I look down at the brown lawn, embarrassed. "Someone told me that."

Alice gazes up at the house for a minute, considering. "If

that's where the supports really were, the house would fall right down." I'm still staring at the sticks and lost in the wonder that is Alice when she points at the foundation. "Check out that crack. It goes right up the side of the house."

A zigzag fissure runs from the bottom center to the top right, just under the gutter, in the shape of a staircase.

"What do you think it is?" asks Alice.

"I don't know. Something's wrong with the foundation. All the rain, maybe." As I say it, a wind picks up and a slant of rain falls from the trees, pelting us.

Alice shivers. "It's like the Gingerbread House is about to crack in half." Alice suddenly looks at me. "What would it take to do one of those well-check things?"

"You mean like they do for old people and shut-ins who don't answer their door? Proof that something is wrong, I suppose. Unless you had a friend in the police department. And I don't think I do, at least not these days."

"Maybe you could do it anonymously."

I bite my lip.

"Or we could ring the doorbell."

"I really just want to make sure she's okay," I say. Because I'm furious with her. But I also need to know she's alive.

"Then ring the doorbell and say that."

I stand there for a minute, shifting around in my coat, shoulders shoved around my ears.

"If you're not going to ring the doorbell, can we go? I've kind of got the creeps."

I laugh lamely. "Worse than when we visited Yvonne Jessup?"

Alice nods seriously. "Actually, yeah."

We trudge across the yard together, feet sinking in the loam. I feel eyes on my back, but maybe it's just the Amityville windows, or the rain that has started again, harder this time. Alice wants to go to the new coffee shop on the outskirts of town where everyone hangs after getting kicked out of the downtown coffee shop for overcrowding it. Alice, with her outsider's curiosity of things insiders do. Socializing is the last thing I'm in the mood for, but she begs, and I'm afraid she's starting to feel like the girl I secretly hook up with when no one else is around. It shouldn't take long to get there, but it does, because miserable cops in yellow slickers are redirecting cars around holes in the street.

Alice slips into the past. I half listen. The skies have opened and my wipers can barely keep up. It's hard not to fixate on the streaming rivulets instead of watching the road.

"I remember Liv's third-grade birthday party so clearly. I thought Mrs. Lapin was the prettiest mom I'd ever seen."

I snort.

"You're not a fan. But all things considered, she is an attractive woman," Alice insists.

I raise my eyebrows.

"Okay, whatever. I was eight. Anyway, I kept wishing I could sneak upstairs to Liv's bedroom to see the carousel horse her father gave her," Alice says.

I laugh. "She never had a carousel horse in her bedroom. That was a rumor."

"You remember it though," she says.

"I remember the rumor," I say.

"Was the canopy bed in the shape of a pumpkin carriage true?"

"She had a canopy bed. It was not in the shape of a pumpkin."

"The slide from the hole in her bedroom floor that led to the playroom?"

"Liv's house doesn't even have a playroom."

"What about the secret eaves through her closet? A whole room where you could play, and no one could find you. Like Narnia."

"All part of the mythology," I lie, a little. I can't deal with Alice's imagination going wild right now, when I'm convinced that Liv is mysteriously holed up in her house.

"Well, her dad is a billionaire, right?" Alice continues. "Royalty, too?"

"More like a millionaire. Maybe a thousandaire. Honestly, I have no idea. He's rich, I guess. I doubt he's royal. Liv never talks about him. In fact, she hates him."

"I guess on some level I knew all that. Still"—Alice pulls down the vanity mirror and adjusts her headband—"why do you think some people inspire so much speculation?"

I pull into a spot in front of the coffee shop and sigh. "You take a little personal attractiveness and add some mystery. Just enough to keep people wondering. Voilà. Instant Fantasy GIRL."

"You know what's funny? I preferred thinking all those stories about Liv's house and her family were real."

"Alice." I turn off the car and shift to face her. "That house might look like a gingerbread house from the outside. But I gotta tell you, there ain't nothing about Liv Lapin's life that's anything close to a fairy tale."

"I guess that depends on the fairy tale," Alice says. She frowns, thinking hard. "It's a shame that Mrs. Lapin doesn't do anything to make the house pretty anymore. It's really dilapidated. Mom said they might even have to have a talk with her, because it's on the historic register and people get mad about those things."

I throw my hood over my head and get ready to run. Alice aims her Hello Kitty umbrella out the door. "I don't get how you suddenly abandon a project you were obsessed with," she yells, fixated, her train of thought unstoppable as we bolt under the rain into the cozy shop, where Christmas music plays prematurely and pretend presents are wrapped near a fireplace.

Looking directly at me is Kellan, standing at a high table with a group of kids, one of whom is the Apple Face girl, perched on a stool. He looks to Apple Face, then to me, and his mouth falls open.

Alice fusses with her umbrella loudly, shaking it out and closing it at her side. "Now that the house is in such disrepair, I guess Mrs. Lapin's more likely to leave it alone."

I spin and face Alice, flipping back my hood. "What was that you said?"

"I said, now that it's not so pretty"—Alice closes her umbrella with a *whoosh*—"Mrs. Lapin will leave it alone."

I grip the back of a wire newsstand. The Christmas carols

sound like demented fun-house music, and the warmth is suddenly stifling. I fumble for my bag, soaked, the notebook inside probably soaked too. It doesn't matter, because I've run out of white space. Alice jams her umbrella maniacally into an overfull umbrella stand, nattering about squirrels in danger of mistaking the chipped paint around Liv's house for butter. I squeeze my eyes tight, and think of

Things Liv has:
- A knife
- A boyfriend with a temper
- A mother who won't leave her alone

When I open my eyes, Alice is staring at me.

"I have to go," I whisper.

"What? You can't leave me! Hey, there's Kellan. Hi, Kellan!" She waves frenetically at Kellan heading toward us.

My heart feels like it's been fitted in a vise compressing slowly. "I have to go see Liv. Right now."

"She's not even home. You can't leave! I don't know anyone here. I'll come with you." Alice fights to release her umbrella from the stand.

I put my hand on Alice's arm. "I have to go alone. Stay here and make new friends."

Her lip quivers.

"You're a true friend, Alice. Anyone would be lucky to have you in their corner." I dash out the front and make it inside my car, slamming the door.

Kellan bangs at my window with the side of his fist. I jump.

"Wait!" he mouths, forearm protecting his eyes from the forming sleet.

"I can't! I have to go!" I yell, already pulling out. Kellan does an awkward jig to get away from my squealing tires.

I take the back roads that wrap around the high school. I can speed this way; the streets are long and straight with no lights or stop signs. Wind gusts sway my car, all 2,750 pounds. Black branches weakened by the rain hang low and lean ominously on power lines. It takes until the first stoplight for me to realize Kellan is in pursuit. When the light turns green I peel out, my tires spinning in slush. I tell myself it doesn't matter if Kellan shows up in Liv's driveway right behind me, he can help set things straight. Shane is skinny but he's still a guy, and a guy Kellan can take, if it comes to that.

Though if Kellan got hurt, I couldn't forgive myself.

Ice pellets fly at my windshield. My wipers can't keep up. Fog makes it impossible to see the next traffic light until I'm on top of it. Yellow turning red. I can make it, but that's a cop on the side opposite, and I have to stop or I'll get pulled over. I slam on the brakes, and Kellan hits his too, missing my bumper by a hair. The cop is a good thing, because now Kellan can't try to run up to my car. He has to stay put; no shenanigans will be attempted by the son of Detective Joe MacDougall.

My phone rings next to me. Kellan. Whoops, can't answer it, the car won't let me, safety feature. I meet Kellan's eyes in the mirror and shrug. His eyes narrow, and he mouths something that is most certainly not romantic. When the light changes, I pull out slowly past the cop, then start to speed again as he shrinks in my mirror.

How couldn't I have known this before?

Donald's purpose. Shane's purpose. What would it take for Deborah to leave Liv alone? Her words haunt me.

I know exactly what I'm doing with Shane.

I take the sharp corner before Liv's street too fast. I am in flight, in this car, super-safe, they say this car is, but that telephone pole is right in front of me; it's taking up my whole windshield.

The crash is harder and louder than I imagined a car hitting a pole could be. The airbag explodes into my wrists and arms, and I choke on white dust and fumes. The pole is inside my car, about four inches from my face, the smell of outside in.

What would Alice do? Pray, probably. How to pray, again?

A *click-click-click* at the door, Kellan yanking the handle. Muffled screams, his.

This goes on forever, or minutes. The sleet runs fast down my windshield and puddles, resting on the wiper blades until they lift and drag the slurry away. It is mesmerizing.

"Shut the car off!" Kellen screams through the glass.

Time moves thick and slow. Too slow. I have somewhere to be.

Sirens. Faint, now loud.

"The ignition! Push the ignition or the door won't unlock!" Kellan's voice, drowned out at the tail end of a siren whine.

The car is still running. I try to press the starter button, but my right wrist feels loose, unattached and unusable. I reach over the deflated airbag with my left hand and shut off the car, and for a second there is only the patter on my roof. Kellan rips open the door and drags me out, but already the EMTs are here, and they are scolding Kellan for moving me.

"I have to go," I whisper, sinking to the ground, the sleet striking my head and shoulders like rubber bullets.

A paramedic kneels in front of me. He is tan and dark-eyed, slender with high cheekbones, wet beads where the rain hit them, more like an actor playing a paramedic than a paramedic. He puts his arm under my back and guides me gently to the ground. "My name is Charlie. What's your name?"

"Julia!" Kellan says.

Charlie the paramedic shoots him a dirty look. "She's supposed to say it. Julia, do you know what day it is?"

"It's late," I whimper. "I have to go."

"Julia, do you know who our president is?"

"You're not hearing me. I have to go!" I beg.

"Do you have any pain or weakness, Julia?" Without waiting for the answer, he opens my jacket and reaches underneath my sweater, palpating.

"Julia, does this hurt?"

I should look toward Kellan, wonder what he is thinking, with this hot guy's hand up my shirt. But instead I flash on Liv, old Liv, imagining her wisecracks, imagining what she would say about the Model Medic pushing on my chest and stomach.

"Does this hurt?"

Old Liv is standing behind him, mouthing *Oh my God*, trying to make me laugh. *Only you, Julia,* she would say. *Only you would get action from an EMT who looks like he stepped out of a telenovela. How funny would it be if you started moaning right now? Imagine the look on his face!*

"How about this, does this hurt?" he asks.

Liv. What are you doing to yourself? When was the last time we laughed at something together, hard? What's going to happen to you? What will it take for Deborah to leave you alone?

"Does this hurt?" he repeats.

I let out a howl.

The medic's perfect features draw together, deadly serious. Kellan tears his hands through his wet hair. Two other medics loom close, blinking rain from their eyes.

"Get her on the spine board," Charlie says over his shoulder.

"I don't need to be immobilized, I have a hurt wrist!" I've been here before, and being strapped to a backboard means they're not letting me go any time soon.

"We're going to move you onto a backboard and splint your neck, as a precaution. You have to start answering my questions, Julia. When did you last eat?"

"No backboard!" I writhe, and they are on me like ants, and Charlie has his hands on both sides of my head, and he is counting, one, two, three, and I am rolled to my hip before being lifted onto a backboard the length of my body. Straps tighten across my hips, legs, forehead, and chin. They slide my arms under the strap across my pelvis. I whimper as my wrist moves, tiny bones shifting and shaking in jelly.

"Are you on any medications?" Charlie asks, hovering in my field of vision now, asking questions while the other two float in and out like disembodied heads, reciting in sharp notes vague things about my color and breathing. The squeeze of a blood pressure cuff on one side, my wrist moved flush against my immobilized body on the other.

"Have you used any illegal drugs in the past thirty days?" Charlie asks, relentless.

I blink against the rain. "Kellan, tell them I'm all right!"

Kellan's face pops into my reduced square of vision. Fat drops drip from the ends of his curls. "You need to follow orders. You need to stay still," he tells me.

Someone murmurs something about possible traumatic brain injury, which makes me even more pissed, because I don't have an injured brain, I have an injured wrist, and a friend who needs me now. I wriggle pointlessly against the restraints. "I have to go! You don't understand!"

"Please stay calm, Julia."

A tiny prick on my arm, a cool rush through my vein. In seconds, I don't want to fight anymore. I love Kellan; he's so worried about me. Listen, he's giving someone my address, he's such a good guy, so responsible. There, now Kellan is speaking in formal tones on his phone, she's okay, Dr. Spunk, it was a super-minor accident, the air bags deployed but she's one hundred percent fine. That car has so many safety features, it protected her like a steel cage. Good.

Kellan shoves the phone into his back pocket and runs beside as they carry me Cleopatra-style on my board. I am loaded into an ambulance for a second time in my life. The dangling equipment is familiar, a sure enough trigger, and yet I won't go anywhere, because all of my memories are on the surface now, where they belong.

Kellan holds my hand. I try to face him, then remember I can't. He realizes I can't see him and gushes apologies.

"I need to see Liv before she gives Shane his present," I whine. It sounds so silly now, listening to myself under the lovely narcotic haze of whatever just entered my bloodstream.

He laughs. "You are most definitely not going anywhere." He's beautiful when he laughs.

"You've been avoiding me," I say.

He laughs again. "I haven't been avoiding you. I've been at a hockey tournament in Lake Placid. My father and me. We thought it might be a good time to get out of town."

I smile. "Placid. Placid is a nice word. Placid sounds . . . placid. Hey. At the coffee place. You were with the Apple Face girl."

"With the *who*?"

"The blonde."

"Kerrie? I wasn't with Kerrie, she just happened to be there. I was saying hello!"

"Of course her name is Kerrie. A Kerrie would like fresh milk. Milk and apples."

"Do you seriously think I'd start seeing another girl because

275

of Paula Papademetriou's stupid interview? We covered this, Julia."

"Papademetriou. Papa-dem-meaty-o's. Like bad canned pasta. With minimeatballs."

"Julia."

"Listen, I'm late, I'm late, for a very important date." I lower my voice to a conspiratorial whisper. "If you unstrap me now, you can come with me."

"You really don't get it, do you? You're going to the hospital. Even if you're mostly fine, that wrist isn't fine. You won't be doing much writing with that hand for a while. You're not ambidextrous, are you?"

"Am-bi-dex-trous. Sounds like dom-in-a-trix. A deviant who's skilled at using both hands." I giggle.

"Oh boy." Kellan casts a look at the medic riding in the back with us, whom I can feel but not see monitoring my vitals.

"It's the Haldol talking," the medic murmurs, unamused.

"My boyfriend likes a girl with an apple face," I tell her.

"I do not like a girl with an apple face," Kellan says.

"I have to save my friend. My friend's name is Liv." It suddenly seems important to get the girl medic on my side. Because even if she's not a GIRL—especially if she's not a GIRL—she will understand that you have to save your best friend's life. It's just what you do.

The strap across my pelvis tightens.

Kellan leans close. "You can see Liv when you get out of the hospital. And you will: if there's one thing you can't do, it's stop saving Liv." He strokes my forehead with his fingertips,

276

and it feels lovely. "When you're done, I'll be here," he whispers. I breathe heavily, and my breathing feels luscious, slow and measured. I have the sense I'm forgetting something, but it's okay, because Kellan doesn't like apples, and Liv thinks Charlie the paramedic is way cute, and I won't be doing much writing for a while.

SEVENTEEN

371 Days After the Woods

Paula took days to confirm Liv's surgical appointment with Dr. Juan Cassio in Bolivia. She was, after all, torn between two major stories now, and she had me to thank for both. The rising number of parents sending their teens to foreign countries for plastic surgery constituted a bona fide trend. And balancing the sensitivities of my personal revelation—girl saw body in pit, remembered later—required a deft hand, and could not be hurried.

Stuck in my hospital bed, with Liv screening my calls and her "surgical holiday" only a day away, I had to spin Alice into action, even if it was Thanksgiving. Alice's official mission was to inform Liv of my car accident, although I doubted Deborah would relay the message. I hoped if Alice made my wreck sound bad enough, Liv might stick around, or at least stop by the hospital on her way to Logan Airport.

Alice thought it odd to find Deborah, rather than packing or fixing Thanksgiving dinner, on the front lawn talking shades of yellow with the owners of Park Pro Painting.

"These people," Deborah had stage-whispered behind her hand to Alice, "don't mind working on holidays."

The next morning, in the wee hours, Alice drove by the Lapins' house again as instructed, and was surprised to see Deborah's car in the driveway and the houselights blazing well past their six a.m. scheduled flight departure. It seemed Deborah and Liv hadn't left for their trip after all. Alice's news of my hospitalization had worked, I declared, stripping off my johnny, ready to be discharged. Alice's conclusion was more mercenary. Deborah had decided that the money for the trip would be better used to finally paint the house, Alice presumed. Either scenario sounded good to me; all that mattered was that Liv's trip wasn't happening. And choosing the perfect historical yellow could be all-consuming.

Call it foolish optimism: I even bet Alice that Deborah would leave Liv alone.

Liv wasn't making any bets. She chose Thanksgiving night to give Shane his early Christmas present. The rest is history.

"He's lucky," Paula said gravely on the phone. "Assault with a deadly weapon can carry a sentence of up to ten years. He was a minor. It happened the day before he turned eighteen. It's an injustice: he just gets charged with a misdemeanor, has a strike on his record, and only has to go to juvie for six months. The system must be reformed."

"It's a clean slash right over the cheekbone, long but not

deep, so it wasn't much more painful than a paper cut," Erik said. His friend was the plastic surgeon who had been consulted, and sharing information with me was okay, because processing is healthy. "Still, it's impossible to repair without stitches. There wasn't much anyone could do, no matter how skilled. Eventually it will scar. It won't be pretty."

Mom said, "Along the way, someone failed her. Someone allowed her to mix with the wrong crowd."

Ricker said, "It is unfortunate to the extent that it hinders your progress." Okay, she didn't say that. But she was thinking it.

Only Alice said, "Go to her. Immediately."

Now I charge past the metal trash can on the curb and up the walk, fly up the stairs, and hammer on Liv's front door. Stacked on the welcome mat are two foil-covered turkey dinners, a fruit-stuffed cornucopia with a tag that says *Saint Theresa's Parish*, and a cellophane cone of autumn-hued carnations. I lift the flowers and peer at the tag: *Wishing you a speedy recovery. Fondly, Ryan Lombardi.* Water saturates everything, tiny beads across the foil and the cellophane. It's classic Deborah, leaving this gaudy, soggy display to show the world that so many people care about the Lapins.

I bang harder. The handle is altogether missing now, but no matter, because the door eases open. Liv wears a ladylike kelly-green peacoat, tights, and gloves, like an old-fashioned traveler ready to board a steam train. Her hair is drawn back into a neat bun. A rectangular plastic bandage stretches across her cheek from under her left eye, nose to ear. "Come in," she says, like it's a regular day, her voice and movements light. I step in, wiping tears of panic away with the heel of my palm. On the round table in the middle of the foyer is a hand-drawn card for LIVVY propped against a bouquet of supermarket flowers: pink carnations losing petals and browned baby's breath. Three pearlized suitcases of different sizes are lined up next to the door.

"It's the holiday season. A time for gratitude," Liv says.

"Oh, Liv." I start to bawl.

Liv throws up her palm. "Stop! You're not allowed to sob. Turn right around and leave if you're going to do that."

I swipe at hot tears with my fingertips. "Tell me. Tell me everything."

"You must have heard by now. I tried to break up with Shane, and he got mad and just started slashing all over the place. Everyone knows he carries a knife."

A gift that goes beyond the recipient, tied with a fat bow. Liv and I both bound our presents with ribbons. Shane got his, but I chickened out and left Liv's stocking alone. If I had let Liv know that I was onto her madness, that I knew, maybe somehow her face would be whole.

Liv snaps her fingers in front of my nose. "Are you saying you didn't hear the story?"

"I just heard. I was in a car accident, in the hospital." I hold up my splinted wrist. "I was discharged an hour ago. I snuck out of my house when my mother went to get the ginger ale I begged for. It doesn't matter, never mind. I called you. I've been calling you," I stammer.

She moves to the burnished-gold antique mirror and turns her cheek to it. "The story got around fast. A matter of hours, really." She touches the edge of her bandage. "I guess the holiday break didn't slow the rumor mill."

"Shane is a criminal. He deserves everything he gets." I search her eyes in the mirror for agreement. There is nothing. I had expected nothing; anything would have surprised me.

Which means it's Go Time.

"I hear he's going to jail for a long time," I say. "Twenty years, maybe."

"Nooo," Liv says, drawing out the word as she tightens the belt on her jacket. "He's going to juvie for six months."

"That's not long enough. Shane is pure evil. Calculating."

"It's over." She moves away from the mirror and drops to her knees at the biggest suitcase, popping the buckles and setting the cover against the wall. She unclicks the crisscrossed straps and removes two sweaters. From a nearby bag labeled Blick Art Materials she slips a set of colored pencils in a wooden box sealed in plastic, along with a tablet of creamy, expensive-looking paper. She places them in the spot where the sweaters were and runs her fingers over them, smiling.

"Thank God it's over." I swallow hard and plow through. "In some ways, I feel like this was all part of Shane's master plan, you know? Get his dream girl, then mark her in some ghastly, irreversible way that will make her forever his."

"That's ridiculous. Shane doesn't have the brainpower to plan his own course load each semester, never mind mastermind ways to keep a girlfriend," Liv says, closing the suitcase and snapping the locks.

"People don't realize," I say. "It takes a lot of courage and strength to break it off with an abuser. The fact that people experience domestic violence doesn't make them inherently weak. Abusers like Shane are able to manipulate and coerce girls like you by chipping away at your self-esteem. It happened so slowly that you probably weren't even aware of it. Then, bam! The violent attack happens."

"Wait." Liv stands and brushes off her knees, the round hall table between us. "What do you mean by 'girls like me'?"

"Statistically, many victims grow up in homes where there's abuse, physical or emotional. It's the norm. It conditions them to accept dysfunction and unhappiness."

Liv circles the table. "Conditions them. The victims?"

"Sure. Victims like you were raised to accept abuse as the norm. So, in some way, your mother orchestrated all of this."

"My *mother*," she says, shaking her head. "My *mother* doesn't get credit here. *Shane* doesn't get credit here."

I reach out blindly and touch the table, trying to blunt the urge to run. "I was thinking. It's a shame you weren't able to hold him off."

"What do you mean by that?"

"Just that he's such a scrawny punk. So soft. Weak-seeming."

Her eyes flash. "He had a knife, Julia."

"Like Donald Jessup. Been there." I laugh weakly, clear my throat, and back away, avoiding her eyes. "I was so afraid of that knife the first time I saw it. Nine inches of serrated stainless steel, I found out later. How big was Shane's knife? Never mind, it doesn't matter. When I pulled Donald Jessup off of you, I was sure he would swing around with that blade and get me. The thing is, with a knife, you have to control the attacker's weapon hand. Kick 'em in the groin, gouge the eyes, strike the throat. Hurt their vulnerable targets. But skills can only get you so far. I didn't have them that day in the woods. Kellan's father says stopping an attacker requires innate bravery."

"Are you saying what I think you're saying?" Liv's voice quivers. She steps closer, her ear resting on her shoulder at an extreme angle. "Are you saying that I'm not as brave as you?"

"I'm not suggesting that at all. I'm devastated about what happened to your face," I say.

"You think brave is answering someone's cry for help in the woods. I call that an instinctual reflex: fight or flight. Some people choose flight. You happened to choose fight. You want to know what brave is? Brave is meticulous planning. Staying with the plan, even when you get cold feet."

My stomach grips. "What plan?"

"Bravery is trading something you love for something you love more. Like your freedom." Liv leans in close and says coolly, "I gave him the knife, Julia. Think about it."

"I have," I whisper.

"You want the real story? An exclusive? We both know you're a fan of those. Fine. You know something? After all this time, you deserve it. Here's the thing: this is for you." She jabs the air in front of my chest with her finger. "Not your fancy doctor. Not your mother. And absolutely not Paula Papademetriou."

I nod slowly.

"He did it fast, like I expected he would. It felt like a paper cut across my cheek. Far worse was watching him fall apart afterward, coke-addled and freaking out over the blood. I didn't scream. He screamed, high-pitched, like a girl. I had to taunt him for over an hour; it was exhausting. First I had to make sure he smoked enough pot to make him impotent, then snort enough coke to get his frenzy going. Throw in some insults about his real mother, then his fake mother, then his manhood, all the while straddling him until my hips ached. A few moans of 'Ryan' instead of 'Shane.' After all my coaching, who would have ever thought it would have taken him that long?"

My bag slips to the floor. I leave it.

"I researched what it would feel like, to be prepared," Liv continues. "The cutters of the world love to blog and tweet. They won't shut up about it. The touchy-feely cutters use words like *release* and *orgasmic*. The more common minds say 'it burns' or 'it stings.' Duh. There's a subset that waxes on about best tools, with a majority in the razor blade camp. I sort of wish I'd done more research before I spent $10.49 on the Grim Reaper, because it sounds like a razor blade would have been the way to go from a precision standpoint. But no one grabs a razor blade in the heat of the moment. It's too awkward. And from the gift standpoint, it wouldn't have worked. Might as well give him a kitchen knife.

"After a few seconds, it felt exposed, like when part of your body gets cold unexpectedly. Imagine dropping trou on a freezing winter day. It was almost refreshing, the moment the air hit that thin line of muscle and blood. I guess that's why corpses are cold, because living blood is warm.

"On the subject of blood and surprises: in case you were wondering, there was very little. All the gauze I bought sat untouched in my bag. I hadn't worked through how I was going to explain carrying what amounted to a first aid kit anyway. Evidence of premeditation, that's what the courtroom dramas would call it. I clasped my hand to my flayed cheek, surprised, which required no acting whatsoever, because even when you're expecting something to happen and are fully prepared for it, getting hurt is always a surprise. No need to fake wide eyes, your eyes just fling open. I made a noise too, but mostly, I kept thinking, my cheek is so cold, and I should get that antiseptic out right now.

"It seems a shame that Shane didn't get to enjoy his Christmas gift a little more. As all future criminals do, Shane has it in his DNA to hide the weapon, so before he even attended to me, he threw open his bedroom window and hurled the knife into the yard. I should have given him a harder time about that. It's funny that his first instinct was to cover his butt, when he admitted his guilt to his mother and the police right away anyway. It just meant some fat cop had to fish it out of the rhododendron next to the Cuthberts' driveway.

"His mother. Oh, God, his mother. She heard his shrieks as she walked in from bunco. How horrid that must be, coming in from Eighties Night. Running upstairs, coat flung open, pink scrunchie hanging halfway down her teased ponytail. Shane pointing to me, her screaming, 'What did you do? What did you do?' like I'd been the one holding the knife. Running to the window and leaning into the darkness, her butt one big tweedy hump, as though an intruder had assaulted me and scaled down the face of her house and was now running down Evergreen Lane. She kept yelling, 'Where is he? Where is he?' and Shane kept moaning 'There was no one,' but pausing for a minute, wondering if she might be onto a good fabrication.

"I was surprised when I started to feel a little woozy, like when you blow your nose too hard and the room tilts and everything sounds muddled. Mrs. Cuthbert yelled at Shane to step away from me then, a motherly move made by someone who had reason and experience enough to be afraid of her son. She forced me to sit on the floor—I don't know why they always force traumatized people to sit on the floor—and hold toilet paper she'd grabbed from the upstairs bathroom against my face to 'staunch the flow' (I expected to find she'd handed me a tampon) while she called Mr. Cuthbert at the bar who advised we go straight to the hospital.

"Even if she hadn't called the police, I knew from TV that the ER doctors would have reported the incident to the cops anyway. It's not like I wanted anything bad to happen to Shane—didn't care, really—I just wanted it on the record, to keep things straight. It was good that I had some time alone with the social worker to recount all the times Shane pushed me and punched me and yelled at me: a quantifiable record of growing violence. There was even corroboration. Half the school had seen him grab my ankle in gym, and certainly Ryan Lombardi had been worried enough by my little bruises that he regretted not saying something sooner.

"I think it's beautiful. When a scar heals, it pulls at the rest of your face like it's clinging to the old skin, as if nostalgic. This morning was hard, I confess. I woke up to itchy stitches, and caught myself about to cry when it all came back to me. Then I heard Mother on the phone arguing with the airline over 'unforeseeable circumstances' and demanding a refund on our flight, and I snuggled back under the blankets and realized it was worth every stitch. I will never second-guess myself again."

The only sound is Liv catching her breath. I have stopped breathing.

"Does it hurt to smile?" I ask, my voice shredded.

"Yes. But I can't help it." She grins widely.

I nod at the suitcase. "You're going somewhere?"

"Yes, right. Those. I'm leaving town. For a hospital in Belmont. A little mental respite. In fact, I thought you were my cab. Mother will follow later, after she drives Crystal home. She was coming anyway, to wish us bon voyage. It all worked out."

"How did Crystal take it? The public version."

Liv frowns, crinkling the dressing on her cheek. "Crystal wasn't really fazed. This is not an unheard-of event in her world. In fact, this very thing happened to her cousin Jessie last year. Except, well. A bit worse. Her boyfriend had a violent history. Unstable," she adds behind her hand in a stage whisper.

Sing-songy voices and splash sounds trail from the kitchen. My ears start to ring and my vision narrows.

"About Crystal and my mother," Liv says, stepping closer, smelling of antiseptic. "Remember your promise."

"I need to use the bathroom," I say, moving drunkenly past her and squeezing into the tiny downstairs toilet in the back hall. I leave the door open an inch and brace myself over the sink. The voices from the kitchen are clearer from here: Deborah, and a younger voice, notes rising and falling, and a cascade of giggles. A strong vinegar-apple smell. I peek through the crack and see Deborah's back, arms bowed, blocking most of Crystal, who leans over the sink. Deborah squeezes a pink plastic bottle in a circle over her head.

"You're going to love it! Your hair will be so pretty and smooth. Try closing your eyes so the fumes don't bother them."

I flush the empty toilet bowl and run the water before stepping out, pausing at Crystal's rush of laughter as Deborah ties her hair in a towel turban and hands her a mirror. "Make believe you're at a spa. If you're good, maybe we'll do your toenails next."

I stumble past Liv as she calls, "Wait, aren't you going to say goodbye?" But I don't stop, because her cab is coming, and Shane is in juvie, waiting for her call, waiting to be told she loves him no matter what, and he is her one true hero, having rescued her in a way Julia never did, and no one can understand that real love hurts, and he will tell her about the visitor's lounge bathroom at McLean that they can use to be together on visits if he ever gets released, and she will tell him that she will, but she won't, because she's done with him.

I pause to breathe in the day. The rain has ended. Much as I hate the rain, the smell that comes after isn't unpleasant.

Liv's breath is at my neck. "This is the end, Julia. You have to say goodbye," she murmurs.

Porch planks groan under my feet as I face her. Liv holds out her arms, and I drop the bag from my shoulder, pressing myself into the brushed weave of her coat, clavicle mashing against a hard button. She squeezes, then shoves me away and holds me, stiff-armed. Her eyes flicker over my face.

"You won't tell anyone. You'll keep your promise?"

I wait, considering. "I'll keep my promise if you tell me one thing. Why did you bring me with you that day in the woods?"

Her cheeks rise with a faint crinkle. "Because I knew if things went bad, you'd save me. The truth is, we're both brave."

I touch the tip of my finger to her bandage. "You're right."

I sink down the porch stairs as the door clicks behind. At the last step, sunlight cuts through the clouds, a momentary, milk-white explosion. I reach for the porch rail and hold on, waiting for the memory of when I topped the crest of the Hill, before the Sheepfold. It comes, and in a moment, I am back. I am in control. I am out of the woods.

I cut through the evanescent haze toward my car, hand in my bag. When I reach the trash can I lift the cover and drop my notebook inside. I don't need to write Donald Jessup in the blank cat's eye, the seed shape, the space common to Liv, Ana, and me. It is no longer relevant. It's not a bad thing, to be irrelevant.

This is the last time I will leave the Victorian. I cross the lawn and touch the edge of the staked sign advertising Park Pro Painting. A contract will be canceled, a stop payment placed on a check. The sign will disappear, because there is a new project to occupy the owner's time. The house will blister and peel into reptilian cracks, then bare wood.

In the parlor window, a silk curtain moves aside, and a bandaged face smiles through pain, waiting to carry her suitcases out the front door and find her own version of perfect.

EPILOGUE

400 Days After the Woods

A flutter of porcine blinks. "Who are you?"

Liv hops from foot to foot, panting and shaking out her hands. "It's me, Liv!"

Jessup presses his palm to his forehead and paces on short legs, three steps, two steps, one step. "You can't be Liv."

"I know you're confused. Listen, I don't have much time. I'm not alone."

He freezes and lowers his head, peering from the rim of a black knit skullcap. "Not alone?"

"Don't you get it? I'm the girl you love! We're finally meeting in person!"

His jowls quiver. "You sound like her. But you don't look like her."

"Describing myself differently was something I had to do," Liv says. "I thought you deserved to know I wasn't truthful. You loved me, and

that proved something I needed to know my whole life. I'm grateful for that."

Jessup stares stonily.

Liv steps closer. "This is the real me. I'm sorry."

"Don't be sorry." He bares small teeth. "You're perfect."

"I—what?"

He touches her smooth cheek. "Perfect."

"Oh my God! You're pleased. You're happy I look this way!"

"Of course I am!"

"Of course you are?"

"I mean, it's better. For the game."

Liv staggers backward. "I'm not here for the game."

"It's okay!" He stalks up to her. "It's more than okay. I think it's great."

She covers her face and groans through her hands. "It's a relief to you, that I look like I do. It's a bonus."

He does a fluttery pantomime to calm her. "No—wait—what?"

"Do I have to spell it out for you? I am not what you fell in love with! If anything, you should be disappointed." Her hand meets his face with a shallow slap.

He raises his palm to his blooming cheek. His eyes slit and spark. "Don't. You. Ever!"

"You prefer that I look this way. You're saying Mother's right. You SUCK!" Liv winds up and gives him another slap, harder.

Clanging buckles. She whirls backward and meets the ground with a thud, him on top. Digs her heels into the earth, kicks up gravel, tries to get out from under him, while he rocks and shifts his weight.

"Let her go!" I scream.

Jessup jerks his head as his body goes rigid. He looks from Liv to me. His pupils jitter. What next, he wonders? Seconds ago, the universe had gifted him a jumbo check from Publisher's Clearinghouse, the winning Megabucks ticket, a girl-sized box wrapped in a bow. But his anger made him blow it, and he succumbed to his worst self. Now she is under his thumb, where for so long he was under hers. The experiment is over. It was unsuccessful. Deborah will always be right.

"Who are you?" Jessup wails to Liv.

Metal at her throat. I howl like an animal. His eyes move between us, hovering on Liv. When she squirms, he pulls the knife away from her neck, for this is not his plan, not her plan. Not at all.

"Walk away and forget what you saw! Now, or her blood's on your hands!" His pitch wavers.

I break into a slow smile, because this time, I know Donald Jessup had it backward. I will remember everything I see, and his blood will be on her hands.

"I'll end her life, right here!" Jessup says.

I laugh, a long, low, glorious, empty-belly laugh. Donald Jessup was so very wrong.

Right here was where Liv's life began.

ACKNOWLEDGMENTS

The following people must be thanked for their guidance, inspiration, help, and love.

Thanks to Janine O'Malley, for her sure hand and deft editing of *After the Woods,* and for understanding Julia from "statistically speaking." I am also grateful to Angie Chen, for her meticulous editing and delightful ways; and to Beth Clark, who conveyed perfectly Julia's predicament and the revelations to come in a haunting, beautiful cover.

Sara Crowe, thank you for knowing exactly the right home for *After the Woods.* You embody high wisdom worn lightly.

I am blessed to have two men in my life who never doubted: my father, Allan Haas, who read to me nightly and nurtured a passion for words; and my husband, Gary, my best advocate and best friend, who, luckily, finds me far more interesting than a Bengal tiger.

Thanks to my mother, Lillian Haas, who inspired none of the flawed mothers in this novel, but who, along with Alice Hall, introduced me to the best of female friendships. Alice, I miss you every day, and I wish you were here for this.

To my incandescent children, Jackson, Charlie, and Lila. Everything is for you.

To the friends and relatives who mothered my children while I was in the woods, most especially Jenny Bernitz, Bobby Brown, Leah Brown, Theresa Brown, Cathy Donaghey, Kim Freund, Dana Garmey, Deirdre Giblin, Diane Hesterberg, Michele Kulik, Amy Legere, Margaret Mack, Liz Mara, Maria O'Connor, Tillie Savage, and Cristy Walsh.

To Julie True Kingsley and Cameron Rosenblum, my first real writer friends.

Lastly, but certainly not least, my deep appreciation and love to my beautiful colleagues at the office. C and L, my bags are packed for you.